LAST STAND

The dull eyes of the Arikara were bright with a wicked light. It was clear that he intended to keep Cleve or kill him, whichever it took.

Suddenly, Cleve felt every bruise, cut, and agonized muscle in his body. He had survived a run of at least twenty miles to escape from the Arikara. He had done all he could do, and he felt with finality that he was ready to die here, but he would run no more. Instead, he gathered his legs under him and sprang right into the face of the astonished warrior.

The body beneath him arched upward, the heels digging into the ground, the head tilted back, away from his choking hands.

Cleve Bennett might die today.

It seemed likely.

But he wouldn't die without a fight.

Mountain Majesty

BOOK ONE

WILD COUNTRY

JOHN KILLDEER

BANTAM BOOKS

NEW YORK · TORONTO · LONDON · SYDNEY · AUCKLAND

WILD COUNTRY

A Bantam Domain Book / April 1992

ISBN 0-553-28885-7

Published simultaneously in the United States and Canada

Bantam Books are published by Bantam Books, a division of
Bantam Doubleday Dell Publishing Group, Inc. Its trademark,
consisting of the words "Bantam Books" and the portrayal of a
rooster, is Registered in U.S. Patent and Trademark Office and
in other countries. Marca Registrada. Bantam Books, 666 Fifth
Avenue, New York, New York 10103.

PRINTED IN THE UNITED STATES OF AMERICA

RAD   0 9 8 7 6 5 4 3 2 1

chapter
— 1 —

The Missouri was running bank-full after the rains of
the past week, and the hooves of his horses squelched
noisily as John Colter turned his mount's head south
from the river that had led him so far away from
civilization. Now he was headed if not for home at
least for blood kin. His cousin and her family farmed
a place they had homesteaded along the Little Sac
River, and he had a hankering to see her again.

It was summer, and his long spell of travel, broken
by intervals of pure terror as he crossed the plains
and headed for St. Louis, had wearied both the man
and his horses. Knuckles, his sorrel gelding, was
grunting with every step as he pulled his hooves out

of the mud and plopped them in again. Behind him Colter could hear the pack animals snorting with disgust at this uncomfortable footing.

The rich wet country around him seemed alien now after so many years in the drylands and the mountains. Closing his eyes, he sniffed the lush earth scents, the grass and leaves that he hadn't smelled for so long. A far cry from that faint spring scent of clover in the hills or juniper and sage, dust and lodgepole pine, he thought.

A shrill yell from beyond the hill to his left made him pull up, ears cocked, eyes scanning the trees for hostiles. Even here, in 1810, there were Indians who were sworn enemies of his kind, and though he had learned in his Western experience to admire some individuals and even a few tribes, he had no desire to lose his hair on the doorstep of his home country. And then he recognized the long *Sooooo-cow* of the call.

Another cry echoed from the right, and this time he grinned and clucked to Knuckles. With a patient sigh, the gelding moved onward, and Colter watched for the boys who were evidently hunting for a lost cow. That long *Soooooook!* was a call he had known in his own boyhood, and he knew that a pair of youngsters must be searching the wooded hills for a stray.

He glanced at the sun, now going down in the west and baking the mud even as the horses plodded through it. He thought the Little Sac was not far ahead, for he could see a line of larger trees as he topped a gentle rise and gazed over wide bottomlands, dazzlingly green.

Behind him he heard running footsteps, and when he turned, he saw a cow splashing heavily down the trail toward him, her swollen udder swinging from side to side. She was pursued by a pair of towheaded youngsters in overalls whose bare feet sent sprays of mud flying as they ran. A bawling calf darted ahead of them all.

He turned his mount to block the trail, and as the cow swung wide to pass, he flapped his arms and yelled. She dug in her hooves and skidded to a stop, looking at him suspiciously. The boys, finding their quarry halted, came panting to his side. The calf, as if losing momentum, paused and turned back toward his mother.

"Thank you, mister. She's a real pest, that Petunia. She'd have gone all the way to the river if you hadn't stopped her." The bigger boy had a halter in his hand, and before the beast could gather her wits, he had it over her head, the rope snubbed around a sapling.

Colter nodded. "You wouldn't be Bennett boys, now would you?" he asked. "Jase Bennett's?"

The smaller one shook his head. "No, sir, we're Oxham's boys. The Bennetts live way down yonder, 'cross the river and back east a ways. You sure you want to go down there? We'd be right pleased to take you home with us. Ma's always got plenty in the pot, and Pa likes to chew the fat with strangers."

Colter could understand that. He had spent months alone in the mountains, and at times he would have welcomed anything that could talk, though he was the least verbose of men. A griz that had the gift of speech would have looked downright beautiful more than once after a long dry spell. But he shook his head.

"Got to git on," he said. "Got a cousin married Jase Bennett and haven't saw her for many a year.

Thought I'd catch up with the family before I settle down."

The smaller boy, gap-toothed and freckled, let out a long *whoosh.* "You watch out for Mr. Bennett, mister. Pa says he was borned mean and got worse. Nobody hereabout can stand him, and when the circuit rider comes through, Miz Bennett goes to preachin' by herself, with the baby."

"Phil, you hush up!" the older boy said, digging his elbow into the skinny ribs of his brother. "Kin is kin. Ain't that so, mister?"

"Reckon it is," said Colter. "Better git along. Watch Petunia. She's fixin' to bolt."

His eye for cow flesh hadn't deserted him in his long association with wild critters. Petunia did bolt, dragging both boys and the uprooted sapling at the end of her rope. This time she was headed in what seemed to be the right direction, for one grimy hand waved a farewell before the trio disappeared into the brush along the hillside, the calf now following instead of leading the procession.

Now what in hell had Mattie got herself into? He'd heard news of her before he went west with the expedition, but those he met seemed to think Jase Bennett was a good catch. Well, everyone to his own taste. God knew, he had strange ones himself.

He chuckled as he turned his mount away from the trail, angling eastward toward the line of huge trees marking the Little Sac. Nobody but a fool would have kept going back for more after the sorts of stunts he'd got tangled up in, out there in trapping country. The crazy old Frenchmen he ran into from time to time, living their entire lives among Indians, tending their traps, tying one on at the slightest excuse, were no crazier than he.

• • •

He came to the Bennett farm just before sundown. The place was easy to find, curving to match the riverbank, its hay meadows freshly mowed and the haystacks sprouting like huge toadstools against the winter. Higher ground was covered with shocked corn, and ripening pumpkins grew among the huddles of stalks, soon to be gathered and protected against frosts by the dried fodder.

He smelled smoke. Raising his head, he sniffed deep and smiled. Hickory-wood smoke; mingled with its fragrance was the scent of meat drippings scorching in the coals of a good fire. Mouth watering, Colter kneed Knuckles into a jog and followed the water toward the source of that compelling aroma, which mingled interestingly with the rich stink of hogs.

He passed a pigpen near the water and counted a dozen young pigs in one part, four sows in the next, and a boar grunting warily from his wallow of mud in the last. There would be no lack of winter meat here, whatever the hunting was like, he thought as he kicked Knuckles into a trot.

Ahead he could see chimney smoke. A stand of oaks surrounded the house, and the yard was fenced neatly with split stakes through which a gray and white dog was threatening instant mayhem to any intruder. Behind him stood a toddler with a thumb in his mouth, and at his side was an older child, four or so, Colter thought, regarding this unexpected visitor with both curiosity and wariness.

"Down, Snip," said the child. "He don't look ornery."

"Much obliged," said Colter. He pulled Knuckles to a halt beside the gate and swung his leg over the saddle. Dropping to stand beside the horse, he loosed the bit in the beast's mouth and eased the cinch. "Got anyplace I could put old Knuckles here?" he asked.

"You want to come in?" The child's voice was skeptical.

"Bein' as I'm your own blood kin, I reckoned on staying a spell with my cousin Mattie," he said. "If that's all right with your Pa, that is."

With a yell, the boy streaked for the porch of the cabin that could just be seen among the flowering shrubs growing up to the eaves all around it. "Ma, a man's come. Says he's your cousin! Come quick!"

The toddler, left with the dog to oversee their guest, removed his thumb from his mouth and said, "Me Timmy."

A square grin accompanied the words, and Colter smiled back. It had been a long time since he'd been around white children, and he felt a little out of his depth. But it was a good feeling, all the same, and he opened the gate, scooped the little fellow up, and proceeded toward the porch with Snip sniffing suspiciously at his heels.

"Gene, who on earth . . ." That was Mattie's voice, distinctive as always.

"Just your cousin John, Mattie. Come to say howdy after all these years. Been off to the west yonder, and now I'm back to settle down. Thought I'd see my kin."

She came out wiping her hands on her apron and stared into the twilight. "John? John *Colter*? My Lord, it's been a long time! Come in here and sit down to this table! I can't get over it—Jase! Come and meet my cousin!"

Colter climbed the steps amid a tangle of three small boys, the dog, and four lanky cats with twitchy ears. Inside the cabin the tallow dips had been lit, and the house smelled of burning oil, woodsmoke, and roast meat.

He sniffed. "Bear?" he asked wonderingly. "You got bear on that fire, Mattie, or I'm a cougar!"

Now he could see her more clearly. The oval face had sagged a bit. There were lines about her eyes, and her hair was no longer the vibrant gold he remembered but had darkened to a tired blond. She looked worn and weary, did his cousin, and he stepped up and hugged her.

"Jase shot it, and it's just now hung enough to be tender. Things will be ready in just a bit, John." She stepped back and stood beside the big man who had risen and turned toward the newcomer.

"Glad to meet you," said Colter, looking into the smoky gray eyes of this man whose inches matched his own and whose hard square body promised to be the equal of any in strength. Their hands met, and the hard grips were well matched as well.

Jase Bennett narrowed his eyes. "Heard of you," he said. "Mattie talks a lot about your ma. Raised her, I take it?"

"We grew up most like brother and sister," Colter assured him. "After her ma died, Mattie lived with us for years. We wasn't educated like her folks, but she seemed to like us, just the same."

He felt that this hard-handed fellow was testing him for something. What sort of man had his cousin hooked herself up with, anyway?

The oldest boy was staring up at him, his eyes round as coins. "You the cousin that Ma says run off from a whole tribe of Blackfeet?" he asked in a voice hushed with awe. "Everybody that comes by, even the circuit preacher, knows about that!"

John felt himself blushing. "We'll talk about that in

time," he said. "For now, let's dig into that tableful of grub!"

Colter woke and stared up at the shed roof. He had slept for so long under stars and fir boughs, in tipis, lodges, and wickiups or caves that the split-log planks above looked completely alien. There was a glimmer of light in the sky outside the open door, and the fresh breeze of a summer dawn stirred about him as he rose and folded his blankets neatly.

As he left the shed, he met the oldest boy, whom he had hardly had time to greet the night before. Cleve carried a bucket and was headed toward a gate that was still just a shadow in the dimness.

"Going to milk?" Colter asked the boy. "I used to do that back when I was a boy in Kentucky. Your mama and me used to do most of the chores 'cause the little ones was too small to do much. You want I should come and help?"

Cleve looked up, his eyes wide. "I kin milk Rachel fine, but I'd be right glad if you'd come and talk while I milk her. I never thought I'd meet you. Ma used to talk about her cousin John, but that was when you was way out in Injun country."

Colter followed the sturdy shape as the boy opened the gate and gave his own call. "Soooook!"

In a moment there came a soft *mooo* in reply, and a small Jersey cow came ambling up from the creek bubbling below. Cleve caught the halter by the short rope and tied her to a bush, squatting beneath her flank and proceeding to prove himself a good milking hand.

As the rhythmic squirts rang into the bucket, John gazed over the glade beside the creek. The morning mist was lifting, and the first rays of the sun struck through it, turning everything to molten gold. A surge of gladness rose in the man. This was much like his old home country in Kentucky, and he was glad to be here.

"You really run off from a whole tribe of Blackfeet?" the boy asked, never slacking his efforts, the level of milk in the bucket rising steadily.

"I really did." John thought for a moment, recalling the desperation of that race. "Buck naked, boy, and barefoot. But it was get away from 'em or die, and no man I ever knowed wanted to die. Not that way, anyway."

"How far did you have to run?"

"Tell you what, boy, you wait and I'll tell you all about it when we have the whole family together. I'm not one for a lot of talk, and I hate having to say anything twice. All right?" He stared down into the gray eyes slanted up toward him past the hairy flank of the cow.

For a moment the boy looked disappointed. Then he nodded. "They'll all want to hear," he said. "But it'll be evenin' before we can. Pa wants to stack the hay in the far meadow today, and he don't wait for nobody or nothin'."

"Then I'll help with that," said Colter. "Its been many a year since I helped with the haying. Too long. I got to get back in practice if I want to make a living here in civilized country. You think he'll mind if I come too?"

Cleve laughed. "Pa'd let the devil help if there was hay needing stacking or a crop needed plantin'."

Remembering the expression in those calculating eyes into which he had looked the night before, Colter found himself agreeing. And the devil, if he was smart, had better look out for Jase Bennett, for the man had an edge to him that made a smart man walk with care.

In the middle of the hayfield, sweated down and sticky with dust and prickles, John decided that if Jase could have roped the devil into his haying, he'd have done it without hesitation. He forked a swath high and laid it in order against the central pole of the stack. The trampler, a young fellow who was trading out work with Jase for similar help with his father's crop, stepped the straw down into a solid thatch as John withdrew his fork and turned to get another load.

It had been too many years. Hard as he was, honed fine and tough by his harsh life, Colter found that this work used muscles he had forgotten he had. When Bennett called time-out for lunch, he was more than glad to sit with the rest in the shade of an elm while Mattie spread a cloth on the tail of the wagon and set out a meal fit for men working their guts out.

The two smaller children were in the wagon playing quietly with an old pot and a tin spoon. Mattie, who had worked along with the men, evidently had cooked half the night to feed the crew. Slices of cold bearmeat were there, of course, but a stew, which could not cool in the blazing Missouri heat, sat in an iron pot; green beans, boiled corn, ripe tomatoes, and peppers from the garden, as well as fresh corn bread, crowded together in the shade.

When everyone was stuffed and only Mattie was clearing away, her work seemingly never completed, Cleve, who had been raking swaths of hay near the men so they could fork it onto the stacks, looked up demandingly. "Tell us about the Indians, Cousin John," he said.

Jase grunted, but he raised no objection. Colter, regretting his lack of words, began one of his tales. But even as he spoke, he was reliving that misty morning on that creek feeding into the Missouri.

They were waiting for an opportunity to approach the Blackfoot on behalf of Manuel Lisa, the fur dealer, and to pass the time they had set traps along the narrow waterway. Being cautious, they ran the traps in early morning and late evening to avoid detection by any wandering Blackfoot. Colter wanted no conflict until he had a chance to meet formally with the chiefs.

It had been a good morning, and several beaver were in the bottom of the canoe, but there were a few traps left to check. The sun was rising, and it was growing too light to risk further exposure on the creek.

Something moved on the other bank of the stream, and Colter prepared to take cover. But it was too late. Now it seemed that almost the entire Blackfoot tribe stood along that bank—warriors, women, and children alike staring down at the canoe and the trappers inside it. The odds were impossible, and he paddled to shore and stepped onto the bank.

His partner, a man who had seemed steadier than that, lost his head, though Colter never had the chance to ask him what was in his mind. He pushed the canoe back into midstream and shot away, sending the Indian who had tried to take his rifle headfirst into the creek. He immediately sprouted enough arrows to quill him like a porcupine.

Of course, it was entirely too late to finish his commission for Lisa—the Indians were shouting and yipping, the women giving their shrill rippling cries of grief. Colter was quickly stripped buck naked and surrounded by angry braves holding a variety of weapons, any one of which could have given him his quietus.

There was a lot of palaver as the assembled Blackfoot tried to decide what to do with him. He understood a bit, although his Absaroka was a lot better than his Blackfoot, but nothing they proposed sounded comfortable. When at last one of the chiefs approached and stared impassively into his eyes, he held his ground and didn't let his gaze shift by so much as a flicker.

"You . . . run good?" asked the chief.

"Some think so. Some don't," he said.

There was more talk, and in the end the same chief led him out onto the plain. "You walk past rock. Then run." He grinned. "We follow."

Colter glanced back at the jostling shapes of the tribe members. There had to be hundreds of warriors there. And the river, with its complex of channels and islands at Jefferson Fork, the only place he could think of that might serve him as a refuge, was at least six miles away. Barefoot and naked—he drew a deep breath—at least he had a ghost of a chance.

He didn't hurry as he approached the rock, passed it, and kept walking. Not until the braves took off did he intend to take to his heels. Entirely too soon he heard their whoops and the thud of moccasined feet, and he dug in and moved.

The creek curved away in an arc, but a straight line would take him to the fork if he lasted that long. He was faced with a long series of rolls that swelled into hills and sank back into flats, and he pounded along, his feet hitting cactus, gravel, and sharp rocks. He kept his gaze fixed on the ground to help him miss what he could of the rough places and kept running.

He had always been a good runner, and he liked the feeling of pushing himself to his limit. His legs took up their rhythm, and he breathed steadily, taking it as easy as he could, given his need to stay ahead of his pursuers.

Although his eyes picked up and helped him avoid big rocks and the larger cacti, his mind floated apart from his laboring body. He remembered Kentucky, fishing or hunting possums in the forest. He recalled a lot of things, some pleasurable, many terrible, but they flowed over him as he ran on, feeling his feet flayed and burned by the terrain.

After something like four miles, he was feeling a stabbing pain in his chest at every step, but he didn't allow that to slow him. He glanced back from time to time and knew that he had left most of the Indians far behind. Only one was still hanging on, some quarter mile behind him.

He pushed his numbing legs into a further spurt of speed, and for an instant he felt he must stop and shit or vomit. No time. He had to keep his rhythm, for to lose it now was to lose the race entirely, though his nose was streaming blood.

He could see the cottonwoods ahead. That had to be the fork. He glanced back one last time. The Blackfoot was almost at his heels. A hard man to outrun, this one.

He whirled in midstep, ducked the lance the Indian flung at him, and plucked the weapon, broken on impact, from the ground. The warrior, still moving with his own momentum, came on, and John met him with his own spear.

For a moment they stood breast to breast, the Blackfoot's blood mixing with Colter's from his bleeding nose as it streamed down his bare chest and belly. Then the man heaved and gasped, and Colter stepped back and let him drop.

Ahead was the river. He forced his feet, now altogether too heavy and reluctant, toward the glint of the stream and plunged deep into the icy water. He swam as far as he could before allowing himself to drift softly to the surface and look back toward the shore from which he had come. So far, no Blackfoot had come into view.

He took time to assess the area. An island lay downstream, and at its head was a tangle of drift brought down in the floods of spring—good cover and within his capabilities for reaching it.

He dived under the drift, shivering now in the snow-water from the mountains, and came up beneath the logs. Not far enough. He ducked under more, working his way beneath the deepest layer of logs and branches. At last he felt that he had enough cover over his head; not even a ribbon of sky showed through the gaps between the dead wood.

Almost frozen now and weary past believing, he heard the Indians arrive on the bank. They splashed about in the water, and before long he felt the tangle rock and surge beneath the weight of men who seemed to be examining the drift closely. He breathed silently, in through his nose, out through his mouth, until the sound of padding moccasins could no longer be heard.

He waited longer as the water grew dark with oncoming night. When he dived under the tangle, swam underwater for a long way, and came up on the other side of the island, it was well on toward midnight. Even then he didn't come out of the cold water but kept swimming down the river until he was certain no Blackfoot would come so far to look for his tracks as he emerged.

He came to himself with a start, staring down into Cleve's wide gray eyes. "And then you were safe, Cousin John? You got away from 'em, and you were safe?"

He chuckled wryly. "Not to say safe, son. I still had a couple weeks' walk ahead of me, naked and barefoot. I sunburnt till you couldn't hardly tell me from a Injun myself. But I made it. After all, I done it before, once on a time, and that with a rifle ball in my leg."

The boy was longing for more, but Jase snorted and rose to his feet. "Time to go to work," he said. "Looks as if runnin' from Injuns didn't set you up too well for forkin' hay, John Colter. You look plumb beat-out." His eyes sparkled with malicious amusement.

"You're right, Cousin Jason. A whole different set of muscles. But it does make me travel fast, and tomorrow it'll be time I take my leave. Just passed by to see Cousin Mattie again." He managed to smile at the man, though he'd much rather have spat tobacco in his red face.

He didn't envy his cousin her husband, that was for certain, though her sons were nice little tads and well behaved. As the day drew on, he managed to stay near Cleve, and they had a few chances to exchange words and even a story or two as they went to the water bottle or paused for a breather while the hay was trampled, but Jase kept an eagle eye on the boy and scarcely allowed him time to breathe.

Colter was more than glad when dawn lit the sky the next morning and he could leave the Bennett farm behind. He was headed for Charette, up along the Missouri, and a certain girl who'd caught his eye years before. Maybe she would still be unwed.

He slung his pack across Knuckles's back and mounted. Mattie was on the porch with the smaller boys, but Cleve stood by his stirrup, staring up with awestruck eyes.

"Come back sometime, Cousin John. We'd purely like to have you!" he said, stepping back to let the horse turn back into the track leading to the main road.

"If I can I will," he said, feeling sorry to leave such a likable youngster behind with such an unappreciative father. "But things often happen that we don't expect, son. So if we don't meet again, I leave you my goodwill."

He fumbled in his possibles bag and drew out a battered rifle slug. "You might like to have this. It's the ball they taken out of my leg, back aways."

The wide grin of pure joy stayed in his mind's eye as he kicked Knuckles into motion and moved back along the track. That was a nice youngun, and he had a notion that rifle ball would be put away with his box of treasures, along with bird feathers and bright pebbles and the sort of trash children stowed away in private stashes.

He had had such a treasury himself when he was young and Mattie was a girl. Still smiling, John Colter rode east and north, toward the short but happy remainder of his life.

chapter

— 2 —

The thong dangling at the end of the bull-pizzle whip hung level with Cleve's eyes as he knelt in the barn. A slow scarlet drop trickled down the darkened leather to drip at last onto the snuff-colored dust of the floor. He knew that before another could gather, his father would swing his brawny arm to cut at him again.

Jase Bennett was a master hand with the whip. All the animals on his farm flinched or shied or kicked when they saw it in his hand, and his sons understood. They more than any other of his livestock suffered the attentions of that stained weapon.

Even as Cleve thought that, the arm lifted, the whip arced up and around and down, and he jerked, biting his lower lip until it bled. It had been years since he had given Pa the satisfaction of hearing him yell.

Snip yelped as if he felt his master flinch, although penned as he was in the farrowing stall, he couldn't get out to help. He'd never have bitten Jase, but he would have showed his teeth in a snarl. Jase would've killed an animal that bit him and most that threatened to.

Someone else gasped in pain as the whip cut into his back, and he knew with sick certainty that his mother had once again come to try rescuing one of her children from her husband's heavy hand. Cleve grunted between clenched teeth, "No, Mama! No. Go back!"

He knew she wouldn't listen. She might be little, and she might be religious almost to a fault, but nobody had ever denied her bravery. That was why her nose was crooked and some of her teeth were missing. Pa's heavy hand was there for anyone who crossed him.

"He didn't do anything, Jase! The mule kicked the shaft and broke it. Nobody could have stopped that!"

His mother didn't whine, he had to say that for her. Her voice was low, husky with anger, cutting as the whip in its own way.

But this time Pa didn't backhand her into the barn wall and knock her out. He turned, his eyes gleaming red in the lantern light, his arm rising, the whip curling high to swing. The lash flicked across her pale face, leaving a track of blood behind it, and he whirled the whip up again. This time Pa was beyond reason.

Cleve had borne a lot, and for himself he might have kept on bearing it, but Mama didn't deserve such treatment. He'd tried to fight Pa more than once

when he took after her, and as a boy he'd been
soundly beaten for it. Now that he had turned nineteen, he felt he might stand a chance with the old
man. Surely his years of field work, woodcutting,
and rock wrestling had hardened him enough. He
surged upward as the whip came down.

He hit Pa with his shoulder, bucking the older man
forward against the wall beside Mama. Cleve heard
her gasp as he grappled with his father, trying to keep
him down. He might as well have tried to hold down
Oscar, the ox that had pulled Pa's wagon to Missouri
from South Carolina. Jase rose as inexorably as the
tide or the wind, carrying Cleve's big-boned but far
lighter frame up with him.

He shrugged the boy off and turned again to his
wife, who had brought this shame on him. A son must
not attack his father, and it was a woman, of course,
who had tempted the boy to sin against the com-
mandment. Cleve knew his father's mind almost
better than the old man did.

The boy, his eyes filled with dust, blood coating his
arms and sides, stared about frantically, for the whip
had laid a red track across Mama's cheek. Pa might
kill her if someone didn't stop him. He was totally
beyond reason this time.

The pitchfork leaned against the stall where they
penned the sow for farrowing. He crawled toward it,
pulled himself up hand over hand, using its handle to
help. Once on his feet, the boy turned again toward
his parents.

Mama lay against the barn wall, her eyes closed, her
face a mass of blood.

"You've killed her, you bastard!" Cleve shouted,
raising the fork. "You've made her life a living hell,
and now you've killed her!"

Without pausing to think, he charged into the downward slash of the whip, his motion stopping only when the tines moved through Pa's upper arm, which was raised for the next blow, and crunched into the wood of the wall. The man jerked, freeing the fork from the plank, and reached to pull the thing out of his flesh. Blood was running down his arm, his side, staining the floor the same shade of red his son's had done. His eyes looked red too in the lantern light as he stared at Cleve, and he shook his head as if to clear his brain.

When his father came at him again, the boy bounced back, laid a hand on the stack of spare ax handles, and used the wood to fend off the fork, now in the hands of a madman. The old man forced him back and back until he in turn stood against the farther wall, holding the tines away from his throat with the handle. Bit by bit, the great muscles in Jase Bennett's shoulders strained to send the metal through his son's throat, and Cleve knew that would happen in time. He was strong, stronger than anyone his age in this part of Missouri, but Pa had the same build, augmented by years and years of muscle-cracking work.

He thought at first that the dull *chunk* he heard was his own flesh yielding to the pitchfork, but he felt no pain. He opened his eyes in time to see Pa rock gently from side to side and then fall flat on his face in the dust.

Mama stood behind him, another ax handle in her hands. She was scarlet with rage and shame and effort, and there was blood from Pa's scalp on the handle. This time he had pushed her too far.

Pa's eyes opened and looked up into Cleve's as the boy bent over him. The pale irises were filled with a vast astonishment, and a bubble of blood curled from the right corner of his lip. "She's kilt me, boy," he said, his voice a gusty whisper. "A damn woman!"

"My mother!" Cleve grunted. He felt tears starting in his eyes but he blinked them back savagely. "My mother, don't you understand?"

"A damn whorin' woman . . ."

Cleve's hands moved before he thought, and he whacked his father over the head with his own ax handle. The eyes rolled up, and the words stopped. He was out completely, and he'd be out for a long time. But things had changed, irrevocably and forever, in the Bennett family. When Jase woke again, he would kill the one he blamed for this, and Cleve knew that he would have to be that one, for he could run, and Ma couldn't.

He turned and found that his mother had fallen into an untidy heap, her bloody face white as paper, her skirts awry about her knees. He knew he must leave, but first he had to tend to Ma. It wasn't fit for her to lie there with her dress up and her face covered with blood.

He staggered to the well outside the wide doors and drew a bucket of water. Taking off his bandanna, he wet it in the bucket and knelt beside Ma, pulling down her spattered calico skirt before he began wiping her face with gentle strokes. He hadn't touched her since he was twelve and Pa forbade any of his sons to touch their mother again. "Ain't fit for a manchild to hang onto the titty too long," he had said. Remembering that, Cleve bit his lip again to keep from hitting his father a few more times.

As he wiped away the blood, tears spilled down his face. He didn't blot them away with his shirtsleeve. He wasn't ashamed of them. Ma had done her best for them all, even Pa, wearing herself to the bone for them. And this was what she got for it!

As he wet the rag again, she heaved a ragged sigh, and her eyes opened. For an instant she looked surprised to find herself there on the barn floor. Then she remembered, and her eyes closed tightly. "How . . . ?" she gasped.

"He's still alive, Ma. He'll be awful when he comes to. He'll kill me if I stay . . . I've got to go, but then he'll take out after you again." Cleve's words came out almost as a sob.

Now that he had had time to think, he could remember Pa lifting him high when he was tiny, tossing him up and catching him in arms as solid as roofbeams. He could feel the stubble of Pa's whiskers when he kissed his oldest son good night. Where had all that gone, that affection and care? Jase had closed himself off from everyone about the time Tim was born, and he never opened up again.

Ma opened her eyes once more and tried to push herself up enough to see the fallen shape in the middle of the floor. "Jase," she mourned. "Oh, Jase, I never thought I'd have to do such a thing to you when first we wed."

"What happened to him, Mama?" Cleve asked, setting his arm under her shoulders and lifting her to a sitting position, propped against a pile of hay. "Why did he stop being the man I remember when I was little?"

She gave a quivering sigh and sagged against his shoulder. "He thought Tim wasn't his," she whispered, as if the words still burned and stung.

The world whirled around Cleve's head for a moment. Mama had never had the time to step out on Pa, even if she'd had the wish, which he was certain she never did. "What made him think that?" His voice rose almost to a shout.

"Shhh! His mother came to visit when the baby came. She said all Bennetts had dark hair when they were born and it fell out and turned blond when it came back in, about the time they turned four. But Tim's was blond from the first. She told Jase the boy couldn't be a real Bennett, and he believed her. Why I will never know." She moved, trying to crawl toward her husband's lax body from which wheezing grunts came at intervals.

Cleve rose and lifted her easily, carrying her over to lie beside Jase. "I'll have to light out, Ma. You let him think I was the one hit him in the head. If he knowed it was you, he'd kill you for certain. I hate to leave you here with him, but there's the other boys. Gene and Tim will take good care of you and the farm if he's laid up for long. And maybe this'll make him careful and you won't get beat up all the time."

As if realizing for the first time what this evening would mean to her son, the woman turned pale. "Cleve! He won't kill *me*, but he will kill you if he comes to before you're gone. We got to get you away from here, right now!"

"You need the doctor, Mama. You're cut bad, and I can't seem to stop the bleeding. At least, I got to get Miz Dolbey up the road to tend to you." He dabbed frantically at the worst of the scalp cuts with his ruined bandanna.

A voice spoke from the dark doorway. "What's happened? Mama? Cleve? Pa . . . Pa?"

Eugene, only fifteen but well grown for his age, stepped into the red light of the lantern and stared at the unconscious man lying on the floor before him.

He turned pale and sat down abruptly on a drift of hay.

"Help your brother, Gene," said Mama. Her hand went out, very gently, to touch her husband's shoulder. "He's got to leave now and get as far away as he can before we let your Pa come to again. We can say I was knocked out for so long that you were scared to leave me, and while you tended me, your brother left. You don't know where he went."

Cleve marveled at her. He had always known she was better educated and quicker witted than Pa, and here she was, battered and bloody, proving it again. "You really want me to go?" he asked her.

He was marveling at the ease with which she, so fervently religious, was inventing lies. For her children, he suddenly realized, she would do anything, including knocking her husband over the head and perjuring her soul.

"Son, you got to. Jase will never forget this or forgive it. As long as he lives, you can't come back. But if you're alive, I can stand having you gone out there someplace, free and making a life, like Cousin John did long years ago. You remember when he came to visit, when you were little?" She caught her lip between her teeth and gave a little sob.

"If Jase beats you to death, I think I'll die too. I've had just about all I can handle, boys, these past years since Tim came. Having my son die would just about finish me off." Her eyes, a darker blue than Pa's, looked almost black in the red light; her pale face was still somewhat tracked with blood.

Gene was a lot like his mother. He glanced up at the saddlebags that Pa had brought from South Carolina, back before Gene was born. The leather was dusty but still strong, and he rose to haul it down and swipe away the musty dirt with a handful of hay. "Got to pack you up some stuff, Cleve," he said. "I'll get food from the kitchen if you'll pick out what you need in the way of clothes. You'll need a heavy coat, don't forget. It may be spring, but winter will come after a while, and you—" his voice broke, "you won't be coming back this way, I'll be bound."

That was true. Cleve sat still, shocked by the abrupt change that these few moments had made in his life. He could never set foot in this part of the Missouri country again. He wouldn't go east, for there were too many people there, thicker the farther east you went. He had to follow the river, he thought, west and north, up into the wild country where his people never went. Where Cousin John Colter had gone long years ago.

Gene was right. He was going to be cold and hungry and lonesome for a long time if he didn't find friends there. And what friends could there be where there were only savages, buffalo, Frenchmen, and the endless scouring wind his cousin had described?

He shivered, the blood, still damp on his back, chilly in the spring air. Gene, noticing, sprang to his feet to get a clean sack and wash his skin, wrapping him in bandages before helping him put on his shirt, laid aside for the whipping.

Pa snorted. Without rising, Mama hefted the ax handle lying beside her and brought it down again on his helpless skull. Jase subsided into unconsciousness, and Cleve went into a fit of hysterical laughter. Gene patted his shoulder and made him lean back against the wall while he brought a dipperful of water.

After gulping down some of the cold sweet well water, Cleve managed to control himself. He'd thought he would spend the rest of his life right here on the farm or nearby, raising a family, helping the folks when they got too old to do field work. Now, in one desperate half hour, everything had changed drastically.

If this night ever ended, it would seem like the wildest dream he ever had.

It was dark by the time Tim and Gene had caught the gelding Socks and packed onto him everything they and their mother could think of that might be helpful in the wild country Cleve was going to. "Take the mule too," said Ma. "You'll need a pack animal if you start trapping. Cousin John told me about bringing in packhorses burdened with almost more beaver plews than they could carry."

"Look, Mama, you're going to be right here, farming, for a lot more years. Coaly is the only mule you've got, and you're going to need him bad. I won't take him. What I'll do is find somebody going out to trapping country and hitch on with them. A sort of partner, you see? They'll have traps and such, I'm positive." Cleve hadn't much hope of that, but if Mama could lie for him, he could lie to save her feelings.

She had cleaned herself, changed her dress for another, more ragged one. Now she stood in the barn door, peeping out through a crack at the road that curved away beyond the lot fence. "There'll be a moon," she said. "At least you can see a little." She turned and wrapped her arms about him as high as she could reach. "Oh, son! I'd give my life . . ."

"It's all right, Mama." He refused to wince when she touched the whip marks. He hugged her close.

"I'll do what Cousin John did, go out as far as I can and trap beaver. Maybe someday Pa'll get better—or die—and I can come home again. You just tell him I done everything that was done—hit him, forked him, everything. You was out cold all the time, and when you came to, I was gone."

Tim came from the back of the barn. "You want Snip?" he called softly. "He'll be mighty lonesome with you gone."

Cleve thought for a moment. His dog, named for old Snip, his first one, had been his best friend since he was a youngun, and nobody else could get a hand on him. Jase had tried to kill him once when he wouldn't fetch a killed possum for him, but Snip had run off into the woods and stayed there until it was safe to come back again. It wouldn't be a good thing to leave him to Pa, and he wouldn't be much good to the others. "Let him loose," he said. "Might as well come with me, else Pa might just shoot him."

When the dog was bouncing about him, frantic with relief and pleasure to be at his side again, Cleve turned again to his kin. Gene looked pale and tense. He was old enough to understand just what this was going to mean to him. If Pa was badly hurt, he'd be the one to do the roughest work of the farm. His gray eyes were steady, however, and his hand didn't shake as he held Cleve's tightly for a moment.

Tim, his hair now the true Bennett faded blond, was only thirteen. Tears were running down his face, but he didn't let loose and cry out loud the way he obviously wanted to. This was something so big and bad and dangerous that the child couldn't quite handle it, but he was doing his best.

Cleve took him into his arms in a bear hug. "You take good care of Ma, you hear? If Pa tries to hurt her any more, you send Miz Dolbey's Tom after the marshal down to Springfield."

The rough head nodded vigorously against his arm. "We'll do it, Cleve. Just you take care of yourself. And . . . and come back, if you can."

Mama opened the barn door, straining at the heavy oak planks. Gene sprang to help her, and the two of them got it open enough for Cleve to lead Socks through the gap. He caught up Mama once again, her feet swinging clear of the ground.

When he set her down, she stared up, her face almost invisible in the moonlight. "Don't forget your Latin," she said, her tone serious. "Or your Bible. I worked hard to teach you, Cleve. Don't waste all that!"

He couldn't answer. He turned and mounted the gelding and rode away toward the river, leaving everything he had ever known behind him.

He headed north into the thin moonlight that managed to slip between the clouds hiding most of the sky. A whippoorwill was crying in the wood beside the road, and an owl fluttered softly over the track and into the trees again, hunting for his supper. As he neared the Little Sac River, he heard the water flowing over the stones of the ford and lapping gently against the reedy bank.

Socks splashed into the stream, hit the deep part, and swam. Cleve didn't bother to raise his legs out of the wet. After the night he had endured so far, what was a bit of water?

Once beyond the river, he kicked Socks into a trot, and they covered a number of miles along the dim trace before he stopped to rest the horse and himself. His back was burning as if Pa had lashed him with fire, and his heart was burning just as hot. Hatred was a bitter dose, he learned, as he nursed his anger and his loss.

He found a spinney and led Socks deep into the young trees, loosing his bit and removing the saddle. There was plenty of grass within reach once he tied him with a long rope, and he had more food than he could eat in a week in the pack Ma had put together for him.

As he rummaged for something easy to chew (his teeth loosened on the left side by one of Pa's blows), he heard a jingle. At the bottom of the pack was a chamois bag, and he knew with fearful certainly that Ma had given him most if not all of the painfully hoarded gold that had been her wedding gift from her grandfather.

He shook his head and munched on a soft biscuit, but the food wouldn't go down no matter how long he chewed. His mouth was dry, and his eyes felt hot and irritated; besides, his bones felt strained and sprung from trying to handle Pa, and he knew he had to sleep or he'd get caught before long. Getting caught by Jase Bennett after the night before was just about equal to wrestling a bear, and he had no intention of doing that.

To his surprise, he dropped into a deep sleep almost as soon as his head hit his saddle. His dreams kept almost waking him again, but he managed to stay asleep until the sky turned pewter-gray beyond the tender spring leaves above him. Socks was chomping noisily at the grass, tugging at his tether to reach beyond the grazed-off circle, and Snip was lying beside his feet gazing mournfully at his master.

He tried to eat again after washing in a brook he ran across soon after starting out, but still he had no taste for food. He kicked Socks, and they moved north and east until they found the main road that went east toward St. Louis.

Following it for a time, he located at last a track that followed a creek northward. It made sense that this big stream would end up at the Missouri, and that was where he intended to go. Surely a fit man who wasn't afraid of work could find a job with some outfit headed west.

Labadie was a tiny hamlet composed of a trader's shanty, four saloons, and a brand-new clapboard church. The wharf where river traffic tied up was its reason for being, and if Cleve was any judge, its time on earth wouldn't be long. Already the shacks along the road were warping, their unpainted boards gray and dingy.

The store was noisy, for a keelboat was tied up at the dock and its hands were busy inside. As far as Cleve could tell, whiskey was the only thing they were buying, and they drank it then and there, smashing the bottles on the floor and yelling for more.

The small man in charge of the place was turkey-wattle red with rage, though he didn't dare offend the roistering crew that was making a bedlam of his store. He kept trying to talk to the biggest man of the bunch, who kept shoving him back behind the counter and demanding more drink.

Cleve pushed into the midst of the chaos and put his broad back between the storekeeper and the keelboat men. "You happen to know anybody's got work for a willin' man?" he asked.

The little fellow glanced up at him, noted what he had done, and looked relieved. "Not to say here. But I got a newspaper out of St. Louis. Not more than two or three months old! Might be somethin' there to interest you." He pulled a sheet of newsprint from beneath the counter and spread it flat, holding it down with his elbows. "Can you read, or should I read it to you?" he asked.

The date on the front page was February 13, 1822. The paper was only a few months old. Cleve nodded and bent to look at the crabbed text, which was enlivened with sketches of fights, riverboats, Indians, and such. The front page was filled with advertisements, and he scanned them closely.

He didn't want any more farm work, that was flat! Nor did he want to cut timber or crew a riverboat. But in the middle of the page, framed in black, he found the thing he had dreamed of finding. A man named Ashworth was looking for enterprising young men to go west with him to trap. Up the Missouri!

FOR THE ROCKY MOUNTAINS, *The Subscribers wish to engage Sixty Men, to ascend the Missouri River, to the*

ROCKY MOUNTAINS

There to be employed as Fur Trappers. As a compensation to each man fit for such business,

$200 Per Annum

Cleve had never seen that much money in his entire life. The bit of gold Ma had sent with him was the only cash he'd ever possessed. He pointed to the ad. "You seen these fellows pass this way yet?" he asked.

The man bent and squinted at the page, then shook his head. "Not yet. They're due to come upriver most any time. I hear tell this Ashworth's a man keeps his word and pays his debts, and that's a thing I value."

Cleve felt a vast sense of relief. After years of abuse and hard work, cussing and slaving, was he about to find something coming out right for him? "There any place to stay around here?" he asked. "While I wait?"

The man shook his head. "You'd be robbed and kilt before you got your saddle off your horse," he said. "No, you better head for Fancher's. He's got a farm upriver about six or seven miles. Usually has plenty of work to go round and likes to have folks drop in and help out, particularly this time of year. If you don't mind a bit of farmin' to keep you supple, that's the place. He's honest, he's fair, and he's so tough, the river pirates don't never go anear him. Besides, he's got three mighty purty girls that are most tough as he is. Fancher's is what you might call a experience you oughtn't to miss."

Cleve grinned his thanks. "Got a blanket I could buy?" he asked. "One a dog would like? Old Snip scootches up so close on chilly nights, I can't get much sleep. Keeps scratchin' fleas and wakin' me up."

The deal was soon made, and a thick drab blanket was added to the pair Mama had packed. Then Cleve, following the directions the man gave, started up the riverbank, watching the ripples shining in the late-afternoon sunlight, feeling the warm breath of spring move out of the woods to touch his face.

He was on his way!

chapter

— 3 —

The Pawnee raiding party crossed the stretch of grassland below, their ponies moving steadily, their lances awhirl with feathers, their dark eyes quick and observant. But Second Son knew they could not see her watching, there on the ridge beneath a clump of brush. Any of the Tsis-tsis'tas, called Shi-hen-na by the Sioux, could dissolve into the soil itself, and she had learned that skill when she was still a child.

The Pawnee were raiding for horses, she knew. It was that time of year, for the winter had been harsh. They had, she felt certain, eaten a number of their mounts, and more had starved. It had been the same in the Cheyenne winter camp. Her people didn't need to lose any more, and she was glad that her hunt had taken her in this direction.

Tomorrow's dawn might see that group headed for her home territory, and it was always good to have advance warning of such danger. Though horses might be their main goal, warriors always became excited if it came to conflict, and often one or the other tribe lost badly needed people in the raids.

She could feel in the air a hint that the weather would change soon. A restless breeze gusted from the north from time to time, and her mare, waiting in the shelter of the cottonwoods along the stream behind her, whiffled uneasily and stamped a front hoof as if to hurry her along. Late spring brought frequent storms from the north, sometimes carrying a burden of unwelcome snow, and she felt that this was such a time.

The Pawnee were out of sight below the swells of prairie in the distance when Second Son rose and returned to Shadow, her gray mare. She should, she knew, ride for home and warn her people, but another, more daring idea had caught her fancy.

Once every month she made a lone hunt, a personal raid, or a long scout. Though she was accepted as a man, a hunter and a warrior, by her people after she was given her name by her father at the age of ten, it was better not to risk defiling the affairs of the other men at such times. Being a functioning female was not something that could be shut off by tribal acceptance.

She resented those enforced absences from her people and her brother, who was now subchief and spokesman for their band. Often she hunted, rode, and scouted more ferociously at such times than was normal even for such an unusual warrior as she. Like that legendary Atsina woman warrior-chief, she feared even herself at such times.

Now an audacious notion had her in its grip, and when she leapt onto the back of Shadow, she set out to parallel the route of the vanished Pawnee. The sun was down beyond the ridge of hills to westward, and she knew they would camp soon, probably at the well-used site near a small river that she knew from her journeys. If she traveled fast, she might well come upon that encampment before moonrise.

Shadow moved through the evening, her pace long and even. When the first blast of chill wind swept down from the north, she twitched her delicate ears and snorted, but her gait did not falter. Second Son, sitting easily and allowing the time to flow past her, paid no heed to the cold or the occasional spat of snow that struck her face. The two of them could cover a long distance before the mare must rest.

They moved in darkness once the last light faded from the sky, and when they stopped, it was at a tiny stream that the warrior had located years before. Both drank deeply before moving on, this time Second Son afoot and Shadow moving at an easy walk.

The storm blew itself out in time, leaving a light frosting on the new grass. The cloud thinned, and a wisp of moon glowed through in the east, glimmering off the patches of snow. Now Shadow ran again, her rider seeming a part of her as they moved across the plain. When they were in the edges of the hills, Second Son turned off to the south and made a long arc to a small valley through which a brook ran. She slipped down and left Shadow to graze while she climbed the rocky outcrops and went over the top of the ridge. Her moccasins were silent on stone and grass as she slid among the scanty junipers crowning

the height and started down toward the cup shelter-
ing the old campsite. She caught a faint trace of
woodsmoke and smiled, dropping to all fours as she
approached the undercut bank that sheltered any
cookfire from observation by an enemy in the flat-
lands.

The horses were in a group in the small meadow
that notched back into the ridge. Grass there was lush
in the spring, and she could hear nickers and snorts
as the animals enjoyed the rest, the water they had
drunk when their riders led them to the stream some
quarter mile distant, and the grass. A low murmur of
talk and an occasional grunt of laughter punctuated
the chilly night.

Lying flat, Second Son snaked through the fresh
leaves of the brush and the cold depths of new grass,
ignoring the ice that dropped into her face and down
her neck. Once, she froze in place as a warrior
stepped into view ahead of her, relieved himself
against a patch of sage, turned, and moved back to
the fire, adjusting his breechclout as he went. She
could see the mist of steam rise where the urine had
struck the cold ground. She smelled the sharp tang of
ammonia on the chilly air, but she didn't move for a
long time.

When the fire was damped and no sound of talk
rose from the cupped space, she moved. Her goal was
the horses, and she knew that several of the Pawnee
would be invisible, huddled into a niche or a shadow,
watching their precious mounts. She intended to
push the herd out of the valley, across the narrow
neck of high ground on which the camp was located,
and out into the prairie. Horses were the wealth of
her people. A great warrior was measured by the
horses he possessed, and stolen ones were best by far.

Her knife, for which she had traded furs long ago with one of the *coureurs de bois* who trapped in the mountains, was in its sling at her side, but she did not take it into her hand. Her bow and quiver were back with Shadow beyond the hills, her lance thrust into the ground beside that distant stream.

Only her coup-stick went with her into the dim reaches, which lay silent except for the sounds of cropping horses and an occasional nightbird's cry. Clumps of prickly growth and reaches of rough brush occasionally interrupted the flat bottom of the valley. She sensed those even when it was impossible to see them, avoiding any sound as she moved smoothly around the obstacles.

From her left she heard a muffled cough. Winter brought breathing complaints, and spring did not always clear them away immediately. One of the watchers suffered from such a condition, she knew at once, and it worked to her advantage. She had him located, and she turned toward the sound.

Lying flat, she listened to the earth beneath her ear. There was the muffled thud of hooves as horses moved about, the grind of grass being bitten off, the creaks and cracks always heard near any large outcrop of heavy stone. The watcher was keeping very still. Had he heard her, seen her, as she moved? She was as quiet as the soil beneath her, breathing silently, listening with all her might. Again there came the faintest hint of a cough, held tightly behind a clamping hand. He was still in place, doing his duty as well as his health would allow.

If another Pawnee stood watch, he would, she knew, be on the other side of the valley observing the other side of the herd. By the time he knew what was happening, it would be too late to stop it.

The inner lip of the valley was curved stone, cropping out from the notch in the ridge. She made her way toward the niche she remembered from her young days when she stood her watch over the Cheyenne horses. He would be there, she knew, keeping himself out of the chill as much as possible.

There was no need to creep up from the lower side of that spot, for she knew a path by which she could approach it from above. She located the shelving rock and stepped up, crawled a bit, stepped up again, moving around toward the little niche. When she was almost directly above it, she slowed even more, and a lizard's motion would have seemed noisy compared to hers.

The strangled cough came again, phlegmy and painful. She could tell from the sound that this one was hardly more than a boy, and she was glad that she had decided to count coup instead of killing him. It was not a brave thing to kill a sick child. Then she dropped through the slot above the opening, almost into the youngster's lap. Before he could move or react, she touched him with her coup-stick and whirled toward the valley.

"Hi-yi-yi-yi-yi!" she yelled, dashing down toward the shadowy shapes of the ponies.

The animals snorted, milled for a moment, finding the direction of the threat. Then she was among them, whacking shoulders and flanks with her stick, shouting, leaping onto the back of a handsome dappled stallion. He flinched, reared, but she forced him down with hands and knees and kicked him with her heels. The animal headed for the opening, out of the trap in which he found himself, urged on by the demon on his back. She grinned into the darkness, hearing the pounding flight of the other horses following the stallion. Nobody could stop them now. Anyone who tried would find himself crushed like pemmican.

Now she could hear above the galloping hooves the sounds of shouts and yips from the low ridge ahead. The warriors were awake and afoot, trying to stop the flood of animals pouring toward them. The stallion was terrified, kept so by her constant pressure. As he seemed to hesitate, she leaned forward and took his ear between her teeth. When she bit down, he gave a scream and tore off again, soaring over the ridge like an eagle. Behind him came the mares, colts, and yearlings, their eyes, she knew, rolled until the whites showed all around, their nostrils wide, their mouths dripping foam. Nothing that men could do would stop them now.

She would ride into her village in two more days with forty new horses in her string. Her brother would keep his coppery face very still, but his pride would shine from his black eyes. Her sisters would look sideways at this strange woman who wanted to be a man and succeeded. Her father, Buffalo Horn, old now and cared for by his two young wives, would nod and tell for the thousandth time how he had known when this one was just a child that she would be a great warrior and hunter. Why else should he call her Second Son? And there would not be one who could argue that he was wrong.

Tearing through the night, gradually guiding the stallion in a gigantic curve that would end where she had left Shadow, she drew a deep breath. It was a good life, no matter that not one woman now alive lived one like it. Others had, in the past, and they had brought honor to their tribes. When the sign of womanhood had left her body, she would go back to her brother's lodge and greet him with no great emphasis. Her own lodge nearby would be empty, for she had no wife, as a warrior should have. With so many horses, she could offer for any woman of suitable age in the tribe.

But this was not a possibility, no matter how her people pretended that she was a man. It would not be fair to the woman, who would want children, and she did not intend to commit such a crime against her secret sex. She was condemned to a lonely life, but she was also young, strong, and skilled. She would worry about loneliness when she was old if she lived so long. For now, she would ride the night wind in triumph.

Three days later, she drove those of her herd that she had been able to keep together into the Cheyenne camp. Some had strayed, and she thought they might have gone back to their former owners, but she still had almost four hands of animals left. She had stopped to bathe in the river some hours' ride before reaching her people, washing away all trace of her monthly inconvenience. There she donned her buckskin shirt, fringed with scalps she had taken with her own hands.

When she rode into the loose grouping of tipis, her eagle feathers streaming from her hair, her many captured horses snorting and raising dust beneath their hooves, those working about the camp ran out to see. She felt a surge of pride that she could bring such wealth to her people as many boys ran out to help her control her unwieldy band of mounts. Soon all were caught with rawhide ropes and tied in a long line about the lodge of her brother.

Singing Wolf was nearby, having been busy seeing to his weapons in preparation for the spring hunt. He came striding toward this warrior "brother" calmly, although Second Son could see the amusement in his eyes as he gazed at her catch. "A good raid, my brother," he said, his deep voice just controlling a chuckle. "There will be rejoicing among the people."

She leapt down and planted her lance in the ground at his side. "Be generous, my brother. I will take the stallion, I think, and two of the mares. The rest you may distribute among those who need them."

Her young nephew, Cub, sidled up to her and looked questioningly toward her choices. When she nodded, he sprang into action, removing them from the herd and leading them, with Shadow, away to the creek pasture where they could rest and fill themselves with the tender grass of May.

She turned toward her empty lodge, set at an angle and some distance from that of Singing Wolf. When she entered, she was surprised to find that her robes had been shaken free of dust and a fire was flickering in the stone firepit. One of her sisters-in-law must have kept it in readiness for her return, and her heart warmed at the thought. They were all busy with their own work; taking the time to prepare her place so that she would not find it cold and dirty was a great favor.

She removed her buckskin shirt and placed it carefully in the pile against the farther curve of the lodge. Her best leggings joined it, then her moccasins, now worn and muddy. She took a jar of tallow from its place and rubbed it into her skin, feeling it smooth the weather-cracks, and when she was done, she put on her usual breechclout and sleeveless shirt, glad to be done for a time with the trappings of victory.

Summer would come soon, with long hunts and weary days of labor. Every year for the past four or five there had been more and more conflict with other tribes that also hunted the great buffalo herds as they rumbled over the prairie. Kiowa and Pawnee, Sioux and Crow seemed to grow more irritable and touchy as time passed, and she wondered why this was so.

But that was true even within a unified tribe like her own—some individuals grated on others, as Long-tailed Beaver did on her. She managed to forget the adopted Pawnee captive each time she went on her lone expeditions, but always when she returned the thought of him waited for her, even when he was absent. When an entire tribe agreed that she was a man, why should a single member keep trying to overturn that decision? She had defeated the boy when they were children—running races, riding wild ponies, hunting rabbits, birds, and other small game. Always she had been better than he at such warrior-skills.

The other boys soon accepted her as one of themselves, but Beaver had objected at every step. When she reached the time of womanhood and her body began to fill out, he had behaved as if she were a normal girl and began watching her with moon-eyes. The strict rules of behavior among her people had forced him to control any overt desire, but his attitude made her most uncomfortable. And now she knew that he would soon return to the village to find it buzzing with her latest coup. He would be furious, and he would once again approach her, begging that she put aside her breechclout and her weapons and become a woman like all the others. That was not a thing she intended to do. She had no desire to spend her days working hides, quilling leggings and shirts, or digging roots and hunting for seeds on the plain.

Anger filled her as she stepped out of her lodge and saw her old enemy waiting near Singing Wolf's. His brows were drawn together, though he managed to control his features well enough. A glitter of something chilling made his narrow eyes sparkle, and she knew from old acquaintance that it boded no good for her. To her surprise, she saw the head chief, the Prophet, standing behind Beaver, with her brother and her father, who looked bent and frail as the breeze flapped his robes about his skinny shanks.

They all looked grave as she approached and said, "I greet you."

With a gesture for the principals to follow him, the Prophet led them toward his lodge, and they went after him, stooping to enter and sitting at once in a circle about the coals of a small fire. This was, Second Son realized, something important enough to require the ritual approach. Though it was hard to control her curiosity, she took her part in the polite talk, the passing of the pipe, the necessary preliminaries to a major palaver.

Then the Prophet spoke. "It is said by one here that the herd brought this morning to our people was not properly obtained. It is said that the warrior who claims to have raided for them took those beasts, instead, from a brother warrior. It is said that this constitutes a crime against our own people, and that demands expulsion from our village and our tribe."

She felt shock run through her body. Who . . . then she saw the glint of triumph in the eyes of Long-tailed Beaver, and she knew. "Who says this thing?" she challenged. Turning her head, she stared into each pair of eyes around the circle, and when she came to Beaver, she found him staring back with no shame in his dark gaze. "I see that it is my brother Beaver who has said this thing. I would like to know where he says this happened, how long ago, and how he captured all those horses? What tribe's were they? Which direction led him to their camp?" She managed to keep her voice perfectly steady and unconcerned.

"I took them from a band of Absaroka to the west. They camped for the night, and I killed four while stealing their herd. Then, while I rested, you came softly to my camp and stole them, in turn, from me."

"That is easily proven to be a lie," she said. "I can lead you east and north, to the old camp we all know where I took these animals from the Pawnee after counting coup only. No blood was spilled, and I waited to gather the beasts together and let them rest before coming home with them. Look at the stallion. You will see the Pawnee markings."

"You lie!" Beaver sprang to his feet. "You want to be a man, but now I will force you to be a woman . . . and not a wife but a woman on the plain, for any man's use."

Singing Wolf rose, without haste but with great emphasis, and turned to the Prophet. "My brother is an honorable warrior, brave in battle, virtuous in life. Is this adopted one, who has no great coups to his credit, no great skill with weapons, and no notable wisdom, to be allowed to belittle him, to cast him out without trial? This one was not even born a Cheyenne! We should ride eastward and north to see the ground where the horses were taken. Then we should decide what is to be done in this matter."

"No," said the Prophet, who had held a murmured conversation with the elder who sat beside him. "That is not necessary. Let us put it to the knife. The victor will stand blameless, whatever the outcome, for both are not of the Tsis-tsis'tas blood. The vanquished shall be cast out of the village and the tribe."

There was a shocked murmur, for it was forbidden for one of their tribe to kill another. But the Prophet held up his hand. "Long-tailed Beaver, though he has lived among us since he was a child, is not truly one of our people. Because of this, if he kills Second Son or if she kills him, there will be no crime committed."

Second Son sighed deeply, though she did not let that show to the others about the fire. This was vindication, for it showed that her brother warriors accepted her fully, no matter what Beaver might say to them.

The sun was almost overhead. Behind the village a circle had been marked off in the grass, and the center of that had been cleaned away to the damp dirt. A post was set in the exact center, topped with two rawhide thongs that hung almost to the ground and a tuft of eagle feathers that flipped in the light breeze.

Second Son stood in her lodge, stripped to breech-clout and a leather band that held her breasts flat to her chest. She greased her muscular legs, her short strong arms, her back, and her belly. Like most of her sisters, she was not a tall woman, making up in muscular development and stocky build what she lacked in inches. Now she hoped that her long years of experience and intense concentration upon making herself strong would serve her well.

Beaver was similar in build to the men of her tribe, tall and long-boned, and his reach was greater than hers. She must substitute skill for length of arm. It had always been enough, before now, to allow her to best her old rival, but he was so angry that his fury might lend him more than his usual ability.

Nesting Bird, Singing Wolf's first wife, came to the door of her tipi and scratched at the hide. "Is our brother prepared for battle?" she asked. Then, in a whisper, she said, "We wish you well, sister. Our hearts stand with you in the ring today. Beaver is an evil man, and we fear him."

Second Son stepped into the sunlight, her skin feeling tight with the oil, warm with the friction of her hands. "I am ready, sister. Let us go to the place where I must fight my enemy."

Together they moved through the village toward the circle. Already there was a crowd of people there—young braves, old women, children, all mixed together but strangely silent as they waited for this conflict to begin. Few had not been given meat or horses or hides through the skill and generosity of Second Son, and they knew well that even if Beaver had great luck at the hunt, he seldom shared with any but his own few cronies. Their faces were impassive, but she knew that many hearts besides those of her sisters-in-law would stand with her.

She went into the ring and stood beside the post. She tied the leather thong that had been painted red about her wrist before testing its limits. She found that she had two long steps in any direction before being brought up by the tether.

There was a soft breath from the watchers, and she looked up to see Beaver coming into the circle. His foster father and his brother Raven-Wing remained beyond the border as the man came to the post and tied his wrist tightly with the thong. Shirtless, he shone with oil in the sunlight, and his muscles coiled like snakes under his skin.

Second Son took her knife from its sling and held it, blade forward, haft solidly in her grip, waiting for a move from her opponent. She watched his eyes, ignoring the rest of him, for she had learned in a harsh school that it is there that one can read the intention of an enemy.

When he charged forward, his knife held low to gut her, she was already moving around the post. Barely in time, he whirled to keep her from stabbing into his kidney, though she managed to open a shallow slash in his lower back.

He paused, watching. She waited patiently, refusing to be drawn into a hand-to-hand situation for which her smaller build made her unsuitable. When he stepped forward, she circled backward around the pole, watching, watching his eyes. Again she avoided his rush, though this time he sliced her hip as she slipped aside. His momentum carried him a step farther than he intended.

Finding him within range, she seized his hair with the tethered hand, and her free one sliced away a long tuft. Then she was gone around the post again, and he was forced to follow, his tether shortening to match hers.

She dropped to her knees and flung herself forward between Beaver's legs. Her tether tightened into his groin as she jerked it hard, and he fell aside, struggling to free himself from the painful position into which she had put him.

That gave her the chance she needed. Second Son flung herself onto his body, ignoring the knife that raked across her shoulder, and plunged her own blade into his throat. The furious eyes glared up into hers as his blood gushed over her hand and puddled into the damp earth of the circle. Still he raked at her with the knife, but the strength was gone from his hand, and the angle was wrong for a fatal cut.

She pulled her blade from the man's neck, pushed backward against the heavy limpness of his arm, and stabbed downward into his heart. The long body quivered and went still, and she smelled the rank stink of urine as his muscles went slack.

Bleeding and sweaty, Second Son rose and slashed the tether from her wrist. The entire battle had taken place within a tight circle no longer than her leg, and now that ring was bright with blood. The post was painted with crimson to match that on the ground.

Singing Wolf raised his gaze to meet those of the Prophet, who nodded solemnly. "This matter is ended," he said. "There has been no shadow cast upon the Scared Arrows by this death, and no purification ceremony will be needful, for the dead man was, when all is said, Pawnee, not Cheyenne. We welcome our brother and his gift of horses. Tend him."

The sisters came around Second Son, not touching her as she walked, straight and proud, toward her tipi. Once inside, she allowed the women to clean her wounds and bind them with soft leather bandages stuffed with dried grass. She felt little pain now, though she knew that it would come in time.

She was rid of Long-tailed Beaver. She had been supported by her fellow warriors. Her sisters were proud of her and stood behind her, silent but solidly there.

What warrior could ask for more?

chapter
— 4 —

All his promises to himself had come to nothing.
Cleve found himself once again following a mule,
splitting rails for fence, and shoveling cowshit out of
the milking lot. He swore to himself that never again
would he make the mistake of swearing never to do
something, but he got so tangled up in all the complications that he quit in disgust.

To make matters even more complex, he was in
love with all three of the Fancher girls. As they had
not yet taken any notice of him, this was not the
problem it might seem, but it gave him many troubled
minutes before he dropped solidly into sleep, exhausted by his trying days.

Henry Fancher had welcomed him, for spring planting was in full swing and the new calves were popping up in the pastures like bluets. Even working his three daughters, his Amazonian wife, and the six variously crippled or incapacitated keelboat men who had taken refuge on the farm after being injured on the river or in knife fights, Fancher always needed more help. A strong nineteen-year-old who had been raised on a farm was something he would have ordered if he'd thought the order would be filled.

As for his daughters, Cleve had learned quickly that those damsels were more than able to hold their own. Now, lying in his blankets in the hayshed attached to the big barn, he stared up into the dimness, thinking of the girls.

Melissa was tall and still, at sixteen just a bit gawky. She was somewhat lantern-jawed like her father, but on her it was attractive. She was very bright and studied by lamplight long after everyone else was asleep. He had peered into the window of the kitchen, seeing the lamplight, to watch her bent over a book lying open on the table. It was a thick leather-bound volume that he later found was concerned with medicine. She bound up all the cuts, breaks, and other injuries on the farm and bade fair to become a pretty good doctor.

Galatea had hair the color of buttercups and a fist that could stagger a mule. He had seen Ramón, one of the keelboat men, get knocked onto his backside after annoying her the day after his arrival at the farm. Her eyes were cornflower-blue, but they brightened with interest only for the livestock and wild things—birds and animals and even fish. She should have been looking for a husband, for she was every day of eighteen, but that never seemed to enter her head.

Susannah looked exactly like her mother but was a slightly scaled-down model. She alone of the Fancher daughters looked capable of holding her own in a free-for-all, and she alone of that group was invariably gentle. He had seen her nursing orphaned calves, tying up the wings of downed hawks and quietly trying to save the lives of the predators that her father was determined to eliminate from his premises. At nineteen, his own age, she was the oldest.

Not one of those girls seemed interested in menfolk except as handy sources of hard labor. It hurt Cleve's feelings to think about that. Back home on the Little Sac, the few neighbor girls had seemed to find him attractive, though he'd never had the time to follow up on their sideways glances. He would love to see if Melissa understood his Latin, sketchy though that was, for all Mama's tutoring. *Arma virumque cano* . . . he wondered if a time would come when the old poem would slide out of his memory. He wondered if his memorized verses of Virgil would impress Melissa. He'd like even more to run his fingers through Galatea's sunny hair and feel her fingers touch his face in the way they did the newborn lambs. He would love to put his head into Susannah's lap and listen to her quiet voice singing a duet with the mockingbirds in the evening while she stroked his forehead. That was just purely the prettiest sound he'd heard since he was tiny and Mama used to sing him to sleep.

That was what his head wanted. With the other end, he wanted to do a lot of things that Mama would never approve of her son thinking about. But that wasn't something it would be safe to hint at with the Fancher girls. They'd peel off his hide and nail it to the barn wall to cure for shoe leather.

The corn and potatoes were planted now, and most of the fence was built. Spring had opened out; already the heat of summer was creeping into the Missouri country, and Cleve felt that it was time for the Ashworth expedition to appear on the river.

Living with three untouchable females, any of whom could break his heart or his neck at any moment, was getting to be a problem.

When, near noon the next day, Ramón called out that men, horses, and equipment were moving upstream along the trail, with keelboats loaded with equipment being hauled behind them up the river, he felt a jolt of excitement that shook him out of his romantic preoccupations. He ran at once to the barn where Fancher was supervising the building of new racks for the hay and waited until the big fellow turned toward him. "Sir!" he yelled above the pounding of hammers and the curses of the two rivermen who were awkwardly wielding them, "Ashworth's coming! I got to go!"

Fancher stopped in his tracks, his mind slowly taking in this news. He nodded to show he understood, and Cleve could see him recalculating the division of work once he left. But he came forward and thumped the boy on his shoulder. "Been good to have you here, son," he said. "Thought maybe one of them gals might take a fancy to you. I'd of liked that a lot. But they're a high-headed bunch, and it may take a tribe o' Comanche to tame 'em down."

Cleve took his callused hand and almost winced at the strength of the man's grip. "Thank you, sir. It's been nice to work here while I waited. You need anything for my keep and Socks's grain?"

"My stars, no, boy! You been workin' your tail off for weeks now. If anybody owes, it's me, but I got no money. Just land and cattle and gals. You go and get ready, and I'll tell Ma. She'll want to load you up with vittles, and the girls'll want to say good-bye."

Cleve had never expected to find such a good friend while he waited on the river. Now he found himself half regretting that one of those girls hadn't fancied him. There could be far worse lives than living here with a ready-made family, farming and raising children and fishing when the crop was laid by. But he smiled and nodded and moved to ready his pack and his gelding.

Socks had been out to pasture for weeks now, and he was more than ready to put his hoof in the road. It was a bit tricky getting him to stand while Cleve loaded him. About the time that was done, in the shady reaches of the horselot he heard a soft whicker and looked up. Galatea stood at the gate, holding the halter of one of the big brown mules that Cleve had come to admire while working them for Fancher.

"Pa thought you might need a pack animal. Gid here is a stout fellow. Carries a big load. And with what Ma's sending along with you, you're going to need him." She led the beast up beside Socks, handing the rein to Cleve. Without warning, not even a flicker of an eyelid, she reached for him, hugged him tightly to her rounded bosom, and kissed him soundly on the lips. He had kissed girls before, but they were very young farm girls who were too shy to say boo to a goose.

Galatea did not suffer from shyness. She smelled like hay and warm grass and girl, and Cleve found his mind going blank. But she pushed him away again and stood grinning at him. "I been wanting to do that but never got around to it. Too bad. We might have made a pair."

She turned and left him staring after her up the shady lane leading around the barn to the house. He had let all that get past him for this long? He had to be wandering in his wits!

It was too late now. Ashworth was in sight and would be passing the river road in less than an hour. This was the thing he was determined to do, following in the track of his cousin John, whose inarticulate stories, thrilling with half-spoken dangers and adventures, had roused something in Cleve that still boiled gently beneath the surface of his mind.

When he rode out into the river trail and waited for the trapping party to catch up to him, Cleve felt something like panic. Would Ashworth take him? Was this dream something impossible and beyond his ability to grasp?

But there was no problem. The party was anxious for strong men to join them, and late was better, the leader declared, than never. Even Snip, frantic with excitement, was a welcome addition to the expedition, for dogs, Ashworth assured Cleve, were valuable to warn against lurking Indians.

"Most of us never trapped," the lanky boy called Bridwell told him as Cleve fell into line beside his piebald mare. "We'll learn the tricks from the old hands with us, and by the time we get to the really serious trapping country, we'll know what we're doin'."

That was the way it turned out. Once past Francher's, the country was almost unsettled as they toiled upriver, mile after weary mile, for weeks. They traveled between wooded banks for a long time, passing the mouths of rivers and creeks, hauling the laden keelboats behind them and watching for Indian sign. When the trees changed to willows and cottonwoods and scrub, the land beyond them seemed flatter, rolling away in long reaches toward the horizon.

Cleve became acquainted with several of the group as they crept painfully along the great river, taking turns driving the string of packhorses or wearing calluses on their hands from the keelboat ropes. The Shooner brothers he found particularly amusing, for they were just alike, both blond, lively, and talkative. What one began to say the other finished, and Cleve found himself making bets with some of the others on what point in a sentence would mark the transition from one twin to the other.

They moved past the mouth of the Platte, and a scary ford that proved to be. Cleve, swimming the horses across three at a time, found himself swept out into the Missouri with the last bunch as an unexpected head of water arrived from some distant upstream storm. The dun he straddled struggled desperately, his head bobbing, his powerful shoulders heaving as he tried to make headway against the current to find land again. Cleve slid off the slick back and swam beside the animal, holding on to the ropes that tethered the other pair. But he soon realized that they would best be left to their own devices and loosed them to swim for it. When he made it to shore at last, he found the rest of the group camped, a fire built high and hot stew for all hands. He ate, but that night he shivered in his sleep at his narrow escape.

On they went, passing beneath tall bluffs on the east shore of the river and fording innumerable

smaller rivers and streams that drained into the
Missouri. Creeks leading down to the river ran deep,
and those they explored showed beaver sign, their
dams and the gnawed-off birches and alders along
the banks proving that this was indeed fur country.
But beyond the plains, in the Rocky Mountains, there
were beaver that made these look puny. Lewis and
Clark had brought back tales of the far country that
quashed any talk of staying here to do their trapping.

Cleve learned to handle the spring traps and to
build others of wood, using techniques he was assured that the Indians had used for generations. By
the time the party reached the area south of the
Arikara villages, he felt that he might give a good
account of himself when serious trapping began in
the distant Rockies.

Ashworth was sitting on a boulder discussing their
further route with Emile Prevot, the oldest and most
experienced of the French trappers, while the Shooner boys cleaned the pots after supper one evening.
The night was quiet, and the horses were grazing
beyond a thicket in a small meadow. Cleve had been
set to watch the herd, but Paul Levreaux called him to
the riverbank to secure one of the keelboats that was
being tugged hard by the current and threatened to
break its tether and float away downstream. The
evening was warm, the breeze fresh off the plains that
would one day become South Dakota.

As they wrestled the boat up short and tied more
lines to her, Cleve thought he heard something
among the willows beyond the river. "Paul," he whispered. "What's that?"

The Frenchman glanced once toward the shadowy
shapes looming over the water. "Mos' likely a frog,
perhaps, or a limb from a tree drop een."

Cleve hauled the knot tight as Paul gave him slack, and the keelboat was secured. He turned to take up his watch again, looking about for Snip, but the dog was gone on an evening rabbit hunt and didn't answer his soft whistle. He could hear the horses chomping grass and snorting softly beyond the thicket through which he must pass.

He was practicing his skills at moving silently through undergrowth, which was why he caught the horse thieves flat-footed. Two dark shapes, slippery and naked in the faint light of the stars, were moving among the gazing animals, and several more sprang up about the startled young man as if by magic.

With a shriek of rage, Cleve pounced on the nearest, bearing him to the ground. It was like trying to wrestle a panther, he found, for the sinewy body was hard as iron, oily and impossible to hold. He grabbed hard with both hands, catching the Indian by the neck, but by then, someone was behind him, and he barely managed to throw himself aside and miss being brained with a war club.

"Hey-y-y-y-y!" he yelled, although he had no time to fill his lungs for a properly loud shout. "Horse—"

This time something came out of the darkness and caught him full in the face. He fell backward, just short of unconsciousness, and felt moccasins brush past his cheek as the raiders rounded up the herd and headed across the river toward Assiniboine country. The splash of hooves, the surge of water against straining sides, came plainly to his ears, but Cleve couldn't raise himself or summon the strength to shout again. He seemed to drift in and out of consciousness, though he strained to remain alert.

Shots sounded from beyond the thicket. His yell had been heard and help was on its way. But the horses were gone! He dropped his head back into the damp grass, feeling the sour taste of failure. They'd been his responsibility. He should have been here on watch. But Paul was one of the leaders. Where had his duty lain?

Someone stooped over him and dragged him upright. "You are well, young Cleve?" asked a familiar voice, Emile's.

The boy sagged for a moment before he could straighten. "Just stunned, I guess," he said. "Head feels like it's been pounded, though."

"Assiniboine," Prevot said through clenched teeth. "Don't geev one damn about us, not even to take the trouble to keel us. They jus' want our horses. *Sacre bleu!* Thees weel make a difference in our plan, eh Guillaume?"

Ashworth was there as well, and now he stood staring into the night after the horse herd while others of the party straggled in from the places where their evening chores had been interrupted. Cleve had learned some interesting new cusswords in his time with the trappers, but now he realized that he hadn't scratched the surface of their inspired profanity. He regretted only that his sore head might not retain the best of this new vocabulary.

There were a lot of men in the group, but most wanted nothing to do with making plans, much less such unwanted and unexpected ones. So it fell to about a dozen of the most vocal to discuss with their leader what to do about this situation.

"We'd better fort up for the winter," Ashworth said at last. "It's summer yet, but timber will have to be felled to build a stout shelter and barricade big enough to hold sixty men. Even with so many hands, that'll take a long time, with construction to follow. We need to be settled in before the blizzards start, and that will happen in just a few months. I'll go back downriver to buy more horses, and when I get back in the spring, we'll start out fresh, well on our way, instead of having to drag up the river so far."

They agreed that this seemed the best plan, though a few were all for tracking the raiders and giving them what-for.

"We're going to have to be dealing with Indians all along the way," Ashworth objected. "If we get the reputation for being warlike, they're going to be the same. Let's take this very cool and calm, boys. Keep our heads, so to speak. This isn't the country we headed for, and we don't intend to stay, so teaching those red bastards a lesson isn't going to do us that much good. Tomorrow we'll scout around for a good place to build our fort. Then I'll head out with a few men to help me bring back the mounts, and that will be that."

They found a spot on a small knoll where a spring bubbled from the ground conveniently near the site of their fort, to be named Fort Ashworth. Along the river there were big trees, handy for the construction of their winter shelter, and again Cleve found himself swinging an ax. *Damn!* he thought. *Looks as if I'll never get away from this kind of work, no matter where I go or what I start out to do!*

The fort was a stout pen of logs, some forty feet by eighty, its rooms roofed with slabs that they sodded over with turf. Notching the ends of the logs, they fitted them together neatly, chinking the cracks with clay mud mixed with straw. It seemed strange to be building so solidly, putting up a pole-and-cat chimney, laying in stocks of firewood cut from the branches of the trees they felled for logs. It was midsummer, but winter came hard and fast in this country. A stock of seasoned wood was necessary if they were to survive the blizzards sweeping in over the long reaches of the plains to the north and west. All this work took time, no matter how many shared its demands.

Cleve knew that and worked hard at helping to provide the necessaries. But he found himself most intrigued by the instructions the old-timers (each of them at least thirty) gave to the greenhorns as they laid out the traps. He cleaned, wiped on the stinking musk, sprung and opened traps until he could do it in his sleep.

He went, along with Bridwell, Barrett, and other greenhorns, with one or other of the experienced trappers up every creek within walking distance of the campsite. As they built near the confluence of the Yellowstone and the Missouri, there were great numbers of streams available for their needs. In time Cleve could spot a promising creek as unerringly as any, and he felt that his life as a trapper was about to begin. The practice they gained while waiting here for Ashworth would teach them their trade better than any verbal instruction from the old hands.

The first blast of winter came early, flinging fine sleet on a rasping wind to patter crisply against the shutters and the logs of the shelter. In a pen on the downwind side, enclosed by log walls, the few horses left from the Assiniboine raid stamped and snorted, backing against the walls to keep the wind off their tough hides.

Cleve, coming in from hunting, moved among the animals, patting necks and smoothing flanks, speaking quietly to them as he went. Socks, in the best corner, which was just what his master would have expected, snorted and pricked up his ears as Cleve neared him. The wily gelding had managed to slip away from the Indians and returned to the camp two days after being driven off. It didn't surprise Cleve. The mule Fancher gave him was gone, he was certain, forever, probably eaten by the Assiniboine.

Snip was tied there in the corner with Socks, and he came out to greet Cleve joyfully. Untying the rope that had kept the dog from following him, he led the way into the house where a huge fire of four-foot logs roared in the hearth.

Prevot was propped in a rude chair of woven branches, his feet near the blaze. His face was red, and his dark eyes snapped as he talked with William Shooner. The youngster was toasting beaver tail on a forked twig over the coals at the edge of the fire, and the smell of the juices dripping and sizzling made Cleve's mouth water.

"By damn, young William, she is terrible, thees storm. I am caught, me, Emile Prevot, too far from home and without my *cheval*. I am freeze *mes testicules* completely *hors de combat*. Should a lovely mademoiselle walk into thees room at thees moment, I should have to turn away and weep."

"Emile, you're pullin' my leg," said Bill. "You Frenchies can get it up for a she-bear in a tornado. I seen a Frenchie back home could come home roarin' drunk, get beat to flinders by his old lady, and get her pregnant that same night. Don't josh me about bein' out of it."

Prevot laughed and turned to greet Cleve, nodding toward the others, who were gathered beyond the hearth, playing cards by the firelight, for the shutters were tightly secured against the searching wind. "You miss nothing, Bennett. We are ver' dull here, when the wind blow cold. You keel anything? Meat, she weel keep for a long time now."

"Got a doe upstream, but it started in to blow and sleet, so I hung her up high in a birch tree. She ought to keep fine there till we can get back to cut her down. Saw a bear, but he was too far-off to shoot. That'd have been a *lot* of meat."

Paul Levreaux left the cardplayers and moved over to sit beside Cleve on the floor. "You be careful how you kill bear when you are with the redskins, young one. Some tribe, they say the bear is brother to them. They never kill, never eat bear and think little of those who do. Just remember, the Indian is a strange fellow, and his ways are not ours. His religions are ver' complicated, and if you wan' to lose your hair, trip up on a *point theologique*."

"I thought they was heathens," the young man said, staring at the Frenchman. "I never heard they had no religion atall."

Both the French trappers laughed. Wiping his eyes, Prevot said, "That is because those back in the East never know Indian, never talk with their great men, never look into their belief. No, they are not Methody or Anglique. Not Catholique, as I, or any other Christian faith, but they have their own God, and he is not ver' different from the one we know. You watch, see with your own eye, young Cleve."

The boy nodded and headed for his blankets in a snug corner, protected from draughts by the piles of supplies that were sheltered in the fort. His boots, damp from the sleet-laden blast, came off with a sigh of relief, and he lay back and tugged the thick wool over himself. Eyes closed, listening to the slap of the wind against the shutters, the tickle of sleet on the wall at his head, he thought about what Prevot had said. Did those red savages actually have a religion of their own? He doubted it would include Sunday school, preaching, stiff collars, and shoes, but those, it came to him suddenly, were not really religion. They were just the outer signs of it. He wondered drowsily what Mama would think of such notions and decided that she would disapprove strongly.

As he relaxed, hoping that no ambitious wolverine would climb up and mangle his doe, he slipped into a half doze.

The people his cousin John had described were interesting if dangerous. They had not killed him at once, though they easily could have done that, as they had his partner. Could it be that some vestige of human kindness lived within those painted skins, beneath the black locks and the feathers?

Could it be . . . But sleep interrupted his questions.

Cold weather didn't stop the trapping. Indeed, it added incentive, for the beavers' fur thickened to keep out the cold, and those plews gathered in winter were prime. It was good to have an excuse for going out to run the traps. Being cooped for too long inside the fort's confines would have driven the motley group of young men out of their wits and tempers.

Cleve was with a group of three who went off every morning to check the cluster of creeks they had found without the aid of any of the old hands. As time passed, the groups entered into a sort of competition for who could bring in the most and finest skins, and Prevot, ready for anything that would maintain good humor and keep the traps busy, proclaimed that the winning team would be given a bonus of fifty dollars to divide among its members.

Cleve, with his partners the Shooner brothers, was determined to win the bonus, and the three were out early and late, even in the bitterest weather. Dawns so dark that they looked like midnight became familiar to the young man as he staggered out into the snow, now hip-deep and drifted in spots over his head, to check the traps they set wherever they could find free water in the beaver ponds along the creeks. Furs were stretched on willow frames and hung from all the walls. It was a good trapping season, Prevot declared, even though they had not yet reached the mountains. These animals were smaller than those they would find farther west, but their furs were prime. By the time all the water was frozen iron-hard, there was little room to store more plews.

Tempers, however, did not fare as well as the trapping. Being confined while the wind shrieked and blew smoke down the chimney and trees cracked like gunshots as they froze in the surrounding woodland was not something young men took to kindly. Fights became almost a daily occurrence, and only the firm hands of the old trappers kept things from becoming explosive.

Cleve had lived with constant dread all his life, and this was nothing new, though it was a matter he had hoped was left behind him in Missouri. Fighting held no charm for one who had suffered as he had, and he moved into one of the storage rooms in a corner of the horse pen. He built a chimney of rocks pried from the creekbanks, or he would have frozen stiff his first night in solitude. But even the smoke and the chill of his new quarters were better than bickering over cards, relative skills, who really should have won that fifty dollars, or just all-around bad moods.

Bridwell joshed him considerably about his hermit-like quarters, but the young man was good-natured about it. Being alone, quiet, with nothing but the occasional stamp or snort of a horse outside his door, was far preferable to the babble and stink of the main room of the fort. He slept deeply, feeling like a bear that had gone into hibernation. Sometimes he slept most of the day, for there was no excuse for getting out of the fort now. It made no sense to risk being lost in the snow and dying uselessly, far from home.

He drifted. Memories of his childhood, the days when his father was still warm and caring, mingled with recollections of his cousin's visit so long ago. Beatings whose scars still crisscrossed his back entered his dreams, but always there was a solid and comforting presence where his mother was, and his brothers. Whatever Pa did or still might do, Cleve was tied to the family. He missed his brothers and his mother with an intensity that was almost pain. A time came when he paid no attention to day or night, just boiled coffee on his smoky fire and toasted strips of venison or beaver tail and chewed them absently, his eyes half closed, his mind far away.

When the uproar in the walled enclosure woke him, he wasn't quite certain whether he had dreamed or actually heard the screams of horses and the rattle of hooves against frozen ground and logs. Cleve rose, dropping the blanket from his shoulders, and grabbed his rifle, which always leaned, fully loaded except for the primer in the pan, close at hand. He primed it, put on the fur cap he had made from a badger hide, and slipped his feet into his boots before opening the door and staring out into the night. It was cold enough to freeze the balls off a panther, but the sky had cleared for the time being. A frozen moon peered over the trees to the east of the fort, and in its anemic light Cleve saw dark shapes boiling about. Snip, at his heels but cautious among the horses, gave a whimper of warning.

Then, at his elbow, he heard an inquiring *whuff!* His nose, even in the cold, caught a rank scent as he turned, his gun coming up, to meet the huge bulk bearing down upon him. A bear! By damn, it was a bear, right in here with him! A faint paler patch showed where the beast had clawed his way by pulling down several logs from the top of the wall.

The roar of his brand-new Hawken (supplied by the Rocky Mountain Fur Company) blended with his shout for help. The bear didn't slow, although there was no way he could have missed him at such point-blank range. Emile had said that bears were hard to kill, but Cleve hadn't really believed it until now.

There was no time to reload, even if he'd had powder and patch and ball to hand. He backed away, stepping on Snip, who yelped shrilly and dodged, almost tripping his master. Cleve didn't blame him— he wanted to yelp himself. He wished he had the nerve to turn his back on that dark shape and run into the fort.

The bear went down on all fours and came toward him a few steps before rising again on his hind legs. His roar held a note of pain, and Cleve knew then that his ball had gone into him. But the upright form was terrifyingly huge against the sky, and Cleve backed cautiously again, feeling for his dog before putting a foot behind him.

Snip dashed between his master's feet, moving toward the bear. Amid a chaos of howls and roars, yelps and snorts, the two became one blurred tangle. The bear's growls rose in intensity; Snip gave an agonized yelp. It was impossible to tell what was happening, and Cleve realized that his dog was about to be torn apart.

He stepped to the chopping block beside the woodpile for the ax and went after the two, hoping that he wouldn't deal a fatal blow to the mongrel. As he went forward, the tumble rolled toward him amid moans of effort and howls of anguish. Snip was not faring well, Cleve knew, and he waded into the fray, trying to make certain that he didn't lop off any part of his dog as he whacked into the tangle of fur about his feet.

By that time, others had come out of the fort, holding up blazing sticks snatched from their fire. The moonlight mixed confusingly with flickers of torchlight, and Cleve found himself blinded by the illumination. Shots rang out, and a slug zinged past his head.

"Hold your goddam fire!" he shouted. "I'm in the middle of this mess!"

A wiry tail whipped against his legs. He leaned the ax against his hip and bent over to scrabble for the wildly waving appendage. At last he found it, grabbed it, and pulled. Snip yowled as Cleve jerked him free of the bear's claws and flung him behind him as hard as he could.

There was no time to wonder if the dog might be fatally injured. The black bear, all three or four hundred pounds of him, was rising to his hind legs again, reaching out with those powerful forelegs to deal with this danger. Claws ripped across the young man's face, and he felt blood slide down his cheek and over one eye. The huffing, stinking beast surged forward again, too close now.

Cleve swung the ax. There was a sound like chopping kindling on a block, ending in the *smush* of smashing a ripe watermelon, and the huge beast fell forward on top of him. All the breath was crushed out of his lungs, and his ribs creaked, unable to rise to refill him with air. His arms and legs were helpless, pinned beneath that dead weight. He felt something hot—the bear's blood or his own, he couldn't tell which—all over his face and chest. He wondered if he was fatally injured, how Snip was, how the news of his death would get back to the family. His head felt as if it were about to burst, and his eyeballs were popping out.

Something cold touched his forehead where it thrust free of the bear. Snip. There came a whimper, a tentative lick, then a flurry of sharp barks. At least his dog wasn't dead. He didn't even sound hurt much, and that was a blessing.

"Now, then, younker, hold still. We'll get you out of there. Just goin' to take a bit of work to move this mountain lyin' on top of you." That was Garner, the oldest of the experienced trappers.

Cleve grunted as some of the weight shifted, settled back again, and then began to move steadily to one side. The light helped then, and he tried to push himself up with both hands. The pain stopped him almost at once as the others pulled him out.

He wriggled arms, legs, neck, and everything worked, though stiffly and painfully. Having so much bear fall on you wasn't something that left you in the same shape it found you. He just hoped that nothing important was cracked or broken, and he dreaded trying to stand up and finding both legs busted.

Two sets of hands caught him and dragged him upright. The scant dozen horses were calming in the hands of their owners now, and Snip, assured that his master was all right, was sitting on Cleve's right foot. He dropped onto the chopping block and steadied himself before taking the time to look at his kill. The ax was buried to the haft in the bear's skull, its handle bright red with blood in the torchlight. One eye of the dead beast stared sightlessly into the torchlight, tiny flames reflected in its glassy surface. That was one dead bear, and no joke.

"Damn!" said Cleve. "What a night!" He reached down and ran his hands over Snip, who was panting, whining, shivering with excitement. Other than ragged clawmarks and a couple of missing bits of hide, the dog seemed to have come out of the scrap without major injury.

Prevot, coming up beside Cleve, chuckled. "Bear-Ax Bennett we must call you, yes? Never have I seen a man kill so big a beast with the ax. You weel carry that *nom de guerre* so long as you are among trappers, *mon brave*." He chuckled wickedly. "And these men, they weel turn it about, so, and in time you weel be Bare-Ass Bennett, or I do not know the breed. How do you like to theenk of that, young Cleve?"

There could be worse nicknames, Cleve thought as he staggered away to his blankets. But he didn't know what they might be.

chapter
— 5 —

Winter lay white and forbidding about the village. Although he had chosen a well-protected spot sheltered by a high ridge that folded like an arm to north and west, Singing Wolf knew that the cold was affecting his people. The days ran slowly in winter, and the old and even some younger warriors were beginning to cough. The very young had begun to grow pale and listless.

The subchief sat beside his fire gazing into the nest of glowing coals. The babble of his own young did not disturb him, nor did the quiet voices of his wives, whose busy fingers were stitching deerhide or decorating leggings with porcupine quills. The winters were not as long for women because their work never ended.

He longed to ride out after wapiti, elk, in the hills beyond the ridge, though the cold pained his bones since his last wound in a raid. He thirsted for the thunder of buffalo hooves on dried earth. He felt the longing of the other hunter-warriors for activity there in the lodges clustered about the central clearing. Hunting or raids stirred the blood to white heat and cleared the mind of musings that troubled the cold gray days of storm.

His brother, Second Son, entered the tipi, along with a blast of frozen air, and Singing Wolf gestured for him to sit. Neither spoke, and he knew that the long dull day had driven this one to seek company. He wondered, not for the first time, how it might be to be both a warrior and a woman. He would not, he thought, have the courage to do that, whatever his skills and ambitions. As he glanced up, his gaze caught that of the one who sat beyond the fire. He felt a chuckle rise in his chest, for they two understood, whether or not they could admit it to others, that theirs was a unique relationship.

At once that of sister and brother, close as that was, and that of brother and brother, it gave unusual dimensions to their regard for each other. In ordinary circumstances, they would not have been allowed to associate more than absolutely necessary, which would have been a sad thing. They had never spoken of it, but he understood her sense of humor, which reflected his own, and both laughed internally at the charade accepted by their village and the entire tribe of Tsis-tsis'tas. Why could they not simply say, "This is a woman who fights and hunts and rides and raids as well as a man," and let it stand so?

Her monthly absences from his lodge and those of their fellow warriors made it easy for men to ignore the problems that might arise from her being female. The women were silent on the subject, as was proper, but not even his own wives ever commented upon his unusual "brother," and often he wondered what they thought of Second Son deep in their hearts.

He sighed. Looking up, he said, "Meat grows scanty, brother. Wingless Hawk sickens, Running Buck coughs and burns with fever. The small ones are thin. Yet the snow is too deep to take a hunting party into the mountains." His tone was tentative, filled with suggestion, which he was unsure whether he wanted her to catch and follow up.

"Then we must go, the two of us, to find meat. The big elk will be pawing the snow in the valleys, and we should find enough to fill these hungry bellies in our village," she said. There was amusement in her voice, as if she knew how he hated the thought of going out into the snow and the icy wind.

"We will take the big mare and the young stallion for carrying back our kill," he said, accepting his fate stoically. "I will ride Pointed-Ear . . . you will take Shadow?"

She rose. The fire glowed on her face, making her eyes shine, and he knew that she was glad to go away from the lodges and the boredom of the long days there. "Yes. I will be ready soon, Na'niha. And let us take three packhorses. Today I feel that fortune will be with us."

The snow on the slopes was not so deep as on the plain, for it had slipped down into fat collars about the slanting boles of scattered spruce and lodgepole pines. The two hunters led their horses up the steepest inclines, but when they reached the top of the ridge, they mounted and moved along the scoured rock on the windward side of the hill.

Beyond the next valley the first mountainside rose, and it took half the day to reach the thin furring of trees there. The horses were exhausted with struggling through drifts by then, and the chief helped Second Son scrape bare a patch of withered grass for them to munch on while the Cheyenne hunted. Such weary horses could not go where they intended going, nor could they move silently through snow.

On the other side of this knee of the mountains lay a valley so lush with grass in summer that the dried forage sometimes lasted the deer, elk, and moose most of the winter. There if anywhere they might find meat for their people.

By nightfall, they were beyond the top of that slope looking down into the cupped valley and the frozen stream winding along its farther side. Outcroppings of rock amid thick spruce offered shelter, and they stamped out the snow to form a protected pocket out of the wind, where they wrapped themselves well in their buffalo robes and dozed through the night.

The morning sky was gray and forbidding. "Go and bring up the pack animals," Singing Wolf told his companion. "We will need them to bring down the meat if we find game down there. I will scout the valley and scent the wind."

She slipped away through the snow, and he turned his face downward, watching his steps, for he did not want to slip down the steep incline to end up dashed against the rounded boulders lining the stream. He angled along the slope, tramping out a path along which Second Son could bring the horses later if they succeeded in finding deer or elk.

Even as he thought that, there came a sound that made his heart bound with excitement. A moose was very close. The great animal would provide meat for many mouths if they could kill it. A snort and a grunt from a thicket below told him where the huge beast must be. Two hunters, afoot, armed only with lances and bows, would be hard-put to kill a moose, even if they managed to corner it. They could not run it down with the horses in such deep snow. No, there had to be a better way.

He moved along the slope toward the lower end of the valley where the stream passed between two enormous icy boulders at the foot of a sheer cliff that soared upward to lose itself in the mist above. Only if the moose went away upstream, toward the mountain slopes, could he escape. Surely they could use this narrow neck in some way to stop the beast, make him turn so their arrows could find his vitals.

It was a terrible effort to move through the snow-clogged forest of the slopes, but Singing Wolf made a circuit of the cup, noting every bit of cover for a hunter, keeping the thicket in sight, for if the moose moved away, he must know and follow. However, the beast, probably a young male, seemed content with his shelter and the browse it contained. There was no sign that it might move.

The hunter moved on, thinking of the best way to kill his quarry. They had to keep him from bolting up the fan of inclines upstream and east of the stream. Beyond the creek on the west was a rocky slope, rotten with shale and ice. If he ran there, he would break a leg, and they would have him.

And what if he broke for the lower route, trying to pass by way of the stream through the narrow neck at the southeast end of the cup? There must be a way to stop that gap, yet there was no time to find logs and pull them down. Only the body of a warrior might hold back the great moose. It would not be a safe or easy task.

When he climbed back to the spruce-sheltered cranny beneath the boulder, Singing Wolf had the nucleus of a plan working in his clever mind. By the time Second Son joined him leading two horses, he had refined it to a workable scheme. But it was getting late again, and this was not a thing to do in the dark, even in the glimmer of snowlight. Another night must pass before putting his plan into action, so the pair built a tiny fire and warmed their half-frozen feet before it while heating their strips of jerked meat and chewing on their scanty ration of pemmican.

"I will watch in the streambed," Singing Wolf said, laying a knot of wood on the coals. "You must come down from the northwest making noise to drive the moose from his covert, yet you must not come so fast that he becomes frightened and breaks uphill, away from us both. Drive him carefully, slowly, keeping him in motion without truly alarming him."

She leaned forward, eyes shining. "It is a good plan. A moose will feed more mouths than many deer or even elk. There will be hide and sinew, brain and bone and gut for making bags to store pemmican. Our people will be glad to see us return. *If* we return."

First light found them in position, Singing Wolf hidden in the cleft between the boulders, Second Son already in the trees to the north of the valley. Both carried bows, and both had short lances thrust into the straps holding their quivers in place. The chief held himself still, although he was chilled deeply and the old wound ached and throbbed as he waited for his brother to bring the prey to him.

He heard the irritable grunts and snorts when the animal realized that someone had intruded into his winter quarters. Then there came the dim plopping of his great hooves in the snow. No sound showed Singing Wolf where Second Son might be, but he knew her too well to doubt that she was well placed and moving with care.

The sky grew lighter, and a hint of silver touched the clouds, which now were higher and less oppressive than they had been before. Against the pale blanket of snow he saw the moose coming toward him, its head cocked so that one eye could observe its pursuer. That meant that it was paying no heed to what might lie in front of it, which was a good thing.

Singing Wolf readied his bow, and when the beast was gathering its legs for the leap down into the bed of the creek, he let fly an arrow. Well aimed though it was, the shaft did not bring down the moose, though it stuck behind its shoulder, caught in the tough muscle there instead of driving through a finger's width farther back and going into the lungs. The animal, losing its concentration in the surprise of its wound, plunged down the bank into the creek and skidded forward, blood marking a plain trail of scarlet on the snow. Blind with pain and fury, he plunged ahead toward the slot between the cliffs, now watching even more closely for the enemy behind.

Again Singing Wolf loosed an arrow, the shaft singing shrilly through the frozen air, and again it went home, into the broad chest that now was only a few man-lengths distant. But this was a huge animal, its hide thick, its pad of muscle all but impenetrable. To kill it, he needed to be horseback, shooting down through the back and shoulder into the lungs to pierce the heart. From this position he was not going to be able to do it.

Then the thing was upon him, and he thrust with his lance as the great body came within reach. Warned by this new wound that another enemy was near, the animal bellowed with pain and rage, and turned to destroy this puny two-legged thing in its path.

A shrill whoop went almost unnoticed as Singing Wolf realized that his death stood there on four legs, head lowered, platelike horns ready to smash him against the rock. He called his death song even as he tried to dodge. Then the head lifted, and the man saw Second Son on the back of the moose, thrusting into those powerful lungs, her lance moving down and down.

The beast twisted sideways, slinging its head to dislodge this new agony. Even as the lance found its heart, it swung those great horns, and they struck the warrior as the moose crumpled forward in death.

Second Son flew though the air and struck one of the smaller boulders beside the stream. Distinctly, Singing Wolf heard the crack of bone, and as he moved toward her, he hoped with all his being that it was not her skull that had broken.

The moose was still kicking reflexively as Singing Wolf edged past the great body and approached his sister. Second Son lay in the snow, her body twisted strangely, her face hidden in a drift. When he bent over her, he thought for a dreadful moment that she might be dead.

However, a thumb thrust hard beneath her jawbone found the steady beat of her pulse, and he sighed and tried to think how best to move her. He had seen injured warriors talk and laugh with those about them until the time came to lift them. At that point, some had jerked and died, and the chief knew that something inside had broken when the wounded men were moved, so he worked so very carefully as he straightened her arms, her legs, and gently moved her head and her neck to align with her body. Hips, back, bit by bit, he worked to get her into a position for tending her injuries.

There was a dark bruise already forming along one cheekbone and the side of her neck where the wide horn had struck her. One arm, the left, was broken near the shoulder. Her legs were undamaged, and no blood oozed from her mouth, which relieved Singing Wolf. That was the sign of an internal injury that always proved fatal.

When he checked her carefully there in the snow, he covered her with his cloak of buffalo hide and moved away, trying to hurry through the deep drifts to where she had secured the horses. He wanted a travois on which to secure her limp body.

The journey homeward would be a difficult one, burdened as he would be with a wounded warrior and a great deal of meat. But Singing Wolf had no intention of wasting his sister's effort. The moose would go with them, and the tribe would wear out the shank of winter with enough red meat to bring health to their bodies and strength to their muscles.

Once he had Second Son warmly wrapped and tied onto the travois, the hunter turned to their prey. His knife worried through the tough hide, letting steaming guts tumble into the snow, and he proceeded to clean and put aside every part of that beast. The meat came first. Both horses were snorting with dismay at the smell of blood and death that surrounded them while he loaded the red haunches, racks of ribs, the huge staring head with its branching plates of horn, onto the other travois. Once that was done, he turned to the hide, which he rolled with the bloody side inward, tying it over the heap of meat and tucking the trailing legs and strips inside the rawhide bindings.

The guts were easier after he emptied their contents into the snow. He cleaned the stomach and used it as a bag into which to pack the remainder of the long stained bowels and the heart, lungs, and other tidbits. It took most of the day, and when he was done, even his tough body was weary. Yet there could be no rest. The smell of fresh blood would draw wolves, bears, and other predators out of the mountains, following their noses toward this feast. He must be gone from the valley before dark if he was to save this bounty for his people.

The two horses that had been brought up the ridge were burdened heavily with the remainder of the kill on their backs and the travois to pull up the slope through heavy snow. Singing Wolf walked ahead, leading them, speaking to them in the language of hope and courage.

Once he reached the other waiting beasts, he shared the weight among the horses, lessening their loads. Even then it was a struggle to go down the slope without tumbling to its bottom, and the valley was even more clogged with snow than the one he had left behind.

It was almost night when he reached the eastern side of that second valley. The horses were stumbling with fatigue, and he knew they must rest, though he could have pushed his painful body forward for hours more. He must camp, and that meant fire.

Absaroka, who might wander here on a mission similar to his, must be risked. He had fought in the snow before, though never with any joy.

There was plenty of wood, although it was never easy to kindle a fire in winter when the branches were damp and cold. He dug under a fallen spruce until he found dried bark and rotted wood, which he piled in a cleared spot sheltered by trees. His fire-drill always traveled with him, but his fingers were chilled and numb, and it took a long while to make the first tendril of smoke curl upward. After that it was easy. He pulled Second Son close to the blaze, tethered the exhausted horses, all of them burdened now, to trees within the circle of light, and sat at last to chew on pemmican and consider his journey for tomorrow.

But his wits were dull with fatigue, and at last he checked his sister, dripped snow-water between her chapped lips, and rubbed her hands and feet hard to prevent frostbite. He built up the stack of branches and sticks that he had gathered in the forest, then he lay close by the fire so he could feed it through the night. As his eyes closed, he heard the first wild wail that told him the wolves had scented meat, horses, and man, and were on his trail. There was time to sleep for a while; the horses would stamp and snort and wake him when the predators drew near.

He woke instantly when the scream sounded uphill among the scattered trees. A great cat of the mountains had decided to join the powwow, he thought, grimly amused. This hunt had not been a very good idea, for he might lose the meat, his sister, and his life. But he rose and cast all his wood into the fire, making the light go deep into the trees while he gathered another great pile of extra fuel—dead branches, small trees, and chunks of deadfall of all kinds.

He stacked it high into a barrier surrounding the side of the fire toward the hill. Almost shoulder-high, it should protect them from an attack from that direction. He pulled Second Son's litter between that barrier and the fire, and brought the horses as near as possible, tying them short and hoping their rawhide halters would hold if they became terrified.

Then, prepared as well as possible against attack, he sat on a chunk of wood and checked arrows, bow, and lance. He added to his own those of his brother warrior.

The subchief hoped the wolves were not so starved that nothing would stop their attempts on this rich store of food. He had seen such things when he was younger, and he had no pleasant memory of them. Only flight had saved the party he had once hunted with.

The pack leader, thin with hunger and winter hunting, watched the flicker of fire beyond the intervening trees. Where fire was, man was, and he made good eating. His horses made better food even than that, and the moosemeat smell that reached the wolf's nostrils was tantalizing. It almost made him forget caution.

A thin cloud cover veiled the half-moon, making the forested slopes about him a maze of black trees and pale drifts. Singing Wolf's ears, tuned closely to the night, detected the first subtle squeak of snow under stealthy paws, and he threw more wood on the fire as he rose to his feet.

Wolves were clever animals, their tactics learned over many generations. He was proud that his totem was that of a wolf singing to the sky as he had seen him in the dream that came to him on his medicine journey. However, now his admiration for the beasts was tempered with caution. He drew his bow, nocked an arrow, and waited, his gaze searching out every firelit stretch of forest about him. Standing beside his sister with the loads of meat, now frozen, piled nearby, he waited for the lead wolf to attack.

Again the scream sounded on the slope behind him, but he ignored it. The great cat did not like fire, and even meat, he was sure, would not draw it down so far. His back was vulnerable if a wolf slunk around to that side, but he had no fear of attack by the mountain lion.

Eyes glowed green downslope. He held his fire, waiting to get a clear shot, for the wolves would fall upon their wounded brother before returning their attention to him. Swift glitters marked the dashes of the beasts across the firelit spaces, nearer and nearer to the barrier of wood and frozen moose.

One moved too slowly, and Singing Wolf's shaft pierced his side, sending the animal down with a yelp of pain. At once others turned, maddened by the scent of his blood, and tore him apart while the subchief waited calmly, bow in hand, and shot and shot and shot as the ravenous animals exposed themselves about the body of their fallen pack-brother.

There was a feast for wolves, for he downed more than a handful while they snapped and growled about the growing number of skinny bodies. Singing Wolf watched, saving his arrows now, waiting for the charge that he knew would still come. These winter-starved beasts would not be satisfied with such a scanty meal.

The pack leader watched for his chance. The confusion as his kindred milled about their fallen fellows was a kind of concealment, and the man who stood behind the wood was watching the starving beasts eat their own kind. It was time, said instinct, cunning, and hard-won experience, to make his bid for a taste of that flesh.

The rich meat of the moose, though frozen, called to the wolves, and the warm and living blood of the two Cheyenne was waiting. Singing Wolf understood them almost as if he were a wolf, and he thanked his long-ago medicine-dream for giving him that knowledge.

The warrior almost jumped as a hand touched his knee. Keeping his eyes alert for any movement toward his position, he backed until he could see Second Son.

"Lance," she grunted. "Watch back. Not . . . much good. Try."

There was an unsettling rattle in the sound of her words, but she was right. Eyes watching the upper slope would be of great value to them both. He handed her the lance that was hers. "I am happy to see you awake, my brother," he said. "Watch well. We have guests tonight."

She nodded, and he turned fully to his task of holding off the wolves.

The lead wolf, furious at the loss of so many of the pack, was a wily animal. He worked his way through the mass of snarling, snapping, red-flecked pack members until he could slip into the trees beyond them, out of the glare of that fire the man had built.

Once he was out of sight, the wolf loped up the slope, avoiding treacherous patches of snow and dried branches, fallen in the winter winds, that might alert his prey to this maneuver. He went a long way, curving up the slope in the cover of the lodgepole pines to keep entirely out of the thought of his enemy, waiting there in the firelight. He would find his back, and he would snap his thin neck with jaws that had brought down elk.

Once above the camp, the animal crept down the slope, keeping in the shadow of the woodpile until he reached the cover it offered. Setting his paws securely in a patch free of snow, he launched himself upward and gained the top of the brushy stack.

There was another man lying beside the delicious scent of mooseflesh, and he knew from experience that one who lay so was no threat. He had crunched the bones of more than one who had looked as this one did. The thing in its hand was of no consequence, for the wolf had no conception of a weapon, even when he had seen the power of the bow.

He balanced himself well, gathered his haunches beneath him, and launched himself down onto that limp figure. But the dark stick in its hand rose to meet him, and once in the air, he had no way to stop. The wicked point, tipped with sharp stone, was coming at him, and with a hopeless howl the wolf felt his belly stabbed deeply, anguish filling his bowels as he impaled himself upon the lance that Second Son held to meet him.

Singing Wolf turned at the sound of a yelp and saw his sister lying beneath the body of the biggest wolf he had seen in many seasons. He moved to lift it from her. Snatching the lance free and hurling it aside, he held the still jerking wolf high in both hands, glaring into the semicircle of green eyes sparking in the light from his fire.

"Here is your chief, brothers! Go home and be done with me," he shouted. "Even a wounded Cheyenne is more than equal to your leader!" He flung the corpse as far as he could, straight toward the cluster of beasts still snapping at their fallen brothers, over the heads of those intending to follow their leader into the camp.

He caught up a flaming branch and sprang past the barrier into the midst of them. Whipping a trail of sparks behind the blazing wood, he flailed right and left, driving the wolves before him, away from his camp. From time to time one of the attackers gave a doleful howl and sped away into the night, and soon the ring of wolves had dwindled to nothing.

"They will not return tonight," said Second Son, her voice weary but audible. She seemed to have gained strength in her long sleep. "I am awake now. Sleep, my brother. Rest yourself, for you have had a very hard and trying day."

He almost laughed, that straight-faced Cheyenne grunt, but he held it in. She was becoming herself again, that brother-sister of his, and she was right. After the struggles and work, the watching and waiting, he was more than ready for sleep. He handed her the bow she had carried, along with a bunch of arrows. "Can you manage, with your arm broken?" he asked.

"No. But I can cry out if there is danger, and an arrow can stab as well as fly through the air. Sleep, Na'niha, Elder Brother, and I will watch through what is left of this night."

As his eyes closed, Singing Wolf relaxed into the depths of his buffalo hide. Sleep was good, and his brother would be alert. Even the scream of the panther high up the slope did not keep him awake.

A stir of motion woke him in the darkness of early morning. The fire was only a flicker of coals now, giving little light. "My brother?" he asked, rising to find his muscles stiff from the struggles of the day before.

There came a grunt in reply, and he felt his way to the travois where Second Son had been lying. It did not surprise him that she had pushed herself up enough to rise and now stood leaning against the depleted pile of wood.

"I will ride for a time when we set out," she said. "There is soreness, but with the arm bound as you have it, I think I can relieve the travois of my weight for a while at least. And riding will be good for me, keeping me from growing even stiffer."

That was good. A warrior kept moving if it was possible, and he was relieved to know that Second Son was able. As she helped, one-handed, to load her travois with bundles of meat, he caught the horses and attached the pack animals to their loads.

Second Son could not leap onto her mount as she usually did. Singing Wolf boosted her onto the beast and looked up into her face, for now dawn lit the sky, though the fire had been smothered in snow.

"I am glad that you are my brother," he said, knowing that she would understand all that he meant by those words. If she had remained a sister, they would have been forbidden the free-ranging companionship they knew, for relations between brother and sister were defined by strict rules.

"As am I," she said, and dug her heels into Shadow's flanks. Although she held her back determinedly straight, beneath her dark skin there was a sickly gray color that told him she controlled her pain and weakness.

The subchief turned his face toward the east and his village, keeping a watchful eye on the laden animals and the erect figure on the mare. This hunt, which might have been a catastrophe, was ending well.

chapter
— 6 —

It seemed the winter might never end. For weeks blizzards roared out of the north and west, smothering the land in snow, freezing the beaver into their dens, burying the walls of the fort halfway up their sides.

Cleve was chilled out of his hideaway and again mixed with the other men in the main room where the fire crackled twenty-four hours a day. Their supplies of food were ample, but tastes grew jaded, and only the inventive cooking of Paul Levreaux kept them from rebelling at its inherent sameness.

Sixty men cramped into those close quarters soon became ill tempered, and even the best-natured showed signs of cabin fever long before winter was halfway done. Whittling and rifle and knife polishing soon palled; endless games of cards and chess with whittled pieces and boards made from soot-marked shingles invoked even more endless bickering. From time to time, there promised to be a fight, which Emile promptly quelled.

Cleve spent as much time as he could out in the horse pen training Socks. The horse learned to stand for long periods of time, reaching for wisps of hay but never stirring from his tracks while Cleve went out of his sight. With the enthusiastic help of Snip, the young man taught the horse to stand, even when the dog snapped at his fetlocks and leapt for his nose. Wolves, the old hands said, were often a problem in the mountains, and if Socks knew how to remain calm under attack, it would be best for both of them.

Most useful of all, Emile told him, would be teaching the animal to come at one whistle and to stop short at another. This wasn't an easy lesson for the gelding, and it took long sessions and a lot of patience before Cleve began to be satisfied with the results. But at last Socks caught on, and though he never became perfectly calm when Snip growled and snapped at his legs, he stopped and started on cue until even the Frenchman approved.

When at midwinter there came a double handful of days that were clear and crystalline, sparkling with sun while yet frozen iron-hard, Cleve took his animals out onto the crusted snow. Another day inside would have seen him go totally crazy, he felt. Another reference to Bare-Ass Bennett (for Emile had been quite right about that) might drive him to murder.

There were fifty-nine others who felt the same, and an array of men fanned out across the countryside, avoiding each other carefully, no matter how close they might be in normal, uncrowded times. Cleve chose a creek that meandered westward, its steep brushy banks now magical with ice-crusted branches and fringes of icicles. The cottonwoods, their fluttering leaves fallen, were now encased in bright sheaths of ice.

In an hour or so he found a small valley, its sides steep enough to shelter them from the wind, that promised to be a good area to train his mount. Every day for a week he rode Socks up the creek, hooves slipping and squeaking on the ice, and every day he went through a ritual of whistles, hand signals, shouts, and calls. After that, Cleve went afoot, wanting to explore what he could while the weather held. Snip at his heels, he roamed the creekbanks while chandeliers of ice glittered in the sunlight overhead. The rolling lands along the creek drainages were deep in snow, and the hills lining the riverbank, when he looked back from a distance, were purple in the brilliant light. Gradually the still, cold landscapes calmed his restlessness.

The cold broke briefly just after Christmas. There had been a lot of merrymaking in the fort, the liquor supply considerably diminished at the end of the festivities. Whittled pegs and chess pieces, packets of flints, and other small gifts were exchanged between special friends.

Cleve held himself apart from much of that. Somehow he felt that he might never become an integral member of this small society, and he missed his family even more than before. Mama had always made magic at Christmas, with nothing much to use but her work-worn hands and her imagination. This rough life was nothing like the festival she managed to create.

But he laughed along with the rest, joined in the joking and the raucous singing of the old songs. It was best, he found, to pretend. No one really cared what his fellows were feeling among this mob of very young men.

In January a warm south wind moved upriver for a brief time, melting a layer of snow, making the walking exhausting. Most of his companions remained indoors, but Cleve couldn't bear the stink of the rooms, the constant bickering of the men, even the flicker of the fire. He had to get out into that cold, clean world to let his personal devils escape. Homesickness was one of those, but by far the worst was his deep-hidden regret that he hadn't killed Pa when he had the chance.

Even Snip was left behind on this day. Cleve felt that any touch, any word, any movement from other creatures might set him off like a bomb, the way he had gone off when Pa whipped Mama. He had been pushing that thought into the back of his mind for a long time now. But something about the slushy surface of the snow, the wind that brought a light mist with it, and the silvery cloud cover that turned the landscape into a featureless glare forced him to remember.

His need to kill Pa was the thing he had to escape from or deal with. The worst, according to what Mama had always taught him, was the fact that he couldn't feel guilty. Even now, he felt certain, Pa was abusing Ma and the boys the way he always had. Tim was the youngest and least able to defend himself, and he knew Pa would still be punishing him for that lie Gramma had told all those years ago.

Stumbling along, his eyes filled with tears of cold and rage, Cleve clenched his fists. He ought to feel guilty. That was the Christian thing. If he didn't, that meant that all the teaching he'd had when he was younger hadn't taken at all. He was a heathen through and through, just as Pa had always claimed.

He crashed through a tangle of icicle-laden bushes that tinkled musically as they broke and the glittering droplets fell. Ahead of him in the shimmering mist of the day stood an animal so large that he stood in wonder, gazing at it.

Dark, the curling hair on its shaggy hump shining with frozen moisture, the buffalo stared stupidly at the intruding man. He snorted, steam billowing from his nostrils, and stamped one massive hoof in warning.

Cleve felt his heart clamp painfully in his chest. Old Nick himself was looking at him from beneath wicked curling horns. He knew he was damned right then. Whatever he did from now on, it was signed and sealed. This was the symbol. He recalled what his cousin John had told him all those years ago: "A Injun goes out when he's young and finds him a sign. May be a hawk or a wolf or a bear. That's his spirit, then, and he goes back home and tells his folks and that gets to be his name. White men don't often reco'nize it when they see it, that spirit, but they got 'em too. It's just best not to tell nobody what it might be, 'cause our kind makes fun of the most sacred things. When you find your totem, young Cleve, you keep it inside and never forget it."

Standing there staring into those wary black eyes, Cleve knew that this was his totem. Those back in the fort might already be calling him Bare-Ass, and the bear might be the thing they *thought* was his sign, but he knew better.

The buffalo was his spirit-totem, and the devil was in it someplace. Now he knew.

When the blizzards swept down again, they froze the drips from that snowmelt into fangs of ice that barricaded the fort from roofline to ground. Cleve, indoors again, kept busy helping Levreaux with the cooking and Prevot with his constant tracing of routes across the plains, using a copy of the old map the Lewis and Clark expedition had drawn of the rivers running into the Missouri.

Cleve's cousin John had added many areas to that map, wandering the mountains, exploring up the rivers, crossing wide stretches of the undulating plains. Prevot ran his finger westward along the Missouri, and Cleve marveled at the branching array of tributaries that were named and noted. The Tongue, the Big Horn, the Mouse, the Milk—strange names for stranger places, he suspected.

"We go all the way up the Missouri, Ashworth say. Plenty water. Probably plenty game, too. Out there in the plain, he is harsh land, no water for many day, sometime. Plenty buffalo, true, but also plenty Indian—Pawnee, Arapaho, Cheyenne, Blackfoot, Sioux, many more." He set his chin in one weather-beaten hand and considered the map. "You be glad when M'sieu Ashworth return, Cleve?" he asked.

"You bet I will. I'm about to go crazy just sitting here with nothing much to do. Can't go out. Can't even train my horse anymore. Next bastard that calls me Bare-Ass Bennett is going to get his chops busted, I tell you that."

Prevot shook his head. "You hol' on, my friend. Keep your temper, yes? That is the biggest thing they learn, *les jeunes hommes*, to keep the head cool when the heart say *keel heem!* That save my life more than once, yes. Train your mind, your heart, to stay still, to watch ever'thing, to wait for their moment. Then you survive out there, where most of these men weel die."

Cleve looked up from the map to stare into those wise dark eyes. "You don't mean that!"

"Ah, but I do. My people, *les Français*, have live, have trap, have trade in thees country for ver' long time. We go out, young and ambitious, yes? And most die. Of a hundred, say, who go out from *la belle France* the same time as I, I think perhaps six or seven still live, these twenty year later." Prevot tapped his pipe against the stone of the hearth, refilled it deliberately, and lit it with a flaming strip of bark.

Cleve found himself feeling cold despite the roaring blaze beyond the Frenchman. "What . . . what killed 'em?" he asked, keeping his voice steady.

"Weather like thees one, yes? No food, no water, perhaps. Indian, yes, often. Sickness, wound . . . many thing kill *les coureurs de bois*. I have myself been shot, all alone, far from camp and companion. Horse run away. Enemy beyond river never know eef I live or die. I crawl for two day, down mountain. Eat grub from dead log, catch cricket in grass weeth my hand. Tie leg to rifle after I take out arrowhead, and ignore the pain. Ai!"

His lined face wrinkled with the memory. "My frien' Henri, he come look after me. Meet me on game trail before I be too far gone to revive. That time, I miss meeting *Le Grand Seigneur* by perhaps thees much." He held up his hand, the thumb and forefinger a scant eighth of an inch apart.

"Is easy to die out there, Bear-Ax Bennett. You are boy, new-come from home, from Mama and Papa maybe. Farming, she is not easy. Make you strong—I know, I see you cut wood, lift log. I see how fast you run . . . not so fast as some I know, but you have great stamina. You have the tough, you have the good mind and the cool hand. Make the head match the hand, and you may be one who survive out there in the wild place."

He nodded toward the nearby chess game, instead of the calm and measured contest known back east, the center of heated controversy at the moment. "Those good fellow. They brave, they strong, they loyal. I say by nex' spring, all but a few weel be dead."

Cleve glanced aside to see the Shooner brothers almost coming to blows with one of the older men. Their noise made him raise his voice. "But why should I live if they're going to die, most of 'em?"

"You *theenk*, my frien'. You train horse, and he come back to you from the Assiniboine. 'Ow many other have that, eh? Most of the horse we have left have stray when the Indian drive them away. Your Socks, he come home to you, because you train heem to and he love you. I see you train heem more, and I suspec' one day that save your life. You have dog that follow where you go and mope when you leave heem behin'. He weel be more to you than a man, I theenk, more faithful, more brave, perhaps. But mos' of all, you keep to yourself. You go out when eet is possible an' run or walk or hunt."

He drew a long puff on his pipe. "Others, they go when the weather it is fine but stay inside and quarrel when it is not. They grow softer than you, here in the winter. When Ashworth return in spring, you be ready to work hard, to haul keelboat, to hunt for food, to explore. Others weel not be so quick, I think. And beyond thees river, beyond the first of mountains, there weel be great wonders that only you, of all these, weel see weeth the eye of the spirit."

Cleve sighed and stared into the fire. "When do you think he'll come?" he asked. "It took us a long time to get this far, dragging those damn boats full of supplies."

"The *riviere*, she will thaw at last. Maybe March, maybe April, for thees is a ver' cold winter. Ashworth, he weel come fast, for he bring only horse, not boat. I think he be here before we see free water. Look for heem when there come no more blizzard from the north, *n'est ce pas*?"

Lying in his blankets that night, Cleve thought of what Prevot had said. Would many of those men—hard, young, skilled, many of them, with weapons—die before another spring? And would he survive, whatever the Frenchman's belief? He was no better or worse than the rest, he knew. Thinking might be something that Mama valued and taught her sons. Latin might be a nice advantage for some beau in the East. But he couldn't see any help in them against winters and Indians.

Death . . . he had never really thought about dying, not for himself. Now he pondered the subject. That old buffalo, wicked-eyed and sharp-horned, might bode ill for him if he did fall in the year to come.

He closed his eyes, listening to the howl of wind about the walls and through the chinks. The same wind, he knew, was pummeling his family's home down the Missouri, howling in the chimney, blowing ash into the big main room. Pa would be half awake, just waiting for one of the boys to whimper. That would bring him up at once, belt or whip in hand, to whale the daylights out of the son afraid of the hand of God. Thinking of Pa, Cleve was reminded once again of the devil he had seen in the eyes of the buffalo bull. Pa was cruel. The devil liked that, he had been taught.

What if he turned around from Pa's way, all the way, and was kind whenever he could be, and it wouldn't get him killed? Would that maybe earn him some credit with God? Maybe. He turned over and closed his eyes.

But when he dreamed, he dreamed of a horned devil in a glare of mist and steely frost.

The ice began to grind in early March, though there was no sign of a real breakup. Ashworth showed up before the snow had melted, leading a string of good horseflesh and another handful of would-be trappers. They hove into view late one afternoon amid crashes of falling icicles and rushing slips of snow from treetops and the roofs of the fort.

Along with the horses he brought packs of fresh supplies—ammunition, coffee, beans, sugar, and rice. Wintering holed up so early in their journey had cut into those necessities. Levreaux welcomed the additions and whipped up a superb pot of venison stew laced with rice and a few hardy herb tops that had thrust their way into sheltered spots where the snow had melted. He spiced it all with a tea made from pine needles, which added a tang and also, according to the Frenchman, prevented scurvy.

The leaders of the expedition sat late beside the fire, and long after he had gone back to his private hole, now habitable again, Cleve heard an occasional exclamation loud enough to carry through the log walls. Prevot seemed to be protesting something, but no straining of the ears could detect individual words, and Cleve had no idea what the argument might be about. Ashworth's voice, lower but agitated, kept interrupting the Frenchman's.

The next morning Cleve leaned against a wall, listening with the others as the leaders laid out their proposed route. Ashworth, as principal organizer of the project, led off with style, marking off the river's course, showing their route, the Indian villages along the waterway, the promising small rivers and creeks leading off the main channel where beaver might well be found in abundance.

"But we will not stop short of our goal, which is the Three Forks of the Missouri in the land called Montana. All the gold in the mines of Peru cannot surpass the wealth to be found in that country," he said. "We must hold to our original course to make our fortunes there."

Prevot allowed Ashworth to finish his talk before rising and setting aside his pipe. "Me, I do not agree with thees route, *mes amis*. The 'Rickara, they still buzz like fly, since your Lewis and your Clark they go upriver long ago. They do not like *les Americains*, not at all. Better far, I theenk, if we go west and south of the river, cut across plains. I have trap and travel these place for many year. There ees danger, yes, but I know where spring rise, where waterhole lie. Emile Prevot can lead you sáfe to your destination."

It sounded sensible to Cleve. Why risk trouble with the Arikara when they might go around and be about their business? But many voices now rose in argument, some insisting that a plentiful supply of water was more important than avoiding Indians.

"What about the keelboats of supplies?" yelled Bridwell. "We got a lot of weight there to haul across country!"

Prevot claimed the extra horses could pack everything. The babble of talk rose so loudly that Cleve, knowing that his opinion wouldn't count for much, moved away into the pasture outside the walls where hints of green were tempting the horses to paw and nibble.

He had a bad feeling about those Indians. Ma had said such foreknowings were the work of the devil, but he had known such times all his life and had never found them anything but helpful. If he had only known what Pa was going to do and had run off into the woods instead of taking his whipping, all this would never have happened. Then he wondered. Would he go back, even if he could, to the abuse, the long hard labor, the tension that lived wherever his father was? No. Never again would he be whipped like an animal. Never again would he endure the sort of suffering that Jase Bennett so masterfully imposed on his family. Given the choice, Cleve would have left, just as he had done. So except for his occasional twinge when he thought about Ma, things had turned out for the best, after all.

Vince Shooner popped up at his elbow. "Them fellows sure going at it hammer and tongs," he said. "I can't see where it makes all that much difference. If'n you're an Injun and white fellows comes up the river, messin' with your women and your game, why it's just naturally sensible for you to get a mite riled. Best I can see is for us to keep our heads down, don't do nothin' dumb, and smile a lot."

Cleve chuckled. Vince was fun, his manner brisk and dry, his words often full of wit. He tended to agree with the young man. This was no country in which to split up their numbers, and whatever the leaders decided was the way the expedition had to go.

They went upriver as soon as the ice broke enough for the keelboats to move. Hauling on the lines or handling horses that pulled the heavy craft along, Cleve watched the country with interest when he had the chance. Off to the west, when he was relieved and moved out to the edge of the trees away from the slope down to the river, the horizon seemed to be at the edge of forever. The sky went from here to yonder, blue with spring, tufted with cottony clouds, busy with flights of migrating birds. Looking up and up, Cleve felt that he might almost fall upward into that endless bowl and never come down again. When he looked back at the undulating landscape, he was dizzy for a while with the immensity of it all.

Prevot, who seemed to have made a sort of pet of him, usually walked or rode near the younger man. Now he chuckled. "You see the endlessness of it, no? It is intoxicating, and I too have known that dizziness. Thees country into which we go, *mon ami*, is unlike anything you ever see or know before." He gazed off into the distance.

"Some, like old Emile, we nevair want to return from it. We go to the high place, look out over country that seem to stand still since time she was born, and we find a—I do not know how to say it. We find something that make us whole men, apart weeth ourself, yes? Not needing othair people. But some do not love such life. They return, in the end, to the town and the family. They do not hear the call of the ghost mountains or the long wind in the canyon or the lonely cry of the wolf in the night. Those thing, they speak only to one kind of man, there in the wild place."

"I wonder which I'll be?" Cleve said. "I certainly don't hanker to go back to my Pa and his bullwhip."

Then a couple of young mares took a notion to bolt, and they both turned their attention to their duties, heading the pair off and herding them back to walk sedately with the string ahead of the teams now hauling the keelboats along.

There were Indian villages along the river, random clusters of lodges, their circles busy with snapping dogs and naked wide-eyed children. Women were working hides and gathering baskets of stuff from the river and the plain to the west. Emile insisted that their odd-looking collections were food and would keep a man alive and healthy, but Cleve found himself gagging at the idea of eating grass seeds and the roots of water weeds. But he deliberately noticed the things he saw gathered as they traveled slowly upriver, hauling the balky keelboats, keeping the horses together, dealing with snakebite, belly-aches, and bad tempers.

By June, they'd come past the ragged remnant of the Menna-kanoza village, which had been all but wiped out by the pox years before. There even the dogs seemed depressed and lacked the energy to snap at their heels. Cleve found it both sad and disturbing. They moved faster now, their habits established, their eagerness growing as summer opened out before them. Nearing the complex of villages beyond the junction of the Cheyenne River with the Missouri, Ashworth slowed the pace a bit, sending Prevot and Levreaux to make contact with the Arikara there.

Since Lewis and his people had passed this way

early in the century, those Indians had been angry with the Americans, and the leader felt that sending Frenchmen to negotiate a passage might work best for all concerned. Cleve, watching closely but keeping silent, had a feeling that this cautious approach was too little and entirely too late. Something nagged at his dreams and made him feel as if an enemy watched him from behind.

They camped well to the south of the villages, and Cleve, after helping to secure the horses, asked Ashworth for permission to go hunting out on the grassy plain to the west of the river. The leader agreed. "You will find small game there, or perhaps buffalo. We can use meat while we wait to see if this passage will be rough or smooth. Go, my young friend, and try your skill. There are many hands here to keep things in order."

Cleve saddled Socks, called to Snip, and slid his Hawken into the boot on the saddle. His heart lifting at the thought of getting away from the noisy encampment, he headed out over the grassy swells, which were scented with summer, new green growth, and purple-flowered plants.

Socks seemed glad too, raising his head and snorting playfully, dancing sideways to show his spirit. Snip took off on the track of a rabbit, invisible in the tall growth. A shifting in the grass, shoulder-high to Cleve as he sat his mount, showed him which way to go.

They moved blindly through the tall growth, and the fresh breeze in his ears sang of adventure, summer, strange places as Cleve rode into the swells. About him the heads of the grasses undulated like waves as the wind swept over them, their shades of green and gold and buff changing from moment to moment. He didn't really care if they found game. Just being alone, free here in the clean open land, was enough to raise his spirits.

Losing the rabbit, Snip returned to walk sedately at Sock's heels, and they forged ahead, topping the small rises from which Cleve could see some distance over the intervening grasses. At last he swiveled about, turning Socks so that he could see the entire horizon through a full circle. Buffalo, even a single one, would show up in the tall grass, but there was no dark blot of muscle and shaggy hide to be seen. Smaller game would be invisible, as the rabbit had been. Even as he thought that his hunt would be futile, he heard a *chakking* beyond the rise, and his Hawken came into his hand with smooth speed.

Now he could load—powder, ball and patch, priming—as quickly as anyone in the company, and he quickly had the gun ready to fire. He rode ahead slowly, watching. Snip worked forward, nose to the ground, tail wagging. Cleve kept his gaze sweeping from left to right, covering the territory ahead of the dog. When the sage grouse came shooting upward from its covert, the Hawken was ready, and the blast of the shot didn't hide the triumphant yelps of the dog as he dashed forward to retrieve the bird.

Cleve dismounted to pat him. "Good boy, Snip! Good dog!" He took the bird, unbruised, its head shot cleanly from its body, from the damp jaws and stuffed it into his saddlebag. "Time to go back, boy. It'll be almost dark by the time we get to camp as it is," he said, turning Socks's head back to the east, the sun now full on his back. As he neared the river again, something began to plague the young man. He reined in the horse and stood in the stirrups to listen.

Was that the sound of shots? Distant, still very faint—
pop! pop! pop!

"Come on, Snip," he shouted and kicked his heels
into the horse's flanks. "They're under attack!"

Socks responded, galloping through the tall grasses,
heading toward the source of the noise, which now
grew louder and more disturbing. Snip stayed at the
horse's side as if alarmed, and Cleve shared his
wariness.

Reaching a small ravine with a creek at its bottom,
he reined in and listened closely. Now that he was
nearer, he could hear occasional shouts, yells, shrill
"yip-yip-yip" that had to be a war cry. He didn't want
to ride in without knowing the situation, but he had
no idea what to do. Could he help his companions?
Cleve sighed, glancing up at the lip of the small
ravine. Four sets of black eyes stared back down at
him from four dark faces, striped with black and
white. Snip gave a low growl and disappeared into the
growth along the edge of the cut, leaving Cleve to
decide what to do in a split second.

He kicked Socks hard, and the gelding headed
down the ravine, breaking through tangles of dried
brush, the overhanging swatches of willows and brittle vines. Cleve ducked his face into the flying mane,
avoiding what he could as branches slashed past. He
felt as if Pa were beating him, so hard were the blows
that hammered at his knees and laid stripes over his
back.

Cries followed him as Socks clattered blindly down
the cluttered gully bottom. His pursuers hadn't descended into the ravine, he was sure, as he whipped
through a tangle of rotted willow branches and got
clear enough beyond to glance backward. They were

running along above, free of the growth in the gully, keeping up easily. Damn!

A game track appeared ahead, coming down from his right. The Indians were on the left bank. Instantly, Cleve kneed Socks toward the steep pathway, which went almost straight up the stony incline. With a great effort, the gelding surged upward, his hindquarters straining, his front hooves scrabbling at the path ahead. Cleve leaned along the horse's neck and clung tightly, feeling the saddle slip backward as the girth slid slightly along the sweaty barrel.

Socks was struggling now, his burden almost overbalancing him on the steep grade. Cleve, feeling the instant when the horse lost his equilibrium, spilled off to one side, and Socks tumbled back down into the ravine, his shriek of terror almost human. Lying flat against the bank, the young man shivered, thinking of what it would be like if he had been beneath the horse when he fell. That bear wouldn't have been any comparison. He'd have been dead or just as near as he could get, for that kind of fall usually was fatal to horse and rider alike.

He could hear the horse thrashing below, and he scooted down on his butt, forgetting his pursuers for the moment. He had to help the animal or shoot him if he was too badly hurt to stand a chance of recovering. Arriving at the bottom, his nose filled with dust and grit, he stood and assessed the condition of his horse. Evidently the gelding had fallen straight back into thick scrub, and he was having a hard time getting himself turned over to stand. His legs were flailing in the air, and Cleve knew it would be dangerous to get too near. From the way he moved, it seemed that Socks had sustained no major injury, although blood where broken stubs had cut him was beginning to show on his brown hide. It was clear that his legs were unbroken, for they moved without any sign of serious injury.

Just as the horse broke down the last of the cushiony tangle that held him, managing to roll and then to stand, Cleve remembered his predicament. But now it was too late to run. Two bowmen stood above him on the bank, their arrows aimed at his heart. The others were already down in the ravine, and one put a rope over Socks's head before the gelding knew he was there. The other was getting ready to tie the trapper hand and foot. Unarmed, his rifle still in the boot, the saddle having twisted halfway around Socks's belly, there was not much Cleve could do but die heroically without achieving anything.

For an instant, he felt a sharp pang of sorrow. Ma would grieve, and the boys would miss him. But they wouldn't know for years, if they ever found out. He would never come home again, and he hoped they wouldn't think it was because he didn't love them. For the moment, he felt that he might have been better off staying on the farm and taking Pa's beatings. The image of the bull buffalo rose in his mind as the cords cut into his wrists and tethered his ankles tightly. Was this what that totem had meant?

He drew a deep breath and stood as straight as possible. He'd die well. He wouldn't disgrace Emile and Paul and Ashworth if he could help it.

chapter
— 7 —

Although she had often been injured as she grew up among her active companions, Second Son had never before broken a bone. Having one arm useless would have been bad enough. The treatment for the broken arm was far worse.

When Singing Wolf brought her into the winter village, dragging the travois of meat and leading the laden horses, she had been riding by will and instinct alone. Her mind was drifting among the snowy reaches of the hills, and her ears heard sounds foreign to anything she knew. When she slipped from Shadow's back, it was the Prophet himself who caught her and set on her feet. Her father, looking frozen in the cold light, came to stand beside her, holding her steady.

Singing Wolf, drawn and weary, turned to his people. "Take her to the medicine lodge," said her brother. "We have killed a moose, but it broke our brother's arm. We must tend it quickly, for we cannot spare so brave a hunter for long."

Prophet led the way, his buffalo-hide cloak dragging behind him in the snow, and Singing Wolf's wife, Nesting Bird, came to put an arm about her waist and help her along. Every movement was exquisite agony as the arm vibrated with her steps, hold it still as she might, but Second Son made no sound as she entered the hut and faced the old woman who was the healer. Beside her stood the shaman who would sing out the bad spirits from her flesh while the old woman worked to set and immobilize the bones.

Those who had accompanied her withdrew and went about their own tasks, leaving Second Son to the mercy of the medicine lodge. She sat, as directed, on a soft scrap of hide before the fire, turning her gaze to the flames.

When Little Otter, the healing woman, came up behind her and with one merciless jerk aligned the bone ends, she almost fainted. Gritting her teeth, she lay back under the thrust of those hard hands. Then the old woman secured her arm, binding it tightly with parfleche.

Now she was growing hot, and Second Son knew that fever was beginning, fueled by cuts, the break, and abrasions. She was not surprised when Otter offered her a bone cup filled with hot bitter tea made from the bark of the willow. She drank it down and waited, knowing that worse was to come.

A young girl entered the lodge carrying a pot filled

with something dark. Kneeling beside the recumbent warrior, she dipped her hands into the pot and brought them out filled with reddish mud, which she dabbed in cool handfuls up and down the bound limb. Again and again she spread the mud, smoothing it with her fingers until the upper side of the arm was covered thickly.

Then all three healers went away, leaving the warrior to lie alone and stare into the soot-stained peak of the lodge, watching the smoke swirl away up the smokehole. Now she was giddy with breaking fever and the willow-bark tea.

Dreams visited her, though she was not asleep. Battles long past, victories, wounds, hunts, raids—all sped past on the milling of her mind. But Second Son did not move, did not call out, did not shrink from this ordeal, which was no worse than many and far better than some, for she had taken her turn hanging from the pole at the sun dance, bone skewers pinned through the flesh of her chest. She had danced there, hanging her full weight against the pain, choosing that course as the appropriate sacrifice to prove herself a man and a warrior. Her skin still showed puckered scars where the skewers had pulled through at last, freeing her from the post, the pitiless sky, and the thirst.

That blazing sun—she could see it still when she closed her eyes. White rings seemed to circle it, and the dark shapes of buzzards circled too. She could feel the nausea again, the weakness in knees and back, the searing as the sharpened skewers pulled at her chest. Only the bravest endured to the end, and she had endured.

This was nothing, this waiting for the mud to harden and hold her broken bone fast. Besides, the dreams . . . the dreams . . . Something touched her face—cool, damp. Otter wiped away the sweat left by the breaking fever before examining the cast. Satisfied, she nodded and motioned to someone beyond Second Son's range of vision. Hands turned her carefully until she lay facedown, the arm positioned correctly, and the application of mud began again.

In time the task was completed, and again the warrior lay alone in the glow of the fire, watching the shadows dance on the tough hide of the curving wall.

She woke deep in the night, listening. It seemed that a distant voice called to her in a tongue she did not know. Someone she had never met stared into the eyes of the huge grandfather of all the bison she had ever seen or dreamed of. Its shaggy coat glimmered in ghostly frozen mist, and its eyes were wicked as it stared at the figure, hidden in frosty fog, that stood before it. She shivered, knowing this must be a dream, wondering what omen this might be for her. Who was this stranger in the cold light? And why did the buffalo face him so boldly?

She opened her eyes and stared up at the smokehole, dark against dark in the flickering light of the fire. She was warmly covered with furs, and Little Otter had crept back into the medicine lodge to tend the flames. Even now the healer dozed on a mat of skins against the wall, and fresh fuel made the blaze crackle.

Second Son wanted to sigh, to turn, but the weight of the hardened mud made her arm unwieldy, and she knew that the slightest movement would bring the healer to tend her. Otter needed to sleep, and a warrior could endure much worse than this. Lying there, the thought of those women who wished her

well made Second Son feel warm comfort for a
moment. Some of her sisters in the tribe were proud
of her accomplishments and did all they could to
make her difficult way easier.

There were others who resented her life of freedom from their constant work of supplying basic
food, clothing, and shelter for the People. Those
were the women who understood that war and hunting were children's games that men played for their
own purposes. Everyone knew, though few admitted,
that without the constant attention and incessant
labors of the women, life in the plains would be
impossible. Meat was a luxury, and delicious, but the
staples of their diet came from small game snared
about the camp, grass seeds, roots of valuable plants,
fruits and berries and herbs that the women gathered
all summer. When those dried and preserved stores
were depleted, as they were beginning to be now, all
the meat would not prevent sickness.

Second Son thought of those she had seen whose
mouths were painful, their teeth loose. Sores broke
out on their bodies, and their bellies cramped. Meat
did not help them. Only when spring brought the
tender green plants whose leaves went into the pot,
the buds that everyone chewed ravenously, did that
sort of sickness go away.

She valued those women, as did all the men,
whether or not they would admit it. Yet many of the
busy sisters resented this one who had escaped their
life of hard work to run free in the winds of the wide
lands. She had hated her tasks at her mother's heels,
going out with parfleche bags to gather seeds,
shaping baskets and pots, working hides, quilling
embroideries on deerhide. The tediousness of the
work had driven her to a frenzy. At last her parents

had agreed, when it was plain how poorly she did such things, to teach her with her brother and his peers. That had been the saving of her mind, she thought.

And there had been no protest. The tradition of women as warriors, chiefs, and hunters was not unknown among the people of the plains. Indeed, it had been a young girl, the orphaned daughter of a man called Bull Looks Back according to a myth told by the tale-tellers about the fires at night, who had given her people their Council of Forty, the peace chiefs who kept the tribes in harmony.

She moved slightly, and the pain made her hold her breath. Then she felt through her body, trying to find the stab of a spur of shattered bone, the faint twinge of some internal injury that might even now be killing her slowly. There was nothing except the pain of her bruises, the dull, nauseating ache in her broken arm. She was healing already, she thought as she drifted back into sleep.

When she woke, there was faint light coming through the smokehole amid the fragrant curls of gray from the freshly fueled fire. Moccasins crunched across frosted snow outside the tipi, and she could hear Otter stirring about.

The door-robe swept back, admitting a gust of icy air, and Singing Wolf stood there gazing down at her inquiringly. At Otter's gesture, he closed the flap over the door-hole and sat on the skin beyond the fire, staring at his "brother" with relief in his eyes. "I thought of you in the night," he said. "But I think you are better now. Otter and the medicine chief are great healers."

She struggled to sit, and Otter helped her to place

her arm to keep from putting pressure on the thick crust of mud about it. Second Son smiled at her brother. "I am well enough," she said, "though I had strange dreams in the night—a great bison confronted a man who was hidden in mist, and the two seemed locked together, not as hunter and game but almost as brothers." The dream came into her mind sharply, though she had forgotten it until this moment. "I hunted on the plain, riding fast, fast, beside a warrior I do not know. When I turned to look at him, he was always too far away or behind or simply invisible. And yet he was there, and his presence was a joy to me."

"A medicine dream" said Singing Wolf. He stretched his feet to the fire and rubbed them carefully through the double-thick moccasins. "Sometimes those are very important. Can you remember more?"

She thought hard, holding the encrusted arm in her lap and bracing it with her other hand. About her the dry sweet smoke curled upward through the hole where it was carried away by the wind, controlled by the flaps at the top of the lodge. "We moved through the hills at the foot of the mountains, just as you and I did when we went to hunt. Always there was a step beside me, someone there who could be trusted, a hand beside my own and a voice to warn me of danger. But never did I see him, and it was not you, which I find very odd. A strange dream, my brother."

He nodded. "But we brought the meat our people must have," he said. "And there are enough stored grains and dried herbs to add to the pot until spring, I think. Perhaps there will be no winter sickness, though the coughing ones have not improved."

Otter came to stand beside Second Son. "If this warrior wishes to return to her—*his* lodge, he may do that," she said. "The fever has broken, and the arm is set. Do you wish to help him, Singing Wolf? Or shall I call his sisters-in-law?"

The subchief stood. "I will be happy to help my brother to his lodge," he said. "My wives have already built up his fire and prepared his robes. It is good to honor one who has helped to feed so many in this terrible winter, and when that one is a brother, it is doubly good."

Second Son sighed with relief. Perhaps in her own place, surrounded by the trophies of her hunts and her battles, the dreams would dwindle and cease.

The winter dragged on, past Snow Moon, past the moon when the wolves howled together. The arm healed. The bruises were now only faint washes of green and yellow against her dark skin. She mounted Shadow in the frozen dawns and often rode out into the snowy plain just to escape from the monotony of the village. In this time of cold there was little chance of meeting an enemy there, for the Kiowa, the Crow, and the Pawnee did not hunt abroad when snow lay deep. Sensible people kept to their own lodges, huddling beside their fires and telling tales through the long days. But Second Son had never been one to be cooped like a trapped hawk in a willow cage, unable to stretch her wings. Though her sisters-in-law shook their heads and even Singing Wolf cautioned her against risking herself in the steely silver waste where even bison sometimes froze where they stood, she kept to her stubborn way.

That was why she was abroad in the dawn, feeling that she was the only living thing in the wide expanse of white. The air was like a blade in her lungs, and her nose hurt. Her breath frosted about her nostrils, and even the heavy buffalo robe she wore about her did not keep her from shivering as she urged Shadow forward. The mare was less enthusiastic than her rider, but she responded, picking up her delicate hooves and snorting irritably. From the undulating white drifts ahead there came an answering whinny. Second Son drew her mount to a halt and listened hard. Once the crunch of the horse's hooves had halted, there was no sound to be heard but the thin hiss of wind over snow. Then the other beast whinnied again, the shrill sound unnaturally loud in the stillness.

The warrior dropped softly from her horse and slid away, circling to the right to come upon the source of that whinny from an unexpected angle. Behind her, she knew, Shadow would stand until wanted, and she moved ahead confidently. Now she felt no cold, all her mind focused on the possible danger there in the drifts. When she moved through the last ridges, hiding her motions amid the undulations of the frozen snowcrust, she looked down at a standing horse. Beside it lay a dark form, featureless in the dawnlight but without doubt a man or woman bundled in fur.

One set of tracks had broken through the crust to that point, and when Second Son stood, she could see no trace of anyone or anything in any direction. She trudged down the slope into the drifted cup and looked down at this unexpected intruder. He was a strange one. When she peeled back the fur from his face, she saw that his skin was pale, his chin sporting hair like an animal or a *coureur du bois*. She had met only a few of those as her people followed their normal route across the plains, and even the one from whom she had obtained her bright-bladed knife had not seemed quite human.

She stood upright, thinking. This was no enemy, for the Cheyenne had no anger toward those newcomers. He would if nothing else provide interesting gossip and perhaps new tales for the tag end of winter when everyone was weary of old stories, old faces, and old quarrels.

Singing Wolf would approve if she brought him back with her. The tribe often brought in stray wanderers, adopting captives from time to time, children and adults. This one might prove to be a welcome addition to their group, even though food was very short.

The horse shied about, avoiding her strange scent as she examined the fallen rider. What he had been doing alone in the middle of the snow in the night was a question that bothered her, but she knew she could find no answer until the man might tell her. She caught the horse, a steel-gray gelding, and managed to make him stand as she loaded his limp rider over his back, tying him to the saddle that was strapped to the animal. Then she led them back to Shadow, still standing patiently though she whuffled inquiringly through her nostrils as she caught the scent of this new animal and the odd-smelling burden it bore.

When Second Son led her find into the village, as the sun rose behind a layer of silver cloud that made the light glaring and shadowless, she found the lodges still quiet. Smoke rose from the smokeholes; there was the smell of cooking, but nobody moved outside. Tracks told her that the young boys had checked the horses down beside the stream, but their elders were saving energy, which the cold sapped quickly.

She kneed Shadow to a stop before the lodge of her brother. "Singing Wolf!" she called. "I have a gift for you."

After a moment, the doorflap moved, and her brother stared out at her. "On such a morning, what sort of—" His mouth remained open, for he was staring at the strange horse, the rider, now stirring feebly against his bonds, and his sister, grinning there on Shadow's back.

"I have brought a stranger who fell in the snow," she said. Then she turned away toward her own lodge and fire, leaving this stray to her brother's whim.

Any new interest there in the depths of winter would have been welcome to the Cheyenne village. This one was particularly so because once he revived under the ministrations of Nesting Bird and Fox-Child, he spoke a bit of their tongue and understood the sign language linking all the tribes.

He was quick, that one, at picking up the language enough to exchange stories with his hosts. Second Son felt that she had contributed a better thing, perhaps, than the moosemeat as he settled into Singing Wolf's family and provided many new tales to be told about fires in all the lodges of the village.

"I am Jules," he told them, "Jules Terrebonne. I trap the mountain stream for beavair for many long year now. But thees winter, I am attack by grizzly—a great, huge bear who tear my shelter apart, destroy my supply, my trap. I run for horse, ride down the mountain fast, but he come after, fast too. Cheval there, he became so frighten', he run away weeth me. We end up out in plain, in cold night so I theenk I freeze to death. Then thees great warrior come, rescue me and bring me here. For wheech I am mos' grateful."

The bearded face turned toward her, and Second Son felt his strange pale eyes studying her. She knew that he understood that she was not a man. But he said nothing, for which she was relieved. It was awkward when one unused to her made a comment that forced her people to step quickly about their own pretenses.

She found, however, that she was uncomfortable in the presence of Shoo-le, as her people called him. Those white eyes, always drawn toward her if she was present, made her neck hairs prickle as if some danger approached, and she made excuses to remain in her own lodge, staring into her own fire.

Even Cub, her favorite nephew, deserted her, for he loved to listen from the shadows behind his elders as the Frenchman told long tales of his prowess as fighter, hunter, and trapper. Those stories also troubled Second Son, for they mentioned no ritual with which to thank the animals that provided food and protection, shelter and bone for tools, for giving up their lives for the benefit of the man who killed them. He had, she sensed, no reverence for the land on which he stood, the mountains, the trees, the waters, and the beasts that gave him his livelihood. She wondered if he might be an outcast because of this or if all his people might be the same. Such lack of gratitude was disturbing, and she avoided him also because of that.

Sitting before her fire, painstakingly flaking flint arrowheads with a wooden awl on a plate of rock, she heard movement outside her doorway. Before she could ask who came, the doorflap moved, and Terrebonne's shaggy face stared in at her. A hot surge of anger rose in her chest. He had not asked to come, and he had not scratched gently at the doorflap to warn her that he was there. She had the feeling, as she stared into those pale hot eyes, that he had hoped to find her naked, as many people tended to be inside their own lodges in the warmth of their fires.

She rose to her feet, silent, waiting for him to explain his presence. Words, she found, were weapons that he could turn against their users, and she would give him no such aid. She had not liked that, and now, looking over the fire into his pink-washed face, she realized that she disliked him for many reasons. Long-tailed Beaver had been a child in wickedness in comparison with this white man.

A warrior was never weaponless. Her metal knife hung in its string holder at her hip. Her bow lay within reach, arrows beside it. A batch of lances, newly sharpened, leaned against the pile of furs that made her bed. She did not fear this one. No. But she sensed a rank danger in him that was like a stench in the close air of the tipi.

He moved forward around the fire toward her, but she held up a hand, palm outward, in the universal sign that meant "stop." He grinned and kept coming. Her knife was in her hand instantly. "What do you want, Shoo-le?" she asked, her tone cool.

"You," he said. "You may be warrior, but you are a woman. I like women. Your people pride themself upon control, upon *chastité, non*? That ees not the way of my kind. I cannot lie weeth the women of the chief, as I would like to do, for he would, I know, keel me. But who weel object eef I take pleasure weeth the *brother* of thees chief?"

"His brother." The words hung between them like

a challenge. "Go from here, Shoo-le. I am a warrior. I am a hunter. I do not lie with man or woman, and I do not like you. If you value your life, go now."

Instead, he leapt forward, thinking to force her back and down. But Second Son stepped lithely aside and caught up a lance in her free hand. The Frenchman rolled away from its plunging point, and as he rolled, he caught up another and whirled to dislodge her weapon from her left hand, leaving only the knife in her right.

Now he was more cautious, and he outweighed her by half. Lunging, he managed to push her flat and flung himself on her.

Second Son had lived among men all her life. She had been captured by those of other tribes, but not one had ever bragged that he knew her as a woman. Some flinched at the mention of her name. There were tricks, and she knew them all. Using the wiry muscles of her tough body, she managed to roll, tangling his legs with her own. With a lightning motion, she snatched away the loincloth beneath his robe, described a brief arc with her knife, and held up his dripping testicles before his stunned gaze.

He gasped, catching himself with both hands, blocking the flow of blood as best he could.

She turned and found a roll of soft-tanned deerskin such as she used every month, and flung the leather toward him. "Tend yourself," she said. "And do not come again to my tipi."

Those pale eyes were wide, stunned, unbelieving as he covered his wound with the stuff and bound it in such an awkward place. Without speaking, he covered himself with his furs and blundered from the lodge, letting the doorflap swing loose behind him.

Irritated, Second Son secured the barrier against

the chill and turned again to chipping flint. In time her brother would visit her and ask what had happened. She was considering what she should say when she heard his scratch at the door. Singing Wolf looked puzzled as he entered and sat beside her fire. He took his time, warming his hands, commenting upon the quality of her arrowheads, mentioning Cub's restless desire for spring to come again before he came to the point.

"Shoo-le is going," he said at last. "First he visited you—to thank you for saving him, he said. Now he is gathering his possessions to leave. Spring is near enough, he says, and he has another camp that he uses from time to time. There he has traps and supplies. But why does he leave so suddenly, while snow still lies deep? Why does he now limp when he did not before? And why just after visiting you?"

She did not reply. Instead, she reached toward the edge of the fire and caught up a twig with which she fished the charred testicles from the ashes. She looked up into her brother's black eyes. "His," she said.

Singing Wolf's face turned to stone. To assault a brother warrior when it was obvious that nobody among her own people considered her a woman was a dreadful insult to the host of the man who committed such a crime. If Second Son had not punished him sufficiently, as she had, she knew that her brother would have done something worse and more painful.

"It is good that he goes," she said, laying aside an arrowpoint and taking up another chip of flint. "He was a good storyteller, but did you notice, my brother, that he never gave thanks when he killed game? Such uncivilized people are best removed from our own kind. He might in time have taught Cub bad manners and immoral ways."

The subchief nodded, looking away from Second Son into the flames where the testicles again bubbled and charred away to ash. She could see the tendons tighten as his hands lay in his lap, and she knew that he longed to throttle that presumptuous white man.

"If your honor is satisfied—" he began.

She held up her hand. "Honor is satisfied. He has paid more than he intended for his try, and there is no need to say anything more to anyone about this." She chipped industriously at the flint.

Her brother rose and stood beside her, breathing deeply. "Then it shall be so," he said at last. Turning, he left the tipi, and she felt a cold swish of air that fanned the flames and stirred the smoke as the flap swung down again and was folded shut against the chill of the day.

chapter
— 8 —

The first thing his captors did after urging Cleve up
the bank with the points of their lances was to fling
him facedown across a horse, which they led at a
jouncing trot across the prairie for several miles. He
felt as if he would lose his breath as the bony ridge of
the horse's back gouged his midriff while his face
scrubbed against the sweaty hide of the paint on
which they had put him.

When they halted at last, the biggest of the Indians
hauled him down and let him drop. They dragged
him forward by his bound hands, almost tearing his
arms out of their sockets, and as they pulled him

upright, he saw that they had come to a rude building made of mud and sticks.

Except for being much larger, the hut into which his captors thrust Cleve was not entirely unlike the beaver lodges he had investigated while trapping in the fall near the fort. Dark and chilly, it stank of something old and nasty, and he suspected that this isolated lodge was not used regularly.

The four painted warriors who had taken him at the creek had not mistreated him . . . yet. Three of them seemed to be in a great hurry to get someplace else, and he suspected that his comrades would see them soon.

They stripped off his woolen shirt and pants, drew off his long johns amid deep chuckles of mirth, and bound him firmly to a stake set in the middle of the small round room. One took the shirt and tied it to the end of his lance. Another tied the pants around his neck by the legs, and a third bound the long johns around his shoulders like a cape, the flap gaping open behind.

The fourth was somewhat older than the others, Cleve thought. He took the rifle, the hand-ax, and the pouch of possibles holding flint, patches, and ball, along with a few treasured small items, including his Cousin John's rifle ball taken from his leg so long ago.

Socks was outside the lodge. Cleve could hear him snort and stamp, still alarmed at these unfamiliar people and their peculiar stink. He pursed his lips and gave a soft whistle to soothe the horse, but the Arikara struck him across the face with his lance, and he stopped at once.

There was a gabble of talk when the four left the lodge. He heard hooves pound away. Had they left him alone, then? He had puckered up again to whistle for Snip, who would be close about, he was certain, when the door darkened and the youngest of the Indians, now denuded of the long-john cape, entered the hut again. This was a very big fellow, almost as tall and broad as Cleve, but he was very young. His lips hung slack, and there was a vacancy in his eyes that told the trapper that he was a lackwit. However, an idiot that big and strong was something to be reckoned with. He wore a steel knife at his waist and held a knotted stick that could have crushed a skull easily, backed by that bulk of muscle.

The guard checked his bindings, going behind the post and pulling roughly at Cleve's arms to make sure the thongs were still tight about his wrists. Unsatisfied with the job the others had done, he carefully untied the rawhides and tied them another way.

Cleve bit his lip in frustration. If they had only left him unguarded, he felt sure that Snip could have gnawed his shackles apart. Rawhide was to the dog's liking, and many a set of snowshoe straps had bitten the dust after he found them hung low enough to reach.

The big boy settled on the floor, his back against the mud wall. The stink of the place didn't seem to trouble him, his own scent of smoke and oil and something wild and gamy being enough to overcome that. Now that Cleve's eyes had adjusted to the dim light, he believed that part of the hut's odor might be caused by the big brown stains on the mat of rotted grass flooring the place.

This lodge, so far from the village and on the other side of the river, must be the place where hot-blooded young warriors played with their captives. He swallowed hard. The light outside grew gold and then

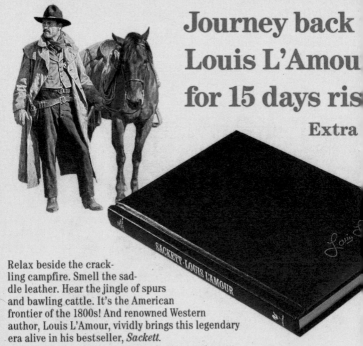

e Old West with
ompelling novel, *Sackett*,
ee!

l: You may keep *Sackett* for only $4.95!*

*plus shipping and handling, and sales tax in NY and Canada.

Detach and mail this postpaid card to preview *Sackett*
for 15 days risk-free and to claim your Free Gift!

RISK-FREE TRIAL CERTIFICATE
FREE GIFT! FREE PREVIEW!

SAVE OVER HALF OFF!

☐ YES. Send my free Louis L'Amour Wall Calendar and my
hardbound Collector's Edition of *Sackett* for a 15-day risk-free
preview. If I keep it, I'll honor your invoice for only $4.95—a
SAVINGS OF OVER HALF OFF the current low regular rate of
$11.95—plus shipping and handling, and sales tax in NY and
Canada. Then I'll continue receiving additional selections
about once a month at the regular rate on the same 15-day
risk-free trial basis. There's no minimum number of books I
must buy, and I may cancel at any time. The Calendar is mine
to keep no matter what I decide.   IL67   41400

Name	(please print)	
Address		Apt.
City	State	Zip

SEND NO MONEY NOW

Prices subject to change. Orders subject to approval. Prices shown are U.S. prices.

In Addition to the Free Louis L'Amour Calendar

. . . your risk-free preview volume of *Sackett* will introduce you to these outstanding qualities of the bookbinder's art—

- Each volume is bound in rich, rugged sierra-brown simulated leather.
- The bindings are sewn, not just glued, to last a lifetime. And the pages are printed on high-quality paper that is acid-free and will not yellow with age.
- The title and Louis L'Amour's signature are golden embossed on the spine and front cover of each volume.

reddish as the sun set. From the wall where his guard sat came a burbling snore.

Cleve didn't hesitate. He whistled very softly just the breath of a note to call his dog. Snip didn't whine, as he usually did. He appeared in the doorway, looked once at the long legs blocking the entrance, and leapt silently over them to come wagging about Cleve's bound legs.

"Ho, boy," Cleve whispered. "Ropes. Chew the ropes!"

It took a long time for Snip to realize that his master was tied with rawhide thongs. Once that sank into his mind, the rest went quickly. Before full darkness had fallen, the young trapper was free, sitting on the floor with Snip poking a cold nose into the nape of his neck while he rubbed life back into his arms and legs.

From time to time, the halfwit gargled and grunted, and then Cleve caught Snip close and held his muzzle to keep him from making a sound. But now it was pitch-dark inside the hut, and even an Indian, he felt, would have a hard time making out their shapes.

When everything worked again, Cleve rose cautiously and moved, one careful step at a time, toward the watchman. Outside, the grass glimmered a faintly paler gray beyond the dark doorway. The legs of the halfwit were silhouetted against it, making it easy to avoid stepping on them. Again Snip leapt over, and the two were outside the hut.

There was no sign of Socks, and Cleve didn't dare wait to hunt for him. One of the other warriors might have ridden the horse when he left, or the guard could have moved him away to tie him at a distance from his master. He wished he could risk the shrill whistle that told his mount to come, but that was out of the question. He glanced about, got his bearings by the dark line of trees edging the bluffs along the river to the north, and set off at a run southward across the rolling swells, thankful that here the grass was only hip-high instead of head-high.

Though resilient to his bare feet, the tough grass was hard on the rest of him. Skin tenderized by a winter of heavy clothing became sore very quickly as the buffalo grass whipped past. Very soon he realized that one hand had better protect his groin. It seemed a long time since he had sat by the fire in the fortress and heard Emile tell him that he was a good runner, not very fast, but very enduring. He just hoped that he could keep running until he was lost in this endless jungle of grass, beyond the chance of discovery by his captors.

From time to time he dropped flat and gasped great lungfuls of the crisp air, resting briefly before rising to run again. Snip, at his heels, lolloped along without a yelp, a sniff, or a whimper. It was as if the dog understood the need for silence, and they ran together, willing to run forever.

Time seemed to swim past, apart from his laboring body. His mind seemed to float above in a dreamy dimension where it could ignore his pain. Yet even there he found pain. He was alone as he had never thought of being. Leaving his home and his kin had been hard, but there had been others, he knew, whom he would meet and learn to know. But here on this endless plain beneath a sky so black and star-shot that it seemed he could feel its folds wrap about him tangibly he was the loneliest creature on earth. Only Snip held him to the world, and the sound of his panting as he pattered along at his master's heels anchored Cleve's mind and kept it steady. He must find, sometime, somehow, a family to replace the one he had lost.

Dawn surprised him. The swells, black before, gradually took on contours, shadings of pewter and gray and green-tan. The sky was appreciably paler than the land now, and he was glad to see that the river bluffs were lost below the horizon. Surely he was far enough from that damned lodge to discourage pursuit.

Then, as the light grew stronger, he saw the great tear in the billows of grass left by his passing, a jagged track that led from the horizon directly to his feet. Only his present position on a long ridge allowed him to see that betraying mark, and he felt his heart grow suddenly cold.

Then he heard the thudding of hooves. Far at the end of that line of tracks appeared a dot, dark against the shimmering grass. Cleve turned and ran desperately again, trying not to leave such a plain trace of his passing but knowing that it was a hopeless task if he was to cover any ground. He crossed a long low-lying area and came again to a rolling ridge, this one sparsely grown with cottonwoods along a dry creek-bed. He concealed himself and looked back again.

Now it was fully daylight, and the sun was only a few minutes from rising. There, much nearer now, was the pursuing horse—with growing excitement, he realized that it looked like Socks—and its large-boned rider. That could be only one person. Idiot or not, the huge young Indian was persistent.

He ran, stopping from time to time when there was cover to peer back. The red rim of the sun rose, followed by its burning circle. The long rolls of grass swayed in the morning breeze, and the tang of something sweet, like clover, came to his nostrils as he ran on, his legs dragging now, his feet like lead.

He tasted blood. Cousin John had said his nose bled after running so far and so long, and now his own nose felt as if it might begin to bleed. Gulping, he looked ahead, straining his eyes to find someplace from which he might ambush that relentless pursuer. He topped a long swell, and ahead, in the distance, he could see a strange conglomeration of sand-red stones thrusting their fingers into the sunlight.

He headed for the nearest, his feet taking on new life, and when he reached it, the hoofbeats were very close behind him. He darted around the stone, the size of a house, and found himself staring at his pursuer, who was now bearing down upon him, riding Socks. Someone, buffalo devil or Christian God, was with him. Wetting his lips with difficulty, he whistled the three-note signal to stop. The gelding set his hooves suddenly, sending the big warrior over his head onto the gritty pebbles around the stones.

Cleve dived on the big Indian, pushing him even flatter. The idiot was stunned by his fall, his lungs emptied of air. The huge Arikara grunted beneath him and began to rise, lifting Cleve's considerable weight on his back. Desperately, the young trapper wrapped his arms about the bulky shoulders and his legs about the waist as the youngster struggled to his feet. *"Agh!"* he groaned as he staggered backward against the sandstone block.

Cleve was crunched between the granite-hard body in front of him and the monolith behind. His hands loosened as he tried to catch his breath again. With a satisfied grunt, the Indian shrugged him off and turned toward him, his hand now holding the knife that had been dangling from his belt thong. Now those dull eyes were bright with a wicked light, and the loose lips had tightened with determination. It was clear that the guard intended to keep his captive or kill him. This was not going to be easy.

Suddenly Cleve felt every bruise, cut, and agonized muscle in his body protest against further abuse. He had survived a run of at least twenty miles. He had escaped from the Arikara. He had done all he could do, and he felt that he was ready to die here, but he would run no more. He bunched his legs beneath him and sprang right into the face of the astonished warrior.

He got in beneath the sweep of the knife before it could move to meet him, and Snip, now leaping and yapping around the fray, bounced up and bit the hand holding it. The metal clattered onto sandstone, and Cleve breathed a sigh of thanks. With that out of the way, things would be more equal.

He tucked his right leg behind the Indian's left and jerked the man's legs from beneath him. This time he landed fairly on top, chest to chest, and he butted the boy in the face, sending his head thudding onto the rocky ground. For an instant the Arikara went slack beneath him, and using that chance, Cleve fastened his hands around the halfwit's neck.

Those tree-trunk arms came up and clawed at his back, pulled his straggling hair, tore at his ears, but Cleve held on, his pounding blood threatening to burst through his eyeballs. If he lost his grip now, it was all over, for he was done, spent to his last wisp of strength.

The body beneath him arched upward, the heels digging into the ground, the head tilted back, away from his choking hands. He found, somewhere deep where he had never been forced to look before, a bit more energy and bore down still harder.

He felt something in the sweaty neck crackle in his grip. The Indian made a terrible sound, dry and retching yet breathless, and suddenly he relaxed.

Socks, who had come near to see what his master was doing, backed away, eyes rolling, and Snip came close to sniff at the dark line of urine trickling from beneath the body. The halfwit was staring up at Cleve, his eyeballs gleaming dully in the harsh sunlight, but there was no life behind them. That flat gaze reminded him sickeningly of the bear back there at Fort Ashworth.

The sun was baking his pale skin as Cleve stripped the Arikara of his breechclout, leggings, moccasins, and deerhide shirt. The bow the boy had carried was a strange weapon to one who had been a farmer, but there was a bark case of arrows tied across one of the limp shoulders, and on Socks's back, tied to a thong (the saddle had vanished, probably cut off by a rider unused to such things), was a bunch of lances.

Cleve's rifle was gone, and he grieved for the fine Hawken and his possibles bag. But it was better to have clothing, even though it stank of urine and Indian, and weapons, awkward though they might be until he learned to use them, than to be naked and unarmed in these wild pitiless lands.

Socks stood, shivering his skin, his ears pricked questioningly as Cleve looked about to find someplace for the body. A Christian burial might not be just the thing, but he could hide him from the buzzards if nothing else. If his fellows came looking for them, it was best to have the body out of sight.

Under one of the nearby rocks was a notch, worn

by wind and weather, and into that he dragged the dead Indian. He pushed up a big stone to close the hole and turned away to mount Socks again. Thinking better of that, Cleve took a tall stalk of bunchy grass and wiped out all he could of the tracks and traces he had left in the bare grit of the soil around the stones. Shooing Snip into the grass, he completed a careful circuit of the tracked area.

When he had done his best to confuse anyone coming after them, he mounted the gelding and whistled to Snip. It was time to make tracks in earnest now. Not back toward the Missouri. Those fellows back there were numerous, well armed, and tough as old boots. They could take care of a bunch of Arikara. And if he went bulling into that area from this direction, he would probably run right into another batch of angry Indians. That wouldn't be sensible. Armed with weapons he couldn't use, he would have to return through enemy forces to get back to his people.

Weighing everything, Cleve decided that he stood his best chance by going south and west. There were rivers there and occasional creeks. Emile had told him of those. If he circled wide, he could approach the Missouri again from the south, much farther along its westward course, with some hope of meeting Ashworth and his people again if they survived the attack and didn't turn back.

He was young and tough, and he would survive. If he failed to make contact with his former group, he might find a lone trapper who needed a partner. Until then, he would ride and ride, and wait to see what happened next. But he was still alone, although having Socks again was some comfort and Snip had become more brother than dog.

Together they would try to survive here in the wide, empty plains.

The land stretched wide about him, its long rolls so shallow that he felt as if the sea his mother had told him about lay around him and his horse was a four-legged vessel plowing through waves of grass toward some invisible goal. Though it was still early in the summer, he found no streams with water in them as he crossed dry beds. Those were lined with cottonwoods, willows, and scrub.

Angling west and south, he passed a dark line of hills covered with a scanty furring of trees, assurance that water could be found. In time he came to a fair-sized river with a sluggish stream, milk-colored with sand. Though it gritted between his teeth, he was grateful for it, and Socks and Snip drank deeply.

He had no way to carry water with him, and that was a concern, but if there was one river, then surely he would find another. That map he had studied with Emile and Paul had been netted with streams, all running into the Missouri. If he kept heading southwest, he must come to something.

They became very thirsty nevertheless. The sun grew hotter as they moved, the land drier, and Cleve took to traveling by night and camping in whatever shade he could find by day. The grass trapped the heat about him, and Socks was suffering too, though there was more grass than he could eat.

Only Snip seemed happy, running down the long-legged jackrabbits and bringing one to his master once his own hunger was satisfied. The juices of the meat and the warm blood didn't satisfy his thirst, but they kept him going.

When at last he came to a river with trees along its

banks and game, principally big tawny deer with large ears, coming and going to drink, he decided to stop and learn to use his weapons. Better to be unarmed than unskilled with what he had.

For several days he rested Socks, let Snip chase rabbits to his heart's desire, and practiced in the scanty shade of the cottonwoods until he was a fair hand with a lance. He learned to throw the flint knife passably well, although it was not balanced as steel knives were and often hit the target sideways or haft-first. Nevertheless, he became a good shot with it. Cleve decided that being hit with something that hard and heavy would kill most rabbits and startle most men enough to let him escape—or get his hands around their necks.

He had nightmares about that. The feel of that deep *snap* between his hands, the jerk of the body beneath him—he had never considered what killing a man would be like. That poor backward Arikara visited his dreams too often. He often felt that he had an invisible companion on his journey to nowhere.

When he attacked his father, he had been in a blind red rage. Though he still felt that the old man would be better dead, he now understood that he would never have been able to live with the feel of his father's death in his hands and his mind.

The bow was a much harder weapon to master than the lance or the knife. Stringing the thing properly was hard enough. Putting one of the flint-headed arrows anywhere near a target proved well-nigh impossible. After two days of constant effort broken only by periods of disgust when he peeled off his clothing and sat neck-deep in an eddy of the river, Cleve admitted that archery was not his best field. He shifted his focus to rock throwing, handling that awkward knife until he became familiar with its feel and balance, and learning to put the point of the lance just where he wanted it, afoot or horseback.

Soon Snip's efforts were joined by his, and he brought down one of the deer as it came to drink in the late evening. He didn't intend to waste any of it. He had helped his family dress wild game and domestic animals all his life, and it took little time for him to gut the deer and skin it out. The stomach and intestine he saved carefully. He didn't intend to lack the means for carrying water in future.

The meat he cut into convenient strips and draped over a stick frame to dry in the smoke of the fire he kept burning for several days. It would be hard when he was done, but Emile had told him of the value of jerked meat to travelers in the wide lands, and he intended to survive there.

Carefully cleaning the intestines and the stomach, he turned them inside out and knotted the openings until they would hold water. The deerhide might have been used as a waterbag, but his sore butt demanded some cushion over Socks's backbone. He wondered what the Arikara had done with saddle and blanket, but that was pointless. He had to have protection, or that sweaty spine was going to saw him in two.

Time passed quickly, for he was very busy tending his jerky and making a sort of saddle of the doubled deerhide stuffed with grass. Strips of rawhide secured under the horse's belly would keep the thing from slipping off.

When at last Cleve looked around his camp undistracted by his many tasks, he realized that the cottonwood leaves, fluttering like frantic hands in the breeze, were now their summer shade of gray-green rather than the tender color they had been when he arrived. Socks was fat with grass and water, and Snip was growing lazy with too much rabbit flesh.

The jerky was dried, shrinking nicely to a bulk that Socks could carry. He packed that into the stomach and the bag he had made from scraps of deerhide laced together with willow withes. The gut he filled with water, tying off with tendon the foot-long lengths like sausages. Anything puncturing one section would not drain his entire store.

When he had covered the ashes of his fire with layers of sand sifted finely through his fingers, he led Socks into the grassland beyond the trees. Then he went back and swept away all the tracks he could find, shooing Snip away so he would not destroy his careful work.

With some regret, he turned his back on the place that had served him so well and headed once again across the waving sea of grass, now seeding in shades of gold, tan, and brown. Far on the horizon was a dim line that he thought might be mountains. That was where he might find a partner if his luck was good, and he turned Socks in a more westerly direction. That would be their goal . . . better than having no goal at all.

Cleve was sparing of his water. He chewed a bit of jerky twice a day and fed Snip only a taste from time to time, for the dog had more rabbits than he could chase. Socks grazed much of the time when they paused to sleep, and he didn't lose much weight as they proceeded. Cleve gave him one gut-link of water morning and night.

The low line of mountains turned from dim gray to

blue-gray to plum, but it seemed that every day passed without bringing them much closer. The sun grew hotter, the grass drier, water more infrequent. Ravines that obviously carried runoff in the spring were grown up with huge fat cottonwoods and willows as thick through as some of the oaks back home in Missouri, but the runnels were dry.

Sometimes he could dig in dampish spots and reach hidden streams still traveling slowly through the underground waterways. At such times he filled his water carriers, letting the water seep slowly, scooping it up, then letting it seep again.

The mountains were now a deeply jagged line, peaks looming up to shine with the sun on their layers of snow. The lower ranges were forested, he could tell, but beyond them there were stark heights that probably held their mantles of white all year.

Sometimes he looked back over his shoulder at the stretches of plains, hills, and dim blue distance he had crossed. How had his companions fared in their battle with the Arikara? He wondered, but he felt no guilt for his escape, though from what he had been taught, he knew that he should. Getting himself killed trying to get to them would have been a fool's game. As it was, he was alive. He had his horse and his dog, clothing that he had finally cleaned of the stink of Indian grease, and enough food for some time. He could have been in much worse shape than this.

Even as the thought crossed his mind, his eye caught motion far ahead and to the left. Deer? There were many here, along with stray buffalo left behind by the herds as they moved across the grasslands. But he needed no more meat at the moment. It required water enough for a long camp if he killed another animal, and that was not at hand.

He rode forward, watching the movement that appeared and disappeared as whatever made it topped the swells and went down into the valleys. By the time he could make out what that moving body was, it was too late to do much but run.

Indians on ponies came up out of the low place to his left. Now they were near enough so that he could make out their shining dark hair, feathers drooping from the bands confining it, the dark skins in which they were clothed, the gleam of bare backs and shoulders in the sun.

Socks turned under his knees and picked up his hooves, but Cleve had a sick feeling that he had been fatally careless. He'd waited too long before taking cover and checking out that movement. Stupid, Emile would have called that, and he agreed.

His horse thundered along through the grass, angling off from the backtrail to head straight away from the pursuers. Snip, wildly excited, ran ahead, his tufted gray tail appearing and disappearing as he bounded through the tall growth. Even above the pounding of the hooves, the swish of grass about his knees, and the thud of his heart, Cleve could now hear shrill yips from the Indians. He had escaped captivity by sheer good luck, he knew. Now he was going to have to face it again, this time without much hope that his luck would hold—if they didn't kill him outright.

An arrow sang past his ear, disappearing into the grass ahead. He ducked, lying flat along the horse's neck, and sped on, urging Socks with every muscle, every nerve, and a set of prayers his mother had taught him years ago. He thought of that demon buffalo, but there was no comfort there. He couldn't pray to an animal, even if it might be Old Nick himself. He might be bad, but he didn't feel that he was wicked enough for that.

The yips came nearer. Socks was cleaving through the heavy grass, and the Indians were taking advantage of the trail he left. The horse was wearying, and there was nothing Cleve could do to help him.

Then the world was flying around him, earth above, sky below, and Cleve hit the ground with a thump that shook all the breath out of him. With sudden clarity, he understood how that hapless Arikara lad had felt when he whistled Socks to a stop.

Socks! Had the horse put his foot into a hole? Was he crippled? Dead? Gasping, Cleve raised his head and stared about. Socks was standing, head down, sides heaving. Lather covered his shoulders and flanks, but he shifted his weight about from leg to leg, and nothing seemed broken.

Even as he sat up, still gasping to fill his lungs, the ponies pounded up and circled him. Moccasined feet hit the ground, and he stared up into a half-dozen coppery faces. They sported no paint, which was a relief. Emile had told him much about the ways of Indians, and one of his lessons was that war paint was used whenever the plains people were ready to fight.

Cleve staggered to his feet and stood facing the oldest of the men, a tall warrior, solidly built, with an aquiline nose and a wide brow. He dropped from his horse last, waiting until the others settled into silence before he stepped from his mount and moved silently over the crushed grass to look closely at his captive. He said something, but Cleve couldn't understand the words. Even the tone was alien, and he tried to read the impassive face that was now within arm's length. Those black eyes scanned him, assessing his pale hair and eyes, his sunburnt forearms and his Indian clothing. A wrinkle formed between the brows, and Cleve realized that this man was both amused and puzzled by the odd combination.

Sighing, he straightened, forced his breathing to slow, and waited for whatever might happen next. He had no idea what sort of Indians these might be. Their intentions were completely unknown. He was once again surrounded by enemies who might well finish him off before the sun went down.

Out of the frying pan was Cleve's first reaction as he rode docilely among the young hunters who had captured him. These were not the same sort of problem that the halfwit back at the Missouri had posed. These were sharp youngsters, on the alert, ready for anything that promised excitement. Not too long ago, he had been the same. That last horrible scene with Pa had quashed most of his youthful spirits, however, and now he felt years older than the Cheyenne hunters.

He found Emile's tales helpful in identifying their tribe, not only by the striped turkey feathers that fletched their arrows but by the markings on their ponies. The Frenchman had said that sign-language for *Cheyenne* was running two fingers along the back of the other hand, imitating the pattern of turkey feathers.

Socks, even after his efforts to escape the pursuers, seemed able to keep up the pace as he followed the rider holding his lead-thong. Cleve sighed and did his best to relax. He tried not to think but found that impossible. Whatever happened now, he knew, was up to him as much as his captors. "These Indian, they admire courage, my young frien'. If ever you are captive, show no fear. Take chance if the opportunity come to you. Be bold. You weel be no more dead brave than cowardly, and sometime that weel make all the difference."

At the moment, Mama's Bible and Pa's hellfire seemed completely unhelpful. That wicked buffalo back in the mist could do nothing to aid him. So he would be silent. He would endure what came and take what risks offered themselves. Maybe, with luck, he might come out alive.

The village they rode into after skirting the edges of a series of hills was unlike the Arikara town. Instead of mud lodges the Cheyenne lived in pole-and-hide tipis, most of which had their walls folded up to let in the breeze on this warm summer day. Decorations had been painted on the skins: deer and buffalo and hunters on horses. Cookfires were kindled at some distance from the lodges, downwind so the smoke did not trouble others.

As the hunting party arrived, there was much interest, although it was controlled, and even the children did not shout and run as they would have back home. The tipi he was taken to was dim with shadow, but he could see a circle of men sitting solemnly about the firepit in which a smolder of coals made tangy smoke. During the long discussion in the lodge he waited in silence, unable to understand a word.

Indians, he found, never hurried their decisions. His captor, who seemed to be of much importance here, talked for a long while, and then a very old man took over and harangued the group for even longer. His only comfort was the elder who sat beside him, intent on the proceedings but also willing from time to time to turn to him in pidgin French-English try to make him understand that the council was deciding his fate.

"Singing Wolf say this strong young man. We lose many in winter, need new blood in tribe. He say give you trial of strength, keep you if you live. He right, *n'est ce pas?* We too few, too weak to go even to summer hunt this year, with all our tribe in plain. But Dancing Bear, he like to see women torture captive, and he want that. Others shake heads, so he maybe not get what he want I think."

The wrinkled mask crinkled into a grin. "Singing Wolf, he good chief, though very young. He will be peace chief, not war chief, and he think for good of all people. I think you get chance to live."

This was the chance Emile had mentioned, presented as if the Frenchman had possessed some foreknowledge that he couldn't explain. Tomorrow he would learn what his trial might be, and he felt a hollow spot beneath his collarbone as he thought of the tales he had heard from the older trappers of such tests of strength and endurance.

When Singing Wolf gestured for him to rise, Cleve stood, his legs stiff from the fall and sitting so long. He nodded solemnly to the circle of old men and glanced cautiously at the middle-aged woman who stood at the rear of the tipi, ostensibly keeping the small fire from going out as she laid the end of a bunch of sticks in the blaze.

She looked amused in some expressionless way, and as Cleve moved through the village behind the subchief and beside Feather-From-the-Sky, he wondered at that. What had she heard, that still-faced woman, that made her look that way?

chapter

— 9 —

The subchief of the Burning-Heart Band was concerned. The long harsh winter had killed not only
horses but people, the very young and the elderly
suffering most, and he was determined to go into the
next winter, distant though it might be, with enough
dried meat, pemmican, seeds, roots, and dried leaf-
herbs to see them through.

For that reason, his band had not joined with the
united Cheyenne tribe for the usual summer hunt. So
many hunters meant smaller shares of meat for each
group, and he knew that he could do better for his
kin and his band if he hunted alone far from the
location of the gathering in parts of his tribal lands

where small herds of elk, mule deer, and buffalo were usually found. In that way he would not risk stampeding the game the greater body was after, but his weakened people would be able to obtain what they needed. Though it was forbidden for a man or a group of men to hunt alone in summer, Singing Wolf knew that he was too distant for his activities to disturb the great hunt. His tribe must store up strength instead of using it to travel long distances.

With a handful of his younger men, he rode out on a bright summer morning to locate strays from the great herd that had gone hammering over the plain two days before, driven by a hailstorm of frightening proportions. There were always young animals to be found that were hurt or separated from their dams and left behind, along with injured adults and those that simply strayed down dry washes or fell into ravines and were lost.

When his hunting party returned with a captive in addition to three mule deer they had killed, Singing Wolf was pleased. This was an interesting man, dressed in the Arikara fashion yet colorless of hair and pale of eye like those white men who sometimes crossed the plains and took shelter with the band.

Long ago, according to the old tales, his people had lived in earthen lodges as the Arikara did. They still traded with them from time to time, journeying to their river villages with horses, buffalo hides, furs, bone ornaments, and other things that could be bartered for the metal tools and weapons for which those people traded with the Fransay. He wondered what this one had encountered that could send him here dressed in this way. He made one of the lightning decisions that had made him a subchief so early in life. This one he would keep. A new face, a new voice, new stories around the evening fires—those were always welcome. This year, without the gathering of the tribe to amuse them, his people were already growing restive. A new distraction might serve them all well. And this one had no sly look, as some of the Fransay had. He had met his captor's gaze straight-on, and he showed no sign of hostility or fear. If Singing Wolf had one fault, it was intense curiosity. He wanted to know about this youngster, how he came to be on the plain alone dressed in garb that didn't fit and carrying Arikara arrows.

There was the summer's work to do, and another pair of hands would be welcome with that. There would be time to learn who and what he was and what tales he might tell of those lands that lay beyond the great river. Old Feather-From-the-Sky spoke many tongues, some of them learned from the Fransay. In time he would talk with this new member of the tribe.

Prophet had led the council parley about the fate of this newcomer, along with Buffalo Horn, the father of Singing Wolf and Second Son, and the healing woman, Little Otter, who pretended to busy herself with helping Nesting Bird about the lodge. Her sharp eyes and sharper wits were valued by those responsible for the welfare of the people, and she was always present at important decision-making meetings.

The prisoner had conducted himself well, keeping his tanned hands folded in his lap, his face still and watchful. His body-smell was alien to Singing Wolf, so the chief could not determine if the odor clinging to his skin had been that of fear or sweat. It was at least not the ripe stink of the French, which was a relief.

The debate had been boring, for he had known the arguments that Prophet would offer before the elder opened his mouth. The women always enjoyed having a prisoner to chivy or to entertain painfully beside a fire at night. Their inventiveness when it came to torture was something that always chilled him. Men were entirely childlike in their methods compared with the ways of women.

But a dead man told no stories. He could not speak of new ways, new people, new tactics in war or hunting. Those were the things that intrigued the young chief, and he suspected that this alien might be a treasury of such matters.

When Prophet's voice died away, one of the elders grunted, sounding as if he agreed, though the sub-chief knew that he was as bored as the rest by the long story. The captive, sitting still, alert, and wordless, glanced up to meet Singing Wolf's gaze. A wry quirk at the corner of his lips said that he too had been suppressing yawns.

As if reading his son's heart, Buffalo Horn tottered to his feet and raised a hand to indicate that he wanted to speak. The young chief felt a surge of hope as his father proposed the very alternative Singing Wolf had been considering. It was not a pleasant one, but if this captive survived it without showing weakness, it would assure him of a respected place in the community as well as freedom to come and go as he wished. Buffalo Horn said, "This is a young man—strong, brave, the hunters tell me. We have lost many in the past winter, and our band is weakened. We need new warriors, new hunters, new women and children, and we have traditionally adopted those we captured if they proved fit to be Cheyenne."

His withered face wrinkled into a crumple as he grinned. "The sacrifice made by those with the courage to undertake it when the sun dance is performed is a test of bravery that many will not venture upon. If this one is willing to undergo a similar torture, it will prove he is brave—or foolish. If he endures as a warrior should, he will prove himself worthy to become one of the Tsis-Tsis'tas. Do you agree?"

The elders and the Prophet glanced around the ring of men sitting in the shade of the tipi. Prophet nodded, and one after another the rest followed suit. Little Otter, from her position in the rear, cleared her throat in a decided manner, and all knew that she agreed.

Singing Wolf rose and gestured toward the prisoner. "We will talk with this one, explain to him what is to be done. He will have the opportunity to prove himself the bravest of men. Perhaps he will become one of us."

Second Son, as a very young warrior, did not attend the meeting, but Singing Wolf informed her of the decision when he returned to his lodge to find her sitting beside his fire talking with Cub, the oldest son of Nesting Bird. "I believe this one will be worthy," he concluded.

She looked up, her eyes dark in the shadowy tipi. "It is no pleasure to me to think of that trial. I will take Shadow and go to hunt in the hills while this is done. My own courage has been proven. I need no evidence that others can endure."

She would return, he knew, when all was settled and the village had returned to its normal babble of talk and barking dogs and occasional yips from playing youngsters.

As it was late by the time the decision was made, the trial was delayed until the following morning. The yellow-hair was given a pad of skins in Singing Wolf's tipi where he stretched out, sighed, and went to sleep at once, seemingly unworried by his impending test. Once he realized just what he was required to do, the young man seemed, strangely, to relax. He even grinned at his captors and said in his odd tongue, "If I could stand Pa's bullwhip and his hard hands when I was just a tad, then I don't think anything you can come up with will be any worse. It sounds nasty, but I've had a lot of nasty in my life already. We'll give it a try, anyway."

Feather-From-the-Sky didn't understand all of that, but he confided to Singing Wolf that he thought this warrior had endured much suffering already, young though he seemed. He sounded confident of his ability to endure, and Feather felt in his heart that he might be correct.

Later, lying in the darkness of the tipi gazing up at the flicker of fire as it tickled the poles and the skins of the walls, Singing Wolf listened to sounds in the night. The steady breathing of the captive was easily distinguished from the familiar noises made by his own people. His curiosity was sometimes troublesome, both to him and to his band. Would tomorrow see some unforeseen catastrophe with this newcomer, or would he react as others did, accepting his fate stoically and without undue emotion? But all of his people knew that there was no way to second-guess fate. One took what came without protest. Knowing that to be the only way, Singing Wolf turned on his side and closed his eyes.

The sun rose in a sky that seemed to amplify its heat. The prisoner, stripped to breechclout and moccasins, stood ready at the door of the subchief's tipi, his expression untroubled. The village was quiet, tense with anticipation as the women and children, the young warriors, and every dog able to walk waited for the trial of courage to begin.

Buffalo Horn led the young man into the space behind the medicine lodge where the post had been set the night before. This was not a part of the regular ritual, and there was no dance lodge in which the test would be endured. The post itself had not been cut with all the attendant ceremony and was not considered sacred. There would be no shade for the sufferer. He must face the power of the sun as well as his agony. The yellow-hair, Cleve he called himself, approached the painted pole quietly, staring up at the thongs hanging from its top. The bone skewers were in place, waiting to be pushed through his chest, and he seemed for the first time to realize just what he had agreed to do. His sunburned face was beyond turning pale, but his eyes went suddenly chilly, though he gave no other sign.

Watching, Singing Wolf nodded. He would go on with the trial. It would be a thing he would remember forever, as the subchief and his brother, Second Son, and many other warriors of the tribe did. Now Prophet nodded, and Singing Wolf moved up beside the young man. Looking into those strange eyes, he saw there a glint of defiance. This one was determined to survive this test uncowed. That was good.

He didn't flinch when the sharp spurs of bone went through generous pinches of flesh and skin just above his nipples on either side of his chest. A bright trail of blood began its journey down his ribs, marking him to match the post.

Feather, standing by to translate, told the victim to lean back as far as he could against the pull and the pain. Without protest, the pale-hair leaned, turning

his face to the sky, a faint clear blue in which no morning cloud promised to mitigate the challenge of the rising sun.

The odd-looking dog that had come into camp with the captive stood at the edge of the crowd staring at his master as if he understood that this was a fearful thing he now did. The animal growled, his hackles rising, but a gesture from Cleve's hand made him sit and still his voice. That was another thing that roused the curiosity of Singing Wolf. Dogs were food, noise, and toys for children in his people's villages. How did one make a friend and an ally of a dog? He hoped that the yellow-hair would live to provide the answer.

Turning aside from the tipi, Singing Wolf stared westward at the distant line of heights, the dusty trees along the stream, the wide sky arching over all. It was summer. Life was good.

And there would, perhaps, be new tales for curious ears in days to come.

chapter

— 10 —

On the morning of his trial Cleve had waked early, relieved himself well clear of the village (followed by one of the youngest hunters), and eaten ravenously when one of the young women who seemed to be wives of this young chief offered him meat and a crunchy bread made of seeds. By the time the sunlight moved past the council lodge, he was ready to face what might be the last day of his life.

Snip, who had followed him and his captors to the village, had already had several fights and established himself as one of the village dogs, was near him. It was a comfort to have him there. This was more frightening, in a way, than being captured by the

Arikara. He was going into it in cold blood, knowing what was to come.

The skewers pricked painfully as they entered his flesh, but he held himself still, expressionless, understanding with sudden clarity why the Indian was considered an emotionless animal by some whites. It was not that they had no feelings. They had simply learned to control them. He was learning that skill too. It gave you the edge in a number of circumstances.

He looked up into the eyes of the young chief. Another poker face, but there was something in those eyes that told him he had done this thing and survived it as a stronger man than he had been before. Cleve drew a deep breath, holding himself still as the old man called Feather had instructed him. Lean back—so be it. He lay back against the tug of the skewers and the thongs, and then he knew what pain lay ahead of him. The raw edges of the wounds felt as if armies of ants stung and chewed there, and the minute tearing of flesh and skin added to that every instant.

But once he settled into the trick of endurance, it was not really any worse than being beaten skinless with a leather whip. The main difference lay in knowing that a beating would end in time through sheer weariness of the arm wielding the whip. This, on the other hand, was something he was doing to himself. Only he could decide when he had enough, and only he could decide to hang there until the sharpened bones tore through his chest, freeing him.

The sun rose above the tipis, burning the sky with brilliance. The shadow of the pole lay across his face for a time, but too soon it moved away, leaving him staring into the intense light, which struck even through his eyelids. *I'll be blind* he found himself thinking as he squinched his lids tighter, shutting out all the sunlight he could. He turned his face aside as far as possible, and the resulting shadow eased him.

His lips grew dry, and he kept his mouth shut tightly to conserve saliva. The burning of his skin went even deeper than his days on the plains had left it until he felt as if he were washed in fire. Never had he known so many miseries as he now found himself enduring.

There was one way to make this go more quickly, and he shuddered when the idea came to him. The skewers were going to tear out a bit at a time. It would take all day, and by evening he would be cooked to a turn. What if he pulled harder, harder yet, forcing the pins to tear more quickly?

He thought of it and pushed the notion away. Not even an Indian would have the guts to do something like that, he thought. And yet the idea was strangely satisfying. If he tore himself loose, the trial would end, and he would have fulfilled the requirements of the test. He had no way to know if they would consider this cheating, but he knew that their tough dark skins could take a lot more sun than he could hope to absorb and live.

He set his feet and pushed backward, the thongs tightening, the skewers twin lines of fire across his chest. There came a rip, both agonizing and satisfying, as the one on the left tore a good-sized gash. It would work. He would make it work!

The morning wore on, the sky a sheet of brilliance and heat. He pushed harder and harder, swinging himself on the thongs, forcing the tearing process to go quickly. There was no sound from the assembled Cheyenne, but when the right skewer ripped free,

there was the sound of many breaths loosed at once into the hot air.

He pushed harder still, swung back and forth with frenzied intensity. The skewer on the left tore again . . . and pulled free, letting him fall to the ground, half unconscious with heat and pain.

He felt dimly that hands were lifting him, dragging him to the shelter of a tipi where they dashed water into his face. He looked up into the amused eyes of the leader of the hunters, who was, he now understood from Feather, an important young chief among his people. Feather was there too, crouching crosslegged on a pad of skins and watching him closely. "You arright? Make good trial. Make new way, too. Very smart!" He laughed silently, his mask of wrinkles crumpling.

Cleve pushed himself up with both hands and accepted a pottery bowl of water from the older of the two wives. She seemed to accept him easily now as one of the family, whereas before she had been wary of him, avoiding his gaze.

Was this the way one became a Cheyenne, accepted as brother by these plains hunters? He felt a sudden excitement at the thought, but his bleeding wounds told him that the price paid was not a small one as he sipped the water and tried to keep his body still.

Nothing was demanded of him for the rest of the day. He lay on his mat, resting from his efforts, accepting water or jerky when offered by the young women, saying nothing even to the oldster who remained there watching him.

When twilight cooled the plain beyond the arm of trees shading the village, Cleve roused himself and sat, suppressing a groan. With the weariness out of his

bones, the torn wounds on his chest, now bound with
tallow and soft moss secured with leather straps, were
far less a problem, and he felt the need of a bath. He
glanced over where Feather sat. The old man dozed,
cross-legged, erect, his sharp black eyes closed now.
As if feeling the weight of Cleve's glance, the old man
grunted and opened his eyes.

"I need to wash. Water—*eau de bain*—wash?" said
the young man. "Is that all right?"

"*Unkh!*" assented the old man. "You go alone now,
warrior of the Tsis-tsis'tas, not with other to watch.
River is there." He pointed down the slope to the
fringe of cottonwoods and willows lining the stream
beside which the horses were pastured. "I know white
man wash with water. Fransay say, but never do."

Cleve wondered what the Indian washed with and
felt comfortable enough now to ask. "How do you
wash yourself?"

"Sweat lodge," said the old man. "Or rub with
grease from elk or buffalo. Keep skin from crack."

Everyone to his own way, but now Cleve understood the source of the odd rancid odor of some of
those Indians he had met so far. Buffalo tallow didn't
keep too well in hot weather. He took up his moccasins and slipped them over his feet. Then, taking the
clothing he had discarded a thousand years ago that
morning, he moved painfully downhill toward the
river, which in Missouri would hardly have qualified
as a respectable creek.

The grass was cropped close by the horses, which
kept to this lush pasture instead of moving out into
the drier grasslands to the east and north. The
willows and cottonwoods were thick-trunked as he
neared the water, promising a deep stream, but when
he arrived at the bank, he found that the melting of

the snows on the ranges westward had decreased, depleting the water. The deepest eddy he could find was barely waist-deep, which was good, for it kept his chest clear of the wet. He wanted nothing to soak those bandages until the wounds healed a bit.

He stripped off his breechclout and moccasins, and waded out, sighing with longing for a cake of his mother's lye soap to cut the ground-in dirt from his days of hard travel. But just to get the sweat of heat and agony off him was a luxury, and he scrubbed with sand and handfuls of grass from the bank until his skin tingled. He combed his long hair with his fingers once it was passably free of grease and dust, and by that time his skin, shades lighter than it had been, was beginning to wrinkle. He felt gritty, desperately sore about the chest, but relatively clean.

The sun had been down for some time, and twilight, long in these latitudes, was gradually dimming, allowing stars to peep through in the east and slowly cover the sky. There was a new moon, just visible above the low mountains to the west, and by its light he moved about, drying himself in the breeze of his motion. A nightbird called among the trees, and a mourning dove whimpered belatedly into the evening. Something yowled at the edge of hearing—not a coyote. Perhaps a big cat in the foothills, he thought.

Up the small valley the horses moved, the sound of their teeth cropping the grass strangely familiar and comforting. He found himself relaxing for the first time since he had looked up to find himself surrounded by Arikara. He was alone among an alien people, but in some way he felt that he had come home. Singing Wolf, Feather-From-the-Sky, and even the grim old Prophet seemed like kinsmen after the long loneliness of the plain.

For the first time, he understood the things Emile had said about his Indian families, wives and children and in-laws. When one was totally removed from everything he knew, all his blood relatives, any human contact was a grateful and warming thing. Here he had other people about him, and that went far to make up for the agony of the trial. He found himself understanding, dimly but with conviction, that the pain he had suffered was not a personal punishment but an offering to these people in payment for a place among them.

From the village came occasional sounds of distant voices, irritable yelps from the motley crew of dogs, yips from youngsters playing at war. If he didn't know better, he would think himself back in Missouri near some village of his own people. After the lonely voice of the wind out on the grasslands, those homey noises sounded wonderful.

He had brought with him a deerhide from his bed, and he spread that along the grassy verge of the river. Stretching himself flat, he listened sleepily to the sound of rippling water, the wind flipping the cottonwood leaves, the whisper of the willows. His eyes began to close.

He slept for some time, lulled by the night sounds and his exhaustion. From time to time he turned in his sleep, waking in pain at the pressure on his wounds, but when he woke, it was not because of any disturbance but the sure knowledge that someone was there, watching him.

He opened his eyes a slit, seeing nothing but dark branches above him, stars peering between the leaves.

He didn't move, sliding his eyes sideways to see what was to landward of him. There a dark shape loomed against the spangled sky. Someone sat hunched on the slab of rock on which he had put his clothing to dry. Leather dried slowly, and he suspected that it was still damp. Was this silent warrior sitting on his wet wash?

Cleve waited, breathing deeply and regularly to simulate sleep, hoping that this stranger would do something to declare himself friend or enemy before the itch along his ribs became unbearable. But at last the thing became impossible, and he rolled to his feet, ignoring the pain of his chest, scratched heartily, and faced the enigmatic shape on the rock. "Who are you?" he asked in the rudimentary Cheyenne he had learned from Feather as they talked.

The watcher rose lithely, shorter than he had expected. The shape against the stars was muffled in a deerhide cloak, shapeless, yet hinting at great strength. Still this stranger said nothing.

"Who are you?" Cleve asked again, striving to catch the pronunciation Feather had tried to teach him.

The answer, when it came, was an unintelligible set of sounds, beginning with *"na."* Cleve thought that meant *son,* or *brother,* though the distinctions seemed unclear. At last there came understandable words, though without his winter with the Frenchmen he would not have understood.

"Il suffit," said a gruff voice. "Near enough."

"Français?" Cleve asked, unbelieving.

"Non!" came the instant reply, tinged with a hint of disgust. *"Allez,"* said the voice, and the warrior turned toward the village.

The young man gathered up his still-damp clothing and followed the dim shape into the random assem-

blage of tipis. When he ducked through the doorflap
into that of his host, the warrior went forward and
entered the next tipi some yards from the back of this
one.

So this was another member of the tribe. Cleve
found himself wondering as he drifted again into
sleep who this French-speaking one might be and
why he had not been there during the excitement of
the day.

It would never had occurred to Cleve back in
Missouri that he could fit so seamlessly into the lives
of those about whom so many bloodthirsty tales were
told. His mother's God seemed narrow and far away.
Pa's ravings and beatings dimmed into the recesses of
memory.

Even that evil-eyed buffalo disappeared from his
dreams, for he found that the lives of the men of this
small band were filled with interest, freedom, and a
total lack of farm labor. As soon as he had healed
enough to ride and use a lance, he joined in the hunts
of the summer months.

The women did all the hard work, which seemed
unfair until he observed the respect in which they
were held. Though this was unstated, almost unno-
ticeable, he learned by careful watching that wives
and mothers, while they seldom spoke, were heeded
when they did. As the women of the tribe seemed not
to protest at the constant labor to provide food,
shelter, and clothing for their families, he soon became used to the idea of riding free over the plains
with the other hunters.

Among those was the one he had thought that first
night to be a Frenchman. And that young warrior was
a mighty puzzle to him, for he had never heard

among his own kind of a woman who chose to live so
or would be allowed to do so if she did. Second Son,
quiet and self-contained, attracted his eye whenever
they were in the same group, whether they hunted,
scouted for ranging Kiowa, or simply rode for pleasure over the billows of grassy swells. He said little to
her, partly because he tended to become tongue-tied
when he tried to talk with her, partly because he knew
from conversations with Feather that chastity was
required of Cheyenne men and women.

To court his friend's sister was unthinkable without
a long process of attendance upon and gifts to her
family. And when that sister was universally considered a man, the complications piled up like one of
those mountains in the distance. Flirting with his
host's *brother* didn't bear consideration. After hearing
some of the penalties for man-woman misbehavior,
he didn't want to know what the other sort of dalli-
ance might bring down upon him. So he kept his gaze
down when she looked toward him, controlled his
curiosity, and hoped that in time he might find
himself on the same easy terms as the other young
warriors. It didn't help his peace of mind that she
seemed to be amused at his confusion about her role
in the tribe. She never offered an explanation. No
one else would admit that she was a woman, and
anyone he asked, including Feather, looked deeply
shocked at the suggestion that she was not a male
warrior just like the others.

Perhaps because she was so constantly present and
yet so completely inaccessible, Cleve found himself
thinking about this strange young woman far more
seriously than he had ever thought about other
women, including the Fancher girls. She completely
displaced the buffalo-devil in his dreams, and instead

of reliving his father's last attack upon his mother he
dreamed of Second Son.

The summer drew out into dry hot days and chilly
nights. The decision not to gather with the tribe for
the annual hunt proved to be a good one, for in these
distant grounds the game, while not abundant, was
relatively untroubled by other hunters, and the hunting parties brought back buffalo, elk, deer, and
smaller game, all of which went into the capable
hands of the women to be jerked, turned into pemmican, or roasted and eaten fresh.

The small children grew fat, and the older ones
kept busy with their work and their games, the girls
working mostly with their aunts, learning the demanding skills they would need as women. The boys
seemed to be left to their own devices, but Cleve
realized that they imitated what the men did, learning
in the process the stalking and weapon-skills they
would need as adults.

So did he. Ashamed to admit his lack of proficiency
with the bow, he slipped into the river meadow with
the striplings and practiced with them, taking point-
ers from Cub, Singing Wolf's older son. The boy
puffed with pride at teaching this large white warrior
a skill that he and his companions had conquered
when still small, but he was a good teacher. Cleve
learned at last to put an arrow just about where he
wanted it.

But all the while he was haunted by the young
woman who rode as recklessly, shot as straight, and
dared as much as her peers. It was troubling, and as
winter drew on, it became painful.

The family sat in the chilling evenings about the
fire in Singing Wolf's tipi, telling tales of hunts, wars,
and adventures with beasts and distant tribes. Now

Cleve understood what was said, for his summer with the Cheyenne had given him a good command of their tongue. He found that learning Latin had made learning other languages less difficult than it might have been. He was grateful that his mother had taken out her worn copy of Virgil every evening and forced him and Gene to comprehend the rolling words and alien phrases. That had smoothed the way for this even more alien language.

Now, sitting silent, listening to Second Son tell of her raid on the Pawnee horses back in the early spring, he marveled at the brightness of her amber-brown eyes, the warm contours of her face, the smooth curve of her shoulder above the deerhide blanket she had wrapped about her. He felt a heat in his loins that made him lower his gaze to the fire and grip himself with harsh control. This was becoming unbearable.

When Singing Wolf took up the tale, chuckling over the knife fight in which the adopted Pawnee had lost his life, it was easier. Yet Cleve soon found an excuse to go out into the icy night and chill his blood in the wind beyond the shelter of the band of trees and the knee of the mountain beneath which they had sheltered this winter camp.

He found himself longing to be truly one of these people. Hard as their lives must be in winter, however harsh their training and their morals, they were more contented than almost any of the white people among whom he had lived back in the East. There was kindness in the family and the band, and quarrels were not allowed to get out of hand. He wished fervently that he were in all ways one of them instead of an alien burdened with other ways.

He walked out into the frozen starlight, shrugging

the robe of supple cougar hide given to him by Feather about his shoulders. Beneath his moccasins the frosted ground crackled under his weight, and the black sky blazed with stars above him, rolling from horizon to black horizon like a spangled bowl. He had a sudden twinge of pain deep inside him in a place that he tried to pretend did not exist in a tough trapper. To belong again, as he had with Mama and the boys, would be good. The thing that hurt most as he watched these families huddle about their fires was the fact that he did not have one that truly belonged to him.

He would, he admitted, have liked to marry one of those beautiful Fancher girls and raise a brood of children there beside the farm their father had created in that wilderness. Since it had not happened, he felt that he might never again be part of a kin group, and that hurt him. He was, at the bottom of his heart, one with a strong feeling for such blood kin.

There was a crackling step behind him, and he turned to see the short, shadowy form of Second Son, standing still now, her face turned up toward the bright-studded sky. She moved very near, as if sensing his unhappiness. For the first time since they had met, she reached to touch him, laying her hand softly on his arm and squeezing it comfortingly between sinewy fingers.

He took a deep breath, and she looked up into his eyes, her face a chill gray in the moonlight. Something in the glint of her eyes spoke to something inside him, and he knew with sudden conviction that she had come out to comfort his misery, which he had thought so well concealed from any observer.

"The night is a fine one," she said, her voice so quiet

that he had to bend to hear her. "On such nights I often ride. Would you like to come?"

He nodded eagerly, following her toward the tethered horses in the shelter of the tipi. Grass pulled in summer by children was piled within their reach. Socks was not happy to leave his rest and supper, but Cleve leapt onto his bare back and turned him with his knees, as he had learned from his tutors.

Together the pair rode softly out of the small village. Once on the plain, Second Son heeled Shadow into a gallop, and Cleve yipped with pleasure as he followed with Socks. Even now, the stresses of riding pulled at his scars, but he had begun to regard them, as the Cheyenne did, as marks of distinction. Few bore such signs of bravery.

The frozen ground flew behind them as the two horses sped forward over the rolling swells leaving behind the dark curve of mountain guarding the tipis. If Cleve had hoped for anything more than a ride in the night, he was disappointed, for after a time his guide turned Shadow in a long arc. Then they were pounding back toward the village, the looming foothills and icy peaks beyond them.

When they parted before Singing Wolf's lodge, Cleve felt disoriented. This ride had meant something more than he could quite grasp, to him and to this warrior-woman, but he had no clue about his next move. She had come to comfort him, and now she was leaving without a word. As she disappeared into her lodge, he turned and ducked through the doorflap to find his bedding, trying to be quiet, for the family was already asleep.

After that night, Second Son came seldom to her brother's lodge at night, and Cleve, trying to understand, found excuses to leave very soon when she did sit beside the fire. He knew now that he must leave the Cheyenne when spring opened enough to travel. He had hoped for a time to remain with these newfound friends, but this was a torture he had not expected. It was not to be borne.

As winter began to wane, Cleve went into the hills after game, riding Socks as far as possible and climbing afoot into the treacherous upper reaches. That was how he came upon Second Son and Shadow, and it was the only time he had ever seen a tear in the eye of the warrior-woman.

Shadow was groaning, long, agonized gasps that held a familiar note. Once a mare Pa bought had foaled too early, the infant arriving with his spindly legs tangled up inside his mother. Both had died, and the suffering mare had sounded just like this. Long years later, a visiting doctor had told the inquisitive young Cleve about delivering a woman of a backward-presented child by cutting it up and taking it out piece by piece. The woman had lived. Now the young man wondered if such a technique might work for a horse.

Second Son looked up as he moved down the slope, his moccasins quiet on the snow-covered pine needles. "She should not have been ridden so far," the warrior said. "I was stupid to do that, but I wanted to get altogether away—" She stopped, as if she were revealing too much about herself.

Cleve touched the mare's side, bumped her flank softly with his fist, feeling the struggling colt moving inside as it tried to escape its suddenly unbearable confinement. He went around behind and saw that she was dilating. He hoped the colt was not as badly twisted as it felt from the outside.

Second Son stared as he got out the keen-edged

metal knife Singing Wolf had given him and sat down to wait. "She will die," said the warrior. "What are you doing?"

"I'm going to save her if I can." He folded his long legs beneath him and set himself to wait.

Second Son was not a talker. She squatted beside him, waiting to see what he intended, saying nothing. Finally the mare gave a harsh groan of effort and dropped to her knees, rolling over on her side.

"Can you hold her head down?" asked Cleve. "I've got to check the colt, see if he's coming out straight. If he's not, I'm going to cut him up so he won't kill his mother trying to get born. All right?"

He could see in her eyes that the entire notion of helping a horse give birth when there was trouble was something she had never heard of doing. But she loved Shadow, as he had seen, and she lay flat across the mare's head, stretching her body along neck and forequarters to hold her as still as possible.

The colt's rump was bulging out of the mare's birth canal. There was no way it could be born alive. Cleve pushed and pushed, forcing the struggling animal back the way it had come before reaching in to feel what was happening. A leg came into his grasp, and he pulled it out and amputated it neatly at the shoulder.

He kept moving the fetus, cutting off what he could reach, until it was reduced to a small enough blob of tissue to come out on its own. By then, he was panting with effort, bloody from head to heels, and feeling sicker than he had in a long time. But once the thing was over, Shadow was able to stand. She sniffed once at the body of the colt, turned sad eyes toward the pair standing beside her, and heaved a terrible sigh of exhaustion.

"She must rest. I will stay here with her if you want," said Cleve.

"No," the warrior-woman replied. "I will stay. You go and hunt in my place. You are becoming skilled with the bow. Take enough meat back to the village to make up for my long absence."

When he rode away, he felt her gaze following him until he was out of sight. They had never seemed so close, even on that winter ride, but this was a torture even worse than remaining determinedly apart.

Singing Wolf, well pleased with his new hunter, did not seem surprised when Cleve spoke to him. "I must go, if you will permit that, when the worst of winter is past," he said to the subchief one evening. "I have begun as your prisoner, but now I feel that I am your friend. If you say I cannot go, I will not try, but I hope you will give me leave to go about my trapping as I planned in the beginning." He tried to keep the strain out of his voice, but he knew he had not succeeded.

Singing Wolf stared into the fire, his skin red-brown in the warm light. No expression disturbed the flat planes of his face, but Cleve felt something like regret between them. "You are now a brother, and what you choose to do is what you must decide to do. You have given us tales this winter that will warm our hearths for many seasons to come, and for that we are grateful. You have hunted as one of us, and no Cheyenne ever turns his back on a friend. If you must go, Yellow-Hair, then so be it. But return, when you can, to the lodges of the Burning-Heart Band. It may be that you will find another trapper, north along the river. Some seasons he traps beneath the very shadow of the Bad Gods' Tower, and he is called Henri. Perhaps you may join him."

Cleve understood that he was free to go when he chose, and perhaps because of that, he delayed his departure longer than he had expected to. The evenings were more cheerful than ever, and even when Second Son came to share the talk, he found that he could speak with her without shyness. It was as if his decision to go had freed him to become her friend, and she smiled and laughed with him without strain.

But the drifts on the plains thawed to slush, and the river rose; the waters began their rush down from the peaks as the sun unlocked the snow. It was time to go if he was to find that Frenchman in time to help with the spring trapping.

There were no tearful leave-takings, for that was not the Cheyenne way. One cloudy morning he rolled clothing, weapons, baskets, pots, and tools onto the packhorse his host had given him as a parting gift and set off toward the north, the river and the black mountain where the lone Frenchman might set his traps this year.

Second Son was not there when he rode away, and Cleve didn't know whether he was sad or glad for that.

The departure of his captive guest did not surprise Singing Wolf. He had watched the yellow-hair watching Second Son. For some time he had been on the alert for any sign of such ideas as the Frenchman Terrebonne had possessed, but there had been no indication of that.

Controlled though his people were trained to be, Singing Wolf knew all the variations of attachments, and he felt some admiration for the control this young stranger showed as they all sat beside the fire through those long cold days of winter. At the first sign of thaw, he knew this must end, and he made no objection when Cleve mentioned going.

What surprised him, though he said little, was the gap his leaving made in the family circle. He found to his astonishment that he had become attached to this chance stranger.

Second Son said nothing. She looked as usual, behaved normally, but something had changed in her, and he knew that his sister-brother had found one who moved her and now she missed him. It didn't surprise him when she began making long lone hunts. She brought in small game from the prairie, sage grouse, woodchuck, and rabbit for the pot. But that soon palled, and she headed for the mountain, determined to find elk. He offered to go with her, but she looked obstinate, and he made no further attempt to go along. What was troubling Second Son was nothing a brother warrior could mend.

Nesting Bird mentioned this to him, obliquely as she did everything, one evening when Second Son had been gone for some time. "Our brother grieves for the pale-hair," she said. "He would like a wife, I think, though none of our young women catch his eye."

Even between themselves, Singing Wolf and his wives never hinted that his sister was not a man, but he understood just what she was trying to say to him. He put a hand on her shoulder and smiled. "Perhaps I should suggest to our brother that he go and find one who does suit his needs. Many of our warriors steal women, as well as horses, and their wives become good members of our tribe. Why should our brother not do the same?"

Nesting Bird almost laughed, but she concealed it

by bending to put a stick of wood into the fire. "That is a fine idea, my husband. Only an understanding chief would have thought of it."

This was polite, but Singing Wolf knew that he was going to carry out some plan his wives had concocted long before. He had no illusions that he was the wisest and best of men. Often his most successful plans and strategies were those worked out with the quiet and unobtrusive advice of the women in his lodge.

He suspected that others, perhaps all, of his fellows were similarly guided, and he wondered at times what the women would do if their men refused to follow their tactful guidance. Recalling their inventiveness and lack of sympathy for captive enemies condemned to the torture, he shivered. No, not one he knew would risk their wrath.

The chief left his lodge and moved to the pasture where the horses slopped about in the soggy grass, finding occasional tender shoots among the winter-killed forage. The foothills loomed beyond the little river, low and furred with juniper and lodgepole pine. Above them rose higher ground, still capped with white. He suspected that Second Son had gone far this time, trying to outrun her unease, but he hoped she would return soon. He might have help for her, after all.

chapter

— 11 —

When Cleve rode away from the Cheyenne village, he felt that he was leaving home again. He had found among those chaste and disciplined Indians the sort of life he would have loved with his own family. Few of those skin-clad men abused their women, and none mistreated children. Those who showed tendencies in that direction were severely reprimanded and sometimes shunned by their fellows.

While the women were quiet and hardworking, they showed no sign of the cowed behavior he had seen too often among the wives of the families he knew back in Missouri. Women were vital members of the tribe; everyone knew that, and no one ventured to think that their work was any less valuable than that of the men.

Far from being the humorless creatures many whites thought them, the Burning-Heart Cheyenne enjoyed a laugh more than most, often inflicting intricate practical jokes upon their fellows. Once Cleve was fully accepted into the tribe, he had found himself, upon walking one morning, face-to-face with a wolf. It was a wolfskin, stuffed with grass and arranged to leer down into his face as he lay on his pallet of skins, but to one still half asleep it was real enough to frighten the stuffing out of him. He did not show how much it disturbed him, but he took care to sleep with one ear open from that time forward.

As he rode across the plain, which was now thawing, the occasional snow thin and dirty, he wondered if other tribes were as friendly as that of Singing Wolf. From Emile's tales, he feared not, though he had great curiosity about the other "red savages," who were evidently human beings, just like those he had known all his life.

He rode Socks, returned to him regretfully by his host as a parting gift. He led a sorrel gelding that carried robes, moccasin and tipi leather, beadwork, pots, and baskets that Nesting Bird insisted would be welcome for his use if he could not find his former group, which by now was probably far past any point he could reach along the Missouri, or any trapper he found needing a partner.

"If you come empty-handed, he will think you a poor man, and he will give you a small share," Singing Wolf said when asked. "But if you come with many things, most of which he will need if he has not been out to trade in some time, then you will be welcomed, perhaps, as an equal partner."

It made sense to Cleve. He whistled softly as he moved through the wind, almost balmy now in contrast to the icy cold of recent weeks. Snip, running back and forth, nose close to the ground, wagged his tail vigorously in agreement. He had, his master knew, maintained his position in the tribe by dint of almost daily fights, and he seemed relieved to be away from the Indian dogs. His torn ears and bitten tail already seemed less tattered.

They camped by night in the highest, driest places they could find, and they built no fires. The most valuable thing he had learned from his hosts was the way to avoid unwanted notice as he crossed the broad expanses of prairie. One of the most important of those was making a fireless camp fairly far from water. Cold jerky was hard on the teeth, and he longed for roast venison as Nesting Bird had cooked it all day, suspended from a tripod over the lodge fire. But he wanted no interference in his journey to the Belle Fourche and the haunt of the reclusive Frenchman. He had been captured twice, and both times he had been lucky. Risking a third capture would be tempting fate to be unkind.

On the fourth morning he rose and moved to the highest ridge of the long swell on which he had camped. Squinting, he stared northward, slightly to the east. A dark mass revealed the hills and the lonely mountain Singing Wolf had described. A faint furring of trees could be distinguished against the silvery sky.

By nightfall, he was skirting that area, recalling Buffalo Horn's warning that it was a favorite winter hunting ground for Blackfoot and Absaroka. Instead of going too near, he curved to the east, then back to the north, crossing a series of steep ridges amid a growth of pines. Now he moved cautiously and mostly by night, for Singing Wolf and Buffalo Horn had warned him of the danger of daylight travel unless one was part of a large and well-armed party. A third dawn found him settling into camp on the north slope of a steep ridge, sheltered by a thicket of pines and alders.

There was water only a mile or so distant, and he made certain the horses had enough after he filled his water jars. Then he returned to his snug spot, invisible to anyone who wasn't standing on top of him. He needed sleep, and the horses needed what browse they could find where venturesome green poked up from the pine-needled floor of the forest. He chewed some tough jerky, ate some pemmican, which by now almost tasted delicious, and rolled himself into his cougar skin, his bow ready at his side and plenty of arrows at hand. Alone, without the alert Cheyenne watchers about him, he was no longer safe. He could not see danger long before it arrived. Who knew what hunters might be in these hills?

He woke with Snip's cold nose against his ear. The dog was making no sound, but Cleve could feel the tension in his wiry body. The rhythm of his breathing held the intimation of a growl.

Without hesitation, Cleve moved silently to make a cloak of his fur blanket, took up his bow, and stood for a moment, allowing his eyes to get used to the sun that now shone blindingly against the chalk-colored stones in the adjacent clearing. A sound behind him sent him leaping into the glare, hitting the pebbly surface and rolling at once into the shelter of an overhanging ledge.

An arrow skittered off the rock overhead and

clattered down the slope behind it. Cleve rolled again, desperately, then crawled along the rocky outcrop to another that ran off at an angle. Putting that between his body and the direction from which the shaft had come, he finally ventured to peer out through the narrow cranny of a stone that had cracked down the middle.

A dark shape stood in shadow at the edge of the trees where he had been standing seconds before. He heard Socks whinny as a strange hand touched him, and he whistled the signal to run, knowing that the sorrel would follow wherever Socks went. Better to lose them both than let them fall into the hands of enemies.

He shot, but by the time his arrow reached its goal, the man had disappeared behind another rocky outcrop. That made Cleve move again to confuse his attacker. He retreated along the stone ledge, keeping his motions silent.

The sun glared down from the sky and up from the powdery dust beneath him, making this late-winter day feel almost like spring. His skin of water was still in its sling on Socks. He had a strip of jerky and some pemmican in the parfleche bag given him by Second Son. His stomach growled, but he ignored it. He had learned from the Cheyenne to ignore the demands of his body when he was in a tight spot. That food might be the last he would see for some time, and a hunted man on foot had no time to stop and shoot game.

He found a place where the rocks were rotted with weather, making many tiny crevices through which he could peer without being detected by the man beyond. He watched closely until his eyes ached, but he saw no movement, heard no sound.

Snip had disappeared, and he had no idea where

the dog might have gone. If he would scout out this unknown enemy and bark, that would be a help, giving another direction to watch, but no matter how Cleve wished for that, it didn't happen. Once the clatter of the horses' flight had died away, only the buffet of wind on rock and through pine needles disturbed the morning.

It was, Cleve decided, a classic case of wait-him-out. He didn't know if his attacker had companions. He didn't know who he might be, although there were several tribes who might claim him.

The sun slid overhead and began its slow descent. Shadows of the ridges to the southwest covered the spot where Cleve lay. As there had been no sign from his assailant in a long while, he risked moving at last. Slipping lizardlike along the gritty ledge, he retraced his route to the point at which he had gone to ground. The rest of the cuplike clearing was shadowy now, and he could see no sign of any intruder, but he had no intention of rising to his feet.

He reached to grasp a pebble and flipped it high, to arc downward beyond the stony ridge that sheltered him, the click of its landing sharp in the chilling air. Instantly there came the subtle sound of a bow being drawn, the stretching of the string all but inaudible, yet unmistakable to a knowing ear. So. The warrior was still there, as patient as the stone, waiting for his quarry to grow restless and show himself. But that drawn bow, the quiet whisper of the arrow being drawn and put into place, had given Cleve a direction. He sank to his knees and squinted into the dust.

He was here—he dotted his position in the dirt. The rock ledge here—a wavering line showed the barrier separating him from the Indian. The other

ledge, against which the man was evidently shelter-
ing, was over there . . . so. He drew a curving line,
the wall forming the other side of the clear spot.
There. That was the exact direction from which the
sound had come. He arrowed a mark into the dust,
straight from his dot to the indentation representing
the other. If he shot to his feet, aimed true, and
loosed a shaft straight at that other dot, he just might
hit the rascal or rattle him enough to allow an escape
from this trap.

He knew that if he hesitated, he'd find too many
arguments against his plan. With infinite caution, he
drew his bow, slowly, slowly, to prevent that subtle
sigh of the string. The arrow in place, he tensed his
knees, took a deep breath, and sprang upright, loosing the shaft at the darker shadow against the stone
the instant he was clear of the protecting ledge.

He dropped immediately and lay against the gritty
rock, listening hard as another arrow sang overhead.
His own missile had not struck stone. A muffled *thunk*
told him it had gone into flesh. Not even by a quick
intake of breath did the wounded man indicate that
he was hit, but Cleve knew. For a moment that one
would be preoccupied with his hurt, and in that
moment he must make his escape.

He secured his bow and the remaining arrows to
his back, settled his cougar skin about him, and
gathered his strength. Then he went flying out of the
cul-de-sac in which he had been trapped and leapt
over a farther ledge, moving down the slope at a
speed that equaled any he had ever made before.

An arrow *whicked* past his head and glanced off a
pine, but he didn't turn. Cleve was fully occupied with
watching the darkening slope, for a misstep, a fall, a
broken bone now would be a catastrophe. Even as he

thought that, he heard off to one side a shrill chir-
ruping cry. It was not a bird. He had learned many
things from Cub and Singing Wolf, and one of them
was to identify a birdcall from human lips. There
were others with that wounded man back there, and
they were moving downslope, getting ahead of him.

Desperately, without real hope, he pursed his lips,
trying to control his panting breath to whistle for
Socks. It was unlikely that the horse could hear him
or was near enough to come in time, but he could
think of nothing else to do.

He plunged ahead. Now the sun was behind a layer
of thick cloud, below the line of ridges, and the
ground ahead was dim to his straining eyes. From
tussock to snowbank to pine-needled thatch he leapt,
hearing those other warriors drawing nearer through
the twilit forest.

Again he whistled, the sound pitifully weak to his
ears. A bundle of gray-striped fur came volleying out
of the trees on his right, crossed his path, giving a
yelp as he passed, and lit out into the forest to the left.

Snip! Bless his hide, he had come back.

Hooves rattled against stony soil, and Socks trotted
into view, followed by the sorrel. Cleve angled to meet
him, grabbed a handful of mane, and got his leg over
the gelding's back. He turned the animal's head to the
north and heeled him hard. The sorrel pounded up
behind the gelding, his bundles of supplies bouncing
on his back.

"Snip!" Cleve yelled. But a flurry of whinnies,
snorts, and wild barking drowned out his cry. The
dog was making himself felt among the pursuers,
Cleve knew. He hoped that Snip would break it off
and follow before some brave skewered him.

Socks was making good time through the timber, angling across the slope toward another ridge farther to the north, and the sorrel was keeping up with him easily. This ridge was lower than the last, and Cleve realized that he must be approaching the grasslands bordering the river.

When they were over that barrier, he could see a long stretch of country, still glowing with light reflected on the undersides of the clouds hiding the setting sun. Far at the western edge, there was a startling shape, gaunt and stark in the strange light. A black mountain rose straight up out of the grassland, its form strangely disturbing. Was that the haunted place the Cheyenne had spoken about?

He wondered why the old Frenchman had chosen to trap beneath the shadow of that forbidding tooth of stone. It gave him the shivers just to look at it, and he hated to think about living every day under its baleful shadow.

Henri. Hadn't Emile spoken about a man who had come out from France with him? Henri—surely that was the name. And if it was the same man, perhaps his knowing an old acquaintance of the trapper might give him some chance at forming a partnership.

There was a light thudding of paws on hard ground, and Cleve turned. Snip, running easily despite a slight limp, was coming fast to join his master. Cleve grinned and heeled Socks into a lope, heading west now, down the last slope into the rolling grasslands.

Ahead, that ominous tower of stone rose black against the last ash-gray of evening from which all color had paled. He twitched his knee against Socks's ribs, angling past the thing, for he had a bad feeling about that place. And it wasn't just the tone in which

Singing Wolf had mentioned it. Something forbidding emanated from the very stone as he neared it.

Socks ran easily, and the sorrel kept his head close to the gelding's flank as if wanting company in those long empty reaches. The sky grew black, the stars hidden by the layer of cloud, and Cleve drew the horse to a walk. Somewhere ahead was the Belle Fourche, the Beautiful Fork if he recalled the French he had learned from Emile. Here it angled north and east to a sharp bend where it angled as sharply back south and east to meet the Cheyenne River.

If he kept going as he was, he must intersect the stream, but before that he must stop for the night. But he dared not use the fire-drill Singing Wolf had given him. A blaze in all this black waste would pinpoint his position. And who knew what unknown enemies might lurk ahead, hidden in the midnight stretches of country?

There was no question of finding water or making a real camp. Cleve pulled up in the shelter of a clump of anonymous bushes and used part of his plentiful rawhide strips to hobble both horses. He would be in trouble if they should stray in the night and those pursuers came up with him.

He felt the slightly springy texture of the new grass that was beginning to show, even before the snow had melted entirely away, and soon the horses were nipping away at the forage. Snip, satisfied with a strip of jerky, turned around four times, curled into a huddle at Cleve's back, and settled down to sleep.

But Cleve stared into the darkness long after he had wrapped his cougar hide about him. A long howl to the west told him that a coyote was calling to others of his kind. Behind him, back in the hills he had left, there was a reply. There couldn't be any more lonesome sound on God's green earth, he thought, closing his eyes with determination.

Sleep was a long time coming. He wondered if he had to worry about his pursuers or if Snip's intervention had delayed them long enough for night to hide his trail. Even then, if they really wanted his hide, they would come tomorrow when daylight showed their keen eyes the traces of his passing. Who had that man been back there in that rocky cup? Kiowa? Pawnee? Sioux? Blackfoot? Cheyenne from another band? He had no answers, for the differences between the plains tribes were matters for one more expert than he.

No matter. Whoever they might be, he was on the wrong side, that was certain. He turned and hugged Snip, as he used to do. That older Snip, back in his childhood, had been much like this one, the dog's grandson. It was comforting to have something left from home. He drifted off to sleep at last, the snoring, twitching dog in his arms.

A distant vibration under his left ear woke him. The sky in the east was turning steely, though the plain was still a mingle of grays and blacks without features. Horses' hooves? He was on his feet instantly, whistling softly to Socks. He could hear nothing standing, which told him that the riders were still distant.

Snip moved about his ankles, whimpering softly and urgently as if in warning. Cleve loosed the hobbles and climbed onto Socks. In two minutes, they were gone, and he knew that only horse droppings and the nibbled grass showed that they had been there. He didn't heel Socks to a gallop. Now he knew firsthand that Indian ears were sharper than those of

white men, and the sounds of his steed's progress
might be picked up by his pursuers. Even at a walk, if
a warrior dropped from his mount and put his ear to
the ground, he would hear, as Cleve had, the soft
thudding carried through the ground. He had to
keep moving, to conceal his movements under the
rising swells that rolled toward the river. He also had
to keep away from the spur of rock that was now, he
discovered, entirely too close. Anyone up there could
command the plain between the river and the hills.

As he glanced toward the looming stone, he caught
a flicker, a glint of something bright there, for one
instant as the sky paled behind him. Was there
someone on the height watching him? He turned
Socks down a long draw that went west and south,
hoping it would hide them until they were out of
range of that excellent lookout.

The sun was touching the sky now, lighting the
high layer of cloud with amber and rose. Deep in
the ravine, he could no longer see the black tower,
and he hoped that nobody there could see him either.
With Snip running ahead, he followed the meander-
ing course of the dry wash, hoping it had not turned
completely around and taken him back toward those
who were pursuing him.

The sun rose, and the high layer of clouds rolled
away, leaving the sky a chill blue. The wind, gusting as
always across the long miles of grassland, whined
about Cleve's ears as he stared over an edge of the
draw, ducking in the saddle to remain unobserved.

Now he was almost due south of that pillar of rock,
and the sun was shining fully on it, turning the
eastern side into a wash of gray-blue, the western to
shadow. Again he saw a glint high up on the south

face of the thing, as if someone with a mirror—or a spyglass?—surveyed the countryside from the height.

He dismounted and led Socks along the wash, now uneven and crooked. Chunks of soil and rock loosened by the thawing snow lay in the sharp angles, and clumps of cottonwood showed that there was water below the channel even when it dried in summer. Peering over the lip from time to time, he moved past the black tower and its unknown watchman until it sank behind a rise in the land as he moved down a long slope to the west.

Then he realized that he must be nearing the river, for there were more clumps of cottonwood and occasional willows. Cleve crawled out of the draw at last, leaving Socks and the sorrel concealed, and looked around. Here the mountain could not be seen, and he knew he was safe from discovery from that direction. Finding a place where buffalo had crossed the ravine, he led his horses out and headed toward the line of trees that marked the river. That stream was wide and flat here, edged with cottonwoods, willows, and an occasional thicket of scrub or patch of reeds.

Three mule deer fled before the approaching cavalcade, and Snip, after an abortive dash, watched them go. Cleve reached down and fondled the dog's ears, grateful to have one companion in this wide reach of country where he would probably find nothing but enemies.

The horses snorted at the scent of water, and he led them one at a time down to drink before tethering them to trees. Too much water might founder them, and he needed those beasts if he was to survive in the wilderness of the plains. Henri might trap these creeks along the river, or he might not. If nothing else, the young man had learned that you couldn't depend on anything—not fate, not yourself, and certainly not God, out here where land and weather and wild men and animals ruled.

Now there was water in plenty. From the tracks and the animals he had already seen, he knew there would be game. He might stay here, build traps of willow wands, gut, and sharpened bone, and trap on his own if he chose. Then he remembered. Those Indians must still be on his trail. He had not taken the time to cover his tracks, even when he entered that ravine to hide from the spy on the mountain. They would come cautiously, for he had given that first member of the band good reason to be wary of him, but they would probably arrive, in time.

He had to move, and this time he must do it with all the care he had learned. He led both horses into the edge of the river before moving back to sweep away, with tufts of fallen brush, any track he could find. Snip, as if understanding what he was doing, scampered along in the shallows, flinging up a spray of small rainbows in the sunlight, which now came from overhead with the turning of the day. Once Cleve moved into the water, he waded forward, feeling ahead with a long branch.

The horses splashed at his heels, seemingly content to be surrounded by water in this arid country. A hawk, downstream and out of sight, sailed up from a dead snag and shrieked into the sky. Cleve paused, stilling the horses by holding their muzzles and quieting Snip with a whispered word. What was ahead that had frightened the bird from his perch?

His heart thudding uncomfortably, he moved forward, his moccasins silent on the damp soil beside the river.

chapter
— 12 —

Since leaving *la belle France* many years ago, Henri Lavallette had lived a solitary life. Only when he returned to the trading fort to barter plews for whiskey, red-skinned women, weaponry, and ammunition he couldn't contrive for himself did he have much to do with other human beings. That had always suited him well enough.

Since a few of his old acquaintances, and some who arrived in the New World later, had decided after a while that taking furs from those who worked for them was easier than trapping, he avoided people. Jules Terrebonne (curses on his name!) had robbed more than one of his former companions in the past four or five seasons, and Henri always kept a weather eye out for any threat from that quarter. Lately, his neck had prickled as if someone watched him, though he had not been able to spot anyone as he went about his work.

The winter that was now intermittently thawing into false springs had been a harsh one, and his bones had come up with nasty twinges in the worst of the subfreezing weather. When one's legs felt as if knives were being thrust down their lengths with every step, it caused even the most hermitlike of men to think about the luxury of having another pair of hands to help him.

It wasn't his habit, fortunately, to go out to trade every year. That was for those effeminate *Americains*, who had outsmarted Bonaparte in their deal to gain these new lands. Only when his horses couldn't carry another bale of beaverskins did Lavallette venture out of isolation.

Against his own inclinations, Henri was beginning to think that he needed a partner, a younger man with strong muscles and not too much brain to pack heavy burdens of traps or plews up mountains and down ravines, to wade into near-freezing waters to secure drowned beavers, and to take on other stressful tasks in return for a share in the profits.

That would mean, sadly, that the Frenchman would have less watered-down whiskey and fewer willing red wenches, but his protesting bones made such rare pleasures a bit wearing, anyway. In his present state, he even wondered if he could show those sinewy women the good time to which they were entitled.

He had settled for the past two seasons in a favorite area, the bend of the Belle Fourche that wrapped about the foot of the Bad Gods' Tower. Sheltered in a shallow cup rimmed with thick brush, his shanty blended so well with the growth around it that from a distance of twenty feet it was all but invisible. No fur thief had found it. He would have known if an alien foot had stepped into his dooryard.

Creeks ran into the Belle Fourche at long intervals, and along them were beaver dams in abundance. He had trapped these over the years, taking care to allow the animals to multiply before he came back for more. These last two seasons had been satisfactory, but he knew that without considerable help, by the time these colonies replenished themselves he would be too old to take advantage of the new crop of furs.

The water had thawed enough to allow the rodents to begin surfacing again here in this warm spell of early March. A few older animals had ventured out, nipping off a fresh supply of willow and alder shoots or felling enough trees to mend small breaks in the dams. Now Henri paddled his canoe quietly along the creek to find one of his submerged traps holding another drowned shape. Not bad for one day at this time of year.

He sighed, hauling the stiff carcass into the canoe. His wrists twinged, his fingers burning with cold and rheumatism. A younger man would be a help, and that was no lie, one without *le rheumatisme* to slow his work and his trigger finger, one who might stand beside an older, more experienced man and fight off fur thieves.

The beaver were not moving about well yet, and he had only a small pile in the bow when he turned the canoe back into the river. The whistled melody that met his ear as he rounded one of the bends made him reverse his stroke and bring the canoe to a standstill. It brought back to his memory a lively lad on the ship bringing a group of fondly remembered adventurers, who would in time become *coureurs de bois*, from Le Havre to this new world. That was so long ago that the thought of those years was almost painful. Forty years—a lifetime!

Emile Prevot had loved that old song, and his talent for whistling it had enlivened many a boring day on deck or seasick night in the hold. Emile was far younger than he. Could this be his old friend come to visit after so many seasons on the off-chance of finding him at this spot that both of them had known?

He moved the light paddle soundlessly in the water, propelling the craft forward without so much as a whisper of overhanging branches or the slap of a wave against the bow. "*Mon ami?* Emile?" he asked in a voice barely audible over the rustle of wind in the leafless cottonwoods. "*Tiens!* Nevair have I theenk to see you again!"

There was a moment of stillness. Then a husky young voice drifted from the scraggy growth along the other bank. "Not Emile. A friend of his, and yours, Monsieur Lavallette."

That was not good enough for the wary Frenchman. He stroked with his paddle, holding the blade silent beneath the water, and turned the canoe into the current to nose gently toward the invisible voice. When he reached the proper spot, he primed his flintlock, always loaded, and aimed it at the point the voice came from.

At his order, the speaker came cautiously out of the undergrowth, his hands held in plain sight. As far as Henri could see, his only weapon was a bow, now slung with a quiver of arrows over his shoulder. But any man alone in the wilderness had a knife. Henri never doubted that for a moment as he herded the young man along the shoreline, keeping his distance in the canoe.

This was a strange one, he knew at once. Dressed in Cheyenne garb, his moccasins the distinctive shape, his arrows fletched with turkey feathers, he was still obviously an American. The toes-out walk, the yellow hair, the flattish accent as he spoke French—all of those told Henri that this not long ago had been a farm lad, now adventuring in the great plains.

The story he told of being the guest of the Burning-Heart Band over the winter was plausible. Lavallette himself had more than once taken advantage of the hospitality of those people, paying his way in tales of peoples and places the wild wanderers would never see. He remembered Singing Wolf, who now seemed to be the subchief who led that group. He had shown promise of good judgment and great strength of purpose, even as a lad. Since his visit, Henri had heard occasional reports of the young warrior, and he was impressed that this newcomer was considered a friend by *le Loup Chantant*.

The fact that the subchief had sent with this youngster a full load of the best pots, baskets, worked deerhides, lances, and other equipment and food-stuffs, including several parfleche bags of pemmican, told him the regard in which he must be held by the Burning Heart. A good relationship with the roving bands of plains hunters was a most desirable thing, and Henri lowered his rifle, laying it still primed over his knees as he maneuvered the canoe closer.

He was listening more to the tone of the fellow's voice than to his words, but the name Terrebonne brought him up short. ". . . nobody wanted to talk about him, and Second Son looked very funny when his name came up," the boy was saying.

Henri brought the canoe up beside the newcomer. "You get een," he said. "Terrebonne . . . thees interest me *beaucoup*. He ees bad man, thief, an' he prey upon hees own kind, that one." He gestured toward the canoe, just aft of the pile of dead beavers.

Cleve Bennett that young one called himself. With the sort of ease that showed how young he still was, he got into the canoe, knowing enough to center his weight and sit at once to keep from tipping the unstable craft.

As cheerfully as if he brought the best of news, he went on. "There's somebody watching from up on that black rock, did you know that? And I may have brought some other fellows with me. I ran into an Indian back in the hills, and I managed to wound him and get out. I never saw him because we both hid out real good, so I can't say what tribe he belonged to. But others came after me, I feel certain. I kept hearing the thump of hooves when I put my ear to the ground. I thought I'd warn you if I caught up with you."

Henri ground his teeth, then spat into the stream. This young idiot brought news of Terrebonne, of a watcher on the Devil's Mountain, and a tribe of angry Indians headed in this direction with all the confident expectation of welcome a child might have showed. But he might prove a valuable ally, nevertheless.

There *was* a watcher on the black stub of rock that was the mountain, and the two of them, after some preliminary plotting and maneuvering, climbed the stub of volcanic rock and caught him between them. Once satisfied that Jules Terrebonne had set the fellow there to spy out Henri's shanty and his store of furs, the Frenchman dropped him off the mountain-top, which, to his amusement, disturbed his young companion considerably.

That task had to be accomplished quickly, for from the top of *le Mont du Diable* where he took up watch once it was cleared of the enemy spy, Henri soon spotted a line of horsemen strung out over the plain between the river and the nearby hills. They were following a trail, for one moved on foot ahead of the rest, straightening from time to time to indicate a direction to the leader of the group.

Blackfoot! That was the worst of it. When he descended to the cabin to alert Cleve, he spat the word into his face. "You breeng *les Pieds Noir* to my ver' door, young Bennett! 'Ow do you propose to deal weeth them, now they follow your track?"

"We know they're coming," the boy said, his pale eyes perfectly calm. "We can either run or fight, whichever you choose. It's your trapping ground, after all, and if we're to move, we'd better pack up your bales of plews and take off. Our horses are fresh, and once we're out on the plain, they can't sneak up on us. I doubt if any horseflesh they're riding after coming so far can catch Socks, and your big dun gelding looks like he might have a turn for speed himself."

"Run? From *une battaille*? Nevair! Eet has been too long seence I feex my sight upon a Blackfoot! They keel one of my women, long ago, an' scalp my child, and I nevair forget! *Non,* young Bennett, we weel fight them, and I know every spot for ambush, every pitfall along thees *riviere.* Run eef you like, but do not theenk to take any of my furs weeth you!"

Cleve looked hurt. "I'd never do anything like that, M'sieur Lavallette. My Ma would scalp me if I did. I just thought, you bein' old and all, that you might prefer to leave."

Henri's temper went off like a fuse. "Old? Henri Lavallette you call old? Like the wine of Provence, I grow bettair weeth age, young Bare-Ass, an' eet weel serve you well to remembair that!"

The boy grinned, though he hated that nickname and had let it slip accidentally while telling the story of his travels. Henri understood in a flash that he had been teasing. If he shaped up well in the coming fray, he would probably be the one (the only available one) to become full partner in his trapping.

"You know the Indian way of fight?" he asked, watching the boy's face closely.

"Not really. I didn't get into that scrap back on the Missouri that separated me from the other trappers. I just got caught and tied up. I killed that Arikara halfwit, but I can't even remember how I did it, I was so tired and winded at the time. And the Cheyenne didn't do any raiding while I was there, just talked about old raids and captives and bouts of entertainment while the women tortured some. No, I don't know anything, and that's about it."

That was good. Too many of the young would not admit that there was anything they did not understand. Henri settled against his rude chairback, prepared to explain the essentials. "These Indian, he do not go up een large troop, face-to-face, like the white man do. He theenk eef he lose one seengle man, eet ees a ver' bad theeng. So those who chase you, they weel not come boldly to the *riviere* and hunt along eet for you. They do not know for sure that I am here, but even so, they would not reesk being keel by one who already have escape them. The man who keep hees nerve, stand hees ground, and catch these red-skeen off guard, he weel send them away fas', for they do not relish the long-lasting *battaille*. *Comprend'*?"

"Sounds too easy to be true," Cleve said, his forehead wrinkling with thought. "If that's all there is to it, why have people like my cousin John Colter had such a hard time of it?"

Henri went into a silent laugh that shook his body and turned his face into a mass of wrinkles. "Because one can nevair be sure how any seengle Blackfoot or Sioux or Pawnee weel react, *n'est ce pas?* Jus' when you theenk you have eet all feegure, you find the *veritable Napoleon* who weel upset all the theeng you theenk you know."

Cleve nodded, his face clearing. "So we don't know just what this bunch is going to do, no matter what anybody says. We just may have a stand-up fight if we play our cards right."

"Much weel depend upon the man you wound back there een the hills. Eef he ees how-you-say small cheeken, they weel not be so anxious to avenge hees wound. Eef he ees dead, eet weel be more fight than before. An' eef he ees chief or shaman, then we weel see action that would not deesappoint Napoleon heemself." Henri felt in his experienced bones that the last was the most likely event, and from his expression, Cleve seemed to hope that would be the way of it.

Knowing his own terrain as he did, Lavallette spent a long while beside the fire, drawing on the dirt floor with a twig to give his new partner an idea of how things lay. "Here ees the *mont*, you see, and here the *riviere* go serpentlike, wiggling north, making sharp turn, then comeeng back to the south of east." He dotted a small hole into the floor.

"An' here we sit, *chez moi*, on the othair side of the stream from those warrior. These creek, eet hide eetself when reach the stream. Nevair have I disturb the bush, the reed, the willow there. The shanty, you have see for yourself, cannot show unless one arrive ver' close to eet. So we leave these out of our mind. So also weeth the horse, who are safe een the pasture where we put them. They weel nevair leave such grass." He drew a wiggly line from the dot to a bulge on their side of the Belle Fourche. "Here there ees the towair, good cover, easy to hide. You hide there weeth bow or my extra fleentlock. Keep watch while I draw those warrior to you, undair the gun, as you say."

Henri felt amusement well up inside him. "These Indian, you see, they terrify of that place. Ees holy place, haunted place, place where bad god live. We have the advantage, you see?"

Cleve's bright eyes met his, and the boy nodded briskly. "Decoy and ambush," he said. "Old Emile told the bunch I started out with about such tactics that winter we forted up on the Missouri. The two of you must've done that sort of thing a lot of times."

Henri felt sadness well up inside. So long ago, those days, so filled with vigor and excitement. And now he was old. . . . But he only shook his head. "Once or twice we do eet. Once eet work, once not. There we lose Pierre Millefois. But nothing ees guarantee, *ne'est ce pas?*"

Cleve nodded again, and from the cocky set of his shoulders Henri knew the young man hadn't the faintest idea how wrong dealings with angry Indians could go. He had been lucky so far, finding himself in the hands of an idiot and a friendly tribe. He had little enough experience of Blackfoot ferocity when those formidable people were angry.

Although it was growing dark and clouds were filling the sky to the northwest, Henri insisted that they set out at once. Spending a night in the open with a storm blowing in and the last storm of winter making itself felt through that false spring of the past few days did not faze the old trapper. Why else did buffalo grow such thick hides?

He took his best robe and checked the quality of the one the Cheyenne had given Cleve as a parting gift. As he expected, it was top-notch, capable of turning the blast of a full-blown blizzard. So equipped, they could dig in and wait for morning with confidence. The Blackfoot did not move by night. Not often.

chapter

— 13 —

The spring turned sour and depressing when Cleve left for the river the Fransay called the Belle Fourche. Once Second Son had traveled there with a war party, and the stark cone of black rock standing guard over that river and the grasslands still struck a chill into her. That was a place of ill omen, she felt certain. The shamans called it a haunted place, best shunned by anyone wanting to avoid danger. Why a mad old Frenchman would choose to trap in its shadow was a puzzle to her. She worried that Yellow-Hair might find peril there.

Or so she told herself in the three days following his departure as she rode Shadow or the young stallion mercilessly across the grasslands or up into the hills, winding among the pines higher and higher until she could see far across the way that he had gone. Then she turned away to hunt, for to justify her long absences to herself, she must return with meat.

But the big elk eluded her, even when she moved afoot through the trees, following game trails to springs where the wapiti usually watered. At last, weary and disgusted with herself, Second Son moved back toward the river. Soon the village would move, for this year her people would join the united tribe for the summer hunt.

The spring evening was growing chilly as she rode across the shallow river and into the grass patch where horses grazed. She slid down from Shadow's back and flipped the rawhide thong from the animal's trunk. Then, trailing that behind her, she walked the half mile to the village.

Cub joined her, slipping from the shadow of a clump of lodgepole pines. "*Nihu*, have you found game?"

"No, Bear-Cub. The elk were not to be located these past days. So I have returned empty-handed tonight to my brother's village." She had to look up to speak to him, for he was growing so fast that he was now taller than she.

He sighed, trudging beside her in the last red light reflected from a bank of cloud in the west. "I wish Yellow-Hair would come again," he said. "I like to hear about the pale-skins and their houses made of wood. They must be strange people to live in one spot for all their lives."

They grunted mutual agreement as they parted to go to their lodges. As she ducked beneath the door-flap, Second Son was surprised to find her brother waiting for her. He sat before her fire keeping the blaze alight, giving the haunch of meat suspended above the coals a twirl from time to time to assist in its long slow cooking.

"My brother!" she greeted him. She shrugged off her deerhide cloak, all she needed now that the weather had begun to warm. "The elk had some great council beyond the peaks, I think, for I found no big game. A woodchuck for meat was not needed, so I returned empty from my hunt."

He nodded, but she could see that he was thinking of something else. When she was settled beside the fire, he turned to her, and she knew something was coming. Seldom did her brother venture to suggest any course of action to her, but on the few occasions when he had, he had looked just so, his face still and expressionless, a glint of amusement lurking deep in his black eyes.

"Singing Wolf, I see words in your eyes. Allow them to come from your mouth. It is easier to understand them when I hear them." She suppressed a chuckle and dropped a bit of wood in the fire.

"A warrior needs one to tend his lodge and work the hides of the beasts he kills," said Singing Wolf.

She nodded, keeping her gaze on the flames.

"A warrior needs children to replenish the numbers of the tribe."

Again she nodded, but she felt her lips quirk uncontrollably at the corners. Between the two of them, this conversation was more than strange.

"Often a young man finds that no maiden of his band takes his eye. He finds no one for whom he is willing to give many horses and long years of courtship. Perhaps he may believe that he must live a solitary life, becoming old without wives and children to comfort him." He glanced up once, slantwise, and she caught the motion and met his gaze for an instant.

"Yet there have always been those who found a way beyond the ordinary one. The stealing of women and horses has been the measure, often, of a warrior's skill and prowess. It is in my mind that you might find, if you look outside our tribe, a wife to suit your special needs." His voice was grave, without the faintest hint of amusement in its sonorous depths.

Second Son did her best to match his solemnity. She folded her hands in her lap and met his gaze squarely. "That is a thing I had not thought of doing. But I find it strangely attractive. It may be, brother, that I will go, taking my horses and my weapons, and try my luck at finding one who fills my eye." She almost laughed. "Is it time, do you think, that I go out and capture myself a wife?"

"It is," he said. "The women in my lodge have spoken of this, and it is their thought too that their brother might go out and by the strength of his arm and the keenness of his wit obtain at least one wife to warm his lodge and his life."

The plan excited her. She had lost her taste for hunting and raids, and even the horseplay among the young warriors had become distasteful. To go away, into the plains and the mountains—that was a thing that she needed and had not understood. If, once there, she followed the path of Yellow-Hair, she should be able to catch up to him. He was not many days ahead of her, and he did not know that he would be pursued.

Second Son had few possessions, for she was the most generous of hunters and had little need for many furs, pots, and baskets. Those she did claim she gave to her sisters-in-law. The extra horses (for those she had given away after the raid on the Pawnee herd were only a small part of her string) she presented to Buffalo Horn, the Prophet, her brother, and those oldsters who most needed them.

On a misty morning she set out toward the northeast, leaving behind her the village and her people. Ahead lay the great mountain and the tumbled hills about it, the forest, and beyond it the looming spire of that forbidding rock she felt waiting for her. Yet she knew that she might find there the one she sought, and she rode Shadow briskly, leading the protesting stallion packed with the supplies her sisters-in-law insisted must be taken.

The country rolled wide about her, the grass now beginning to show a tender green that tempted her horses as they traveled. The air was sweet, tanged with a faint cloverlike scent, and she relished it, breathing deeply as she rode. Three days of steady travel would take her into the hills about Great Stone Mountain, standing alone as outrunner of those higher, colder mountains that rose in the west.

She knew this country. Only one who had spent her life ranging over it could understand it so well. Every dry runnel, every seasonal stream, every rise and fall of the countryside was a part of her, and she kept to low-lying areas as much as possible. In spring, others traveled and hunted and raided. Every high point held a watcher. This was the time for replenishing food supplies, and other tribes moved into the plains, their bellies lank after the long winter. They would be gathering wild stuffs, hunting for the mule deer and the smaller game that ranged its endless reaches. Some of those were allies, some very old and devoted enemies. Often alliances changed suddenly and with little warning.

When she came within eyeshot of the rounded twin hills that were the first indication of her approach to the lone mountain, she circled wide to keep out of sight if anyone kept watch there. Covered with pines and rows of rocks, the hills' lines of stony outcrops grinned, skull-like, between layers of trees on the steepest side. That was a favorite spot for those who watched the prairie, for it commanded a view over many miles in all directions. Below and to the north were the ridges beyond which lay the Belle Fourche. To the east lay the rough lands about the mountain, and to the west ran long ranges of hills grazed by jackrabbits and mule deer.

She would have liked to climb it, to survey the stretches lying between that hill and the distant river. It would save time if she could cut straight across, but even as she lay in the grass, her horses tethered in a draw at some distance and hidden from anyone on the height, she saw a wisp of smoke rise from the highest part of the hill, followed by a dark puff. Others already were camped there, sending messages to scouts or hunters out on the plain or in the pine forests. It would be best to remain in that hidden draw with her horses until night provided cover. She must go the long way around, no matter how her instinct urged her to hurry.

Instead of heading west, she moved in a long arc eastward, gaining the cover of the forest. Then, keeping to shelter as much as possible, she crept forward under a half-moon much too bright to suit her taste. Instead of moving along the bottom of the canyon, constantly risking detection by those camped nearby, she chose to climb over the ridge that curved to the north over pale outcrops that looked under the moonlight much like a horse or a man to an inattentive watcher.

She did not know who those people on the height might be, but she felt they might well be a Blackfoot band. If that was true, they were good ones to avoid. She had no time for personal battle, and she needed no horses. One who had counted coup as often as she needed no more such honor. As young as she was, six eagle feathers dangled from her hair. Besides, it was stupid for a single warrior to risk battle with a group of those formidable fighters.

Yellow-Hair had been gone for three days. She hoped that he had gone another way, avoiding contact with the Blackfoot. However he had chosen to go, if he kept moving, he was getting farther and farther away with every passing day. If he had located the old trapper and joined forces with him, however, she felt that she could locate him fairly rapidly. She knew the creeks where beaver built their dams. Her people sometimes ranged widely through these lands, risking contact with enemy tribes, and she had explored even more than most of her kind. She knew the creeks where the builders of small houses made their homes. The Fransay was wise in the ways of the beaver, and he would work along those best creeks. Now that she was past the camp of the unknown band, she could hurry. Every impulse urged her on.

She slipped like a mist through the evening, passing the hill in darkness, keeping her mounts hidden among trees or in ravines. Once they had to hole up in a crevice washed into the face of a ridge while ten riders made their way down a steep trail beyond a dangerously thin screen of pines. She held the stallion's nose in both hands, trusting Shadow to remain quiet until the peril passed.

She watched those passing warriors, her keen eyes assessing each one as they led their horses down the perilous track. An old brave, wearing the otterskin anklet that denoted a member of the Kit-Fox society. A younger one with a single scarlet feather trailing from his long tail of hair. Two youths, hardly more than boys, who were helping a wounded man as he made his painful way down the incline. Behind came two more, and the one in the rear was instantly recognizable. Jules Terrebonne.

For a moment all her instincts told her to take up her weapons and run yelling her war cry until she could skewer that Frenchman with an arrow or a lance. But that would be foolish. He had paid with his hope of future children for the insult he had offered her. She remained still as death there in the conceal- ment of the trees as the line of men went downward.

She had heard from time to time of white-eyes who lived with tribes, fought with them, hunted with them, and she saw nothing wrong with that. Some- times they were able to supply their friends with the noisy weapons that could kill a deer or a man from a distance not to be thought of by one armed with a bow. But something about this made her uneasy. Blackfoot were enemies. Terrebonne was her sworn enemy for as long as either lived. The combination was a dangerous one, and for some reason she felt a sudden concern for Cleve.

She waited patiently for the last of the men to go beyond sight and hearing, which they did so quickly that she knew they had some important business in hand. Then she moved quickly. Turning back west- ward once she had the first of the ridges behind her, she moved down a wooded slope, going with great care because of the stony soil. The moon had set long since, and she went cautiously, feeling her way.

Reaching a flat place that offered a chance for rest, she paused and let the night speak to her. The air was still for once, scented with spring bloom and the distant smell of water. But nearer, at once fainter and more startling, was the odor of dried blood, which her keen nostrils picked out of the mingled aromas of stone and soil, pine and grass and horses.

Ahead glimmered a rank of pale stones edging the level spot. Reaching it, she sniffed that faintest possible tang of blood. Not fresh—no, this was several days old, dried and powdering into the dust. There had been death here, and she felt apprehension in her bones as she led the horses into a thicker growth of trees beyond the clearing and settled herself to wait for dawn.

Had Cleve blundered into scouts or been caught by a war party? Alone, he would stand little chance against those warriors, undoubtedly Blackfoot. The wounded man she had seen might be one result of such a meeting.

If Yellow-Hair was dead, there was no need to go forward. Yet she had no intuition that this might be true. She knew that she must read that battleground by daylight to know what to do next.

First light came at last, revealing a sky marked with high trails of cloud. As soon as she could see well, Second Son moved into that bare patch, first scouting in a wide circle to make certain no other hunter or warrior was within eyeshot. There was no sign of anyone; only birds called their trilling spring songs into the morning.

There had been a fight in that flattened area edged with rock, which on the downhill slope was rimmed with a snaggle of huge stones. She found a fragment of a feather caught in a crack, still attached to a broken arrowshaft. Blackfoot, she saw at once. Where those warriors fought, few survived. What had happened to the enemy he had found here? She knelt and peered along the pebbly ground, looking up at the slopes of jutting stones.

Caught in a sheltered crevice and held by a tooth of rock, a wisp of something fluttered in the breeze. She took that into her fingers and stared down, her heart chilling. This was a bit of fur from a cloak made of cougar skin, the color the same and the texture like that given to Yellow-Hair by old Feather-From-the-Sky. She had been present when the gift was made. Second Son let the wisp flutter away on the morning wind. Cleve had been here. Was it his blood that tainted the place? Or was it that of the enemy he had fought here?

She knelt again and crawled over every inch of the space, seeking through the pebbly grit, between the stones, for any answer she could find. Kicked beneath the overhang of a rock she found the blood-stained remnant of an otterskin anklet. Kit-Fox Society again, oldest and deadliest of the Blackfoot societies.

If her intended wife had fought and died here, it was with a worthy enemy. She felt amid the premonition of grief a surge of pride.

She rose at last, took the horses, and headed toward the country guarded by that grim black tower of stone that her people dreaded. She would learn at least if Yellow-Hair had reached the Frenchman. If he had not, she would know that he had died here, hand to hand with those whom even the Cheyenne avoided.

She would have vengeance upon them if they had killed this white man.

She heeled Shadow into motion and headed away from the sun toward the distant line of the Belle Fourche. In a short while, even sparing the horses, she would be there, and it should be short work to ferret out that old trapper and find her answers. But deep inside herself Second Son felt a needle of apprehension. Moving with the horse, she scanned the countryside for enemies, looking for a promising place to rest the animals again before noon while that desolate feeling nagged at her. She had found the one who might share her life. She knew that in her deepest heart. Was she to lose him before he understood her feelings?

She felt a vast impatience to find Cleve and ask about his encounter with the Blackfoot, but she had problems of her own. There were others in the hills, and she had avoided them only because she was skilled and cautious. If she was unlucky, they would be on her heels. A lone warrior with good horses would be considered a gift fallen into their laps. While she would normally enjoy a brisk skirmish with any number of enemy warriors, she had no time to waste, so she crept and hid, and came at last out into the open.

When she was clear of the hills, she camped in a shallow cup where many buffalo had wallowed over the years. There she waited for night to conceal her movement over the plain. The wind fluttered through the grass and the brush, and behind her the hills loomed with their scent of pine and aura of danger.

The weather had cleared, foreshadowing the longer days of spring, and there were no clouds to speed the coming of darkness. Off to the north and west the stark shape of the haunted mountain rose alone in the waste, and she shivered to see it silhouetted against the sunset sky. She had been here before, and always she had felt some dark spirit waiting there, watching the land below. Now she felt that even more strongly, and she kept her horses close until it was fully dark. She feared no ghost, but she wondered, as always when she was near this place, if there were gods in the earth who had no patience with man.

The sky held light for a long while, the plain a glimmer of shades of gray stretching in shallow billows toward the west, but at last she was sure the shapes of her animals would blend into that mixture of shadows. Leading her mare, followed by the young stallion, she set out again, keeping to the low places between the swells, following washes and ravines that ran where she wanted to go.

She felt as if enemy eyes watched her, though no tricks she knew revealed anyone following. The black tower was lost to her sight here in these low and overhung places, and even if she had been in the open, anyone atop the spire should see nothing in the blackness. The moon would not rise until after midnight.

She dared not go quickly, for the footing was rough, and she wanted no injury to either of her mounts. Walking ahead, feeling out the way with sure moccasined feet, she crossed the expanse toward the river, listening for the rattle of a sidewinder before she ventured around bends or over rocky outcrops.

The waning moon cast its reddish light over the country, but it was too dim to imperil her journey. Even things very near, brush or stunted cottonwoods in the washes, were distorted in that light, and anyone watching at a distance would never be able to make out what it was he might see. When the sky turned palest gray in the east, she stopped and found a fairly well-concealed slope of grass for her horses. Then she lay with an ear pressed to the ground, but only the occasional stamp or step of her own animals could be heard. There seemed to be danger abroad tonight, but she could not identify it, and she closed her eyes at last and allowed herself to doze.

chapter
— 14 —

When the east grew silver, then gray, then pink with dawn, Cleve had managed to sleep a bit. Henri snored away as if he were at home in his own bedroll, but Cleve was too keyed-up to relax, and he had listened tensely to every sound in the night as he lay in his blanket.

Henri had chosen a good spot. A long column of basalt, flat on its upward side, had fallen from the face of the tower, lying aslant like a roof over an even floor of sandy grit. Tough shrubs grew about the dripline where dew fell from the rock, concealing the long narrow cavern it formed. Even a Blackfoot, he felt, wouldn't detect anything if some scout should slip this way to scout the terrain.

But now the darkness had thinned, and Cleve rose when he heard Henri move. "Where do you want me to hide?" he asked in a whisper.

"First, we go up and look, eh, *mon ami?*" The Frenchman yawned widely, spat, and stretched. "Find out where those Indian put themself, yes?"

It made sense, though Cleve had no great yearning to climb the rocky stub. However, it proved to be easier than it looked, and except for avoiding brittle spots where the rock had rotted and was treacherous, they made it to the top before dawn lit the sky.

When he was concealed behind a protruding tooth of stone, Cleve surveyed the mosaic of grays that formed the grasslands below the height. Only the movements of horses told him at last where the Blackfoot camped. He touched Henri's elbow and pointed.

The older man squinted into the dimness. "Yes. There the horse, but the Blackfoot, they already send scout to river, follow your track, young Cleve. So I go to meet heem, eh?"

Cleve nodded. "You intend to take out the scout?"

"*Oui,* but more. Much more. You see the small ledge above where we sleep?"

He nodded again.

"You hide there. I breeng our guests to your feet, and you welcome them weeth joy, *eh bien?*" Henri grinned, showing snaggles of broken teeth that Cleve hadn't noticed before. The glint in those strangely assorted eyes, one blue and one green, was visible even in the tenuous light of dawn, and Cleve almost shivered. He felt a sudden surge of sympathy for those warriors who thought they were after a single man and were about to find themselves toe-to-toe with a devil.

They crept down the mountain, careful to dislodge

nothing that might make their presence known to the
Blackfoot. Cleve crawled up the sloping stone to his
perch and concealed himself among scrubby growth
that was just putting on lumpy buds. With the buffalo
robe over him, he was both warm and invisible from
below, Henri assured him.

The Frenchman disappeared behind the tower,
and Cleve knew that he would move upriver to meet
the scout, if one there was. He settled himself into
cover, keeping an eye on the flatland below through
a slit between the robe and the rock on which he lay.
The light grew stronger, although low clouds still spat
snow from time to time. The horses were now gone,
moved, Cleve assumed, into the same gully he had
used to escape detection from the watcher on the
tower. They were headed right down his track toward
the place where he had met the river.

His head drooped, and Cleve dozed there beneath
the robe. The wind whistling around the organ-pipe
rocks of the tower waked him from time to time, but
the morning seemed to creep with leaden slowness. It
took time to slip upriver toward the place where the
Indians would reach it. They were moving along his
tracks, watching for a possible ambush springing
from the scrubby growth around them. They didn't
know he was a white man, Cleve suspected, and they
were never careless.

He woke fully to a long scream, more fury than
pain, that came from the south and west. A spot of
motion surged up from the line of cottonwoods along
the stream, and it was with some surprise that he
recognized Lavallette's dun mare. The wily old fox
must have gone after his horse before moving upstream to meet the Blackfoot. Now he rode hellbent
for the tower, waving something triumphantly above

his head. Cleve narrowed his eyes and realized that it was a scalp. He could see the long tail of hair trailing behind in the wind. So this was the way Henri intended to invite their guests to his position.

He pushed back the robe, wrapped his cougar skin closely about him, and tied it to keep it from interfering with his aim. His powder and shot, his ramrod and a spare frizzen, he laid out neatly beside him, ready for fast loading. The flintlock rifle that Henri had provided was a good weapon, though still unfamiliar, and he practiced aiming and dry-firing while the chase drew nearer.

Then he loaded powder, ball, and wadding, priming the pan, checking the flint, and positioning himself for accurate shooting, the barrel resting in a handy notch in one of the boulders lining his perch.

Behind Henri, other running horses appeared from the shelter of the riverbank. Deliberately, Cleve counted the riders, wondering if any remained behind as a backup force. Probably not. Indians didn't seem to think that way. Seven . . . eight . . . nine. There was a hint of motion nearer the river, but it disappeared into the trees.

Now Henri came within rifle range, dashing toward the tower. The horses behind him slowed minimally as if their riders had lost some of their enthusiasm for the chase. Cleve didn't blame them. He didn't like sitting up here on the black stub of rock either. It had bad omens written all over it if you knew how to read them.

The nearest rider, a stocky warrior on a paint, kicked his horse into faster motion, and Cleve drew a bead on his chest. The blast and the cloud of black-powder smoke hid the scene below until the wind carried it away in a swirl. Then he saw the paint running riderless, and a blot of darkness against the light frosting of snow showed where its rider had fallen.

Once again he had blood on his hands. The feeling was fleeting, for the Blackfoot now urged their mounts onward in a frenzy of anger. Carefully reloading, priming, aiming, Cleve shot again. The smoke hid Henri as he reached the tower and his horse scrambled among the stones at its base as he rode around toward the river on the north side. Cleve could hear that, even above the shrill yells of the surviving Blackfoot.

A third fell before Cleve's flintlock, but now combined arrows and badly aimed balls began to patter against the stone below him. It was time to move, for his smoke betrayed his position, and there was no way to hide it. He scrabbled backward, down the sloping stone, and slipped between it and the abutting curve of upward-looming rock. He peered out under the slab, watching the riders divide, one group of three dropping off their horses and running toward the shelter of the boulders at the tower's foot, the other trio taking off around the curve after Henri.

After a moment, Cleve heard the deep bellow of the Frenchman's army-issue flintlock musket. Nothing the Blackfoot carried seemed loud enough to make the Bad Gods' Tower shake.

He had pulled his buffalo robe, along with his bow and quiver, with him, and he fumbled in the dimness and found the long shaft, the bundled quiver. Hastily he strung his bow and set an arrow into place. Then he watched the slit, waiting for another victim. He loosed the arrow at a skinny shape that momentarily blocked off the light. The Blackfoot stumbled to his knees and dragged himself out of sight, badly hurt, from the way he moved.

Much better! The bow didn't betray its user as a rifle did. He crept along the long slot, making for the larger opening where the end of the slab had broken away, leaving a ragged gap. As he reached his goal, the musket bellowed again, very near this time, and a cry of agony told him the Frenchman's aim had been true.

That left how many enemies to cope with? Two had fallen as they came, and another lay very near the tower. He had at least wounded that skinny fellow. If Henri hadn't missed his first shot, he had taken out two, leaving only three more, unwounded and fighting mad.

It evened the odds, Cleve thought, as he strained to see over the intervening snaggles of rock. Henri lurched into view, strangely misshapen. Then Bennett realized that he was dashing himself against the rocks, trying to dislodge a man who clung to his back trying to hold on to his knife long enough to stab the big Frenchman in a vital spot.

Cleve dropped his bow and sprang toward the struggling pair. Henri backed heavily into a stub of broken stone, and the Indian gave an agonized grunt just as Cleve reached them. With one heave, he broke the Blackfoot's hold on the Frenchman and raised him high before slamming him into the ground. Henri turned with an agility strange in one so big and heavy and stamped on the man's neck. The cry that had been struggling for release died in his crushed throat, and his eyes glazed over.

Something rattled behind Cleve, and he turned to find, too close to him, a tall, heavy fellow with a lance. The brawny arm went up, and the tip of the weapon gleamed wickedly. This had to be it, Cleve realized.

The end. The bad end Pa had always said he'd come to. He closed his eyes and gulped.

But nothing happened. He opened his eyes cautiously to find the Indian lying flat, his skull curiously misshapen, blood running from his mouth onto the pale grit.

"Henri? Did you do that?"

The Frenchman staggered toward him and pulled him into the shelter of the stone slot under the slab. "*Non, mon ami.* I was behin' you when you turn. Someone come up *behin'* heem and smash heem flat weeth a war club. *Mon dieu!* I do not know who thees friend may be, but he ees paint in stripe, black and white, all down the face. And then he go, *pouf!* like *un esprit.* We go too, before that last Blackfoot surprise us again, eh?"

"Where do you suppose *he* is?" Cleve asked.

"I do not know, but you can be certain that he ees close by and he know what have happen here. We go to ground like fox, *n'est ce pas?* Take time to theenk and to spy out the land." Henri dragged his bulk to the very end of the slanting cave formed by the slab and lay flat to peer under the overhang.

There was nothing to be heard except the ever-present wind, which became inaudible once the ear grew so used to it that it blanked out the sound. Cleve remained near the wider entrance at the end, watching and listening intently, but he could detect no movement nearby except for the scutter of an insect or animal in the rubble of stone. Then, from the invisible area concealed from them by the bulk of the tower, there came a bubbling grunt, followed by a shriek of rage and triumph.

The voice was shriller than Cleve had heard yet, and the message seemed to be clear. Someone had died out there, and he had no idea if either of the combatants had been a friend, though at least one was an enemy.

There was nothing more. Even the horses, now riderless, had gone still or had moved back into the dried grass beyond the tower's shadow. Cleve waited as long as he could endure the stillness, then he said, "Henri, I've got to know. If that was the last Blackfoot dying, who killed him? Anyway, I'm going out to see. I've missed death by a hair's breadth already today, and if I'm supposed to go, I don't begrudge it. How about you?"

Lavallette drew a long breath. "You move more easily than I. That Blackfoot, he almost strangle me, eh? You go, and eef you need help, call. Maybe by then I have my breath back."

Cautiously, quietly, Cleve crawled out through the rear slot, climbing onto the slab again instead of sticking his head out into danger. When he was higher, he could see around the front of the tower, and there, in an uneven line, lay the three he had killed as they chased Henri, with a fourth, at some distance, who lay motionless in the thin scattering of snow and stubble of dried grass.

He counted on his fingers. Three. Two for Henri. One wounded—where was he, by the way?—one killed by Henri's foot, one by an unknown and unseen warrior, and this last. Nine.

But where was that other who had killed him? Cleve shivered in the wind, which had gained an even sharper edge of chill. Snow again touched his face, too light to see but icy on the skin. He turned back and called down to Henri. "All gone except for the one I wounded. No sign of the one who killed those last two."

There came a grunt as the Frenchman struggled out of the cramped slot. "Then, by damn, we keep watch, my frien'. There are plews to trap, now that the water ees thaw, as well as those that wait to be sold, and we must waste our time een look for enemy. But eet must be done. Now we clean up thees mess, eh?"

For a moment, Cleve didn't know what he meant. Then he understood. They couldn't leave all those bodies to shrivel and rot. Besides, it would be far better if no one of the band back in the hills ever learned what happened to their fellows down here on the Belle Fourche.

chapter

— 15 —

Second Son rose with the advent of dawn and went forward, keeping low, watching when she found a suitable place from which to peer for any activity on the flatland or around that forbidding black tower. By nearly full dawn, she had located the tracks of Blackfoot, who seemed to be following the steps of Yellow-Hair. She looked carefully when she came to the site of their first halt, finding a single set of Terrebonne's distinctive tracks. He still limped from his encounter with her.

There were other ravines cut into the grassland, draining the snows from the hills into the Belle Fourche. She found one and descended into it, mak-

ing her way along its sinuous length toward the river
and its black sentinel. All day she traveled, listening
frequently for any human sounds, crawling up to
scan the horizon for horses and riders, but she saw
nothing. Those others were also keeping to low
ground, making for the river, she was certain.

At nightfall she crept out of the ravine, leading her
horses, and made for the black tower in the distance.
From there she could see down into the river and along
its wriggling length. It would help no one if she stumbled into the Blackfoot and was captured or killed.

By midnight, she was in the tumbled area about the
rock's foot, her horses left safely tethered to trees to
the north and east of the tower. Now she was able to
move freely, for she was hidden by great broken
blocks and columns of stone. Surefooted as a lizard,
she went up the slanting ramps where parts of the
stumplike shaft had broken away, around groins of
warped and twisted stone, up narrow crannies in the
dark basalt.

Nearing the top, she paused to listen hard. No
sound came to her except the constant whine and
buffet of wind through teeth of weathered, hardened
rock. Unable to locate the source of her uneasiness,
she lay flat on a ledge near the top of the tower and
waited for dawn, dozing lightly but alert for any
unaccustomed sound.

When the sky turned faintest gray in the east, she
crawled to the edge and looked over the gray-black
expanse below. Motion caught her eye directly under
her position, and she stared down, her keen eyes
recognizing the shape of a man who was taking up a
position among the bushes growing along a fallen slab.

His head came up, and he moved the fur that
covered it as if to hear something said to him from

below. The pale hair told her that she had caught up with Cleve, and she knew he had found old Henri. They were waiting for the Blackfoot to attack.

There on the side of the black tower, Second Son took out her pouch of war paint and lined her face with long black and white stripes. She pulled her hair up into a scalplock and bound it with a cord from which dangled an eagle feather. She would do nothing, allowing the white men to show their mettle against the wily warriors who pursued her intended mate. Only if he was in danger would she enter the battle to come, for she had no intention of returning to her lonely life in the Burning-Heart village.

The morning moved forward, and she watched the slaughter below until both of the whites went to ground. At that point she descended the rocky height, taking a route that kept her out of sight from below, and moved around the curve of the tower until she could see what was happening. Only when a tall Blackfoot crept up behind Cleve, his lance ready to skewer the yellow-hair, did she drop softly from the boulder on which she had lain flat.

Her war club was a heavy one, given her by Singing Wolf when she proved herself as a warrior. It smashed with a satisfying crunch into the skull of the Blackfoot with the lance, and then she darted back into the concealment of the boulder from which she had leapt. Cleve would manage now . . . this had been a danger that could happen to anyone who was occupied with one enemy and unable to look about for others.

But she climbed back up the tower, watching. She had not seen Terrebonne, and he had been among those warriors. She had not seen him come from the shelter of the river's edge, and she watched it closely.

As the two below located and dragged away the bodies of the dead and stumbled at last over that of the wounded man, another rider came up out of the trees, staring intently toward the tower.

Terrebonne. Grinning through her war paint, Second Son stood on the edge of the cliff. The rider looked up as she shook her club at him. He could not recognize her, she knew, but she also knew that this one was a coward and would flee if he thought other enemies were at hand. She was correct. Terrebonne listened, looked, cast about for tracks, but learning nothing from his efforts, turned his horse at last toward the distant hills and rode away as if the winds of all the north propelled him.

Second Son returned to her horses and rested beside the river for a long while. After eating, she rubbed her skin with oil as she shivered, naked in the icy wind, yet warm excitement welled up inside her, for soon she would confront Yellow-Hair. Before another day wore away to night, she would know if he felt as she did.

It did not surprise her when one of the white men returned to the top of the Bad Gods' Tower. They would be foolish after learning that still another unknown person lurked about the place to fail to keep watch.

She left the mare and the stallion again and moved up to a brush-grown niche sheltered by sharp edges on either side and shaded from above by a slab of rock. There she settled to wait. The sun would not reach far under the looming overhang, for to the west there was an outthrust knee of frozen lava. It would be a good place of concealment, commanding the sweep of grassland to east, south, and west.

She would wait in her hidden cranny, silent and

resting, until some sound told her that her quarry was climbing to his perch. Then she would meet this watcher, Cleve or Henri, and neither would recognize her because she had again donned war paint, as was proper when raiding for a spouse.

The scream of a hawk brought Second Son to attention. The sun, now far down in the west and below the overcast, had poked long fingers into her hiding place. It laid a golden haze across the country below the tower, which cast a long shadow eastward. A hawk cried high above, and the Cheyenne knew that someone was coming.

She lay still, peering through the screen of gray-green brush. A step gritted on stone. Someone breathed heavily, cursing as pebbles rattled down the height from some dislodged foothold. He was coming, that one who watched above.

Second Son again felt excitement rise inside her, but she pushed it down. From childhood she had learned not to heed her feelings or her impulses. She tensed slightly, leaning forward, her knife in hand, ready to spring down if the opportunity presented itself. She had no intention of being killed by a friend surprised by her arrival.

A small bird shot from a patch of brush below, chirping shrilly. Looking down, the Cheyenne could see the faint trace marked into the dust and the scanty vegetation by cautious feet. He was coming now. The sun moved lower, and long shadows stretched across the grasslands, each ridge and swell extending its shadow eastward. The man came nearer, and at last she saw his dark shape very close.

Pausing in a crook of the dim path, he took from the roll at his back a long tube that shone with a bright glint in the last reflected light of the sun. Putting it to his eye, he gazed down over the country commanded by the mountain. Yellow-Hair had mentioned a thing one of his people had used that gave long vision, and she suspected this might be such a tool. But the man was not Yellow-Hair. It was the old Frenchman.

He was absorbed in scanning the land from east to west. While he was preoccupied in this way, she crept to a lip of rock extending above his hiding place, put her knife between her teeth, and leapt the three man-heights downward, landing beside his shoulder.

She tripped him as he turned toward the sound of her landing, and at once she was kneeling on his chest, the tip of the knife blade, that wonderful metal knife, at his throat. A bead of blood rose from the pale skin, and a pair of astonished eyes, one green, one blue, stared up at her.

"Sacre bleu!"

She eased her weight back a bit, staring down into the face, bearded as were those of most white men. *"Vous êtes Henri.* I am the one you called the small warrior. Do you remember?" she asked.

The man squirmed, his bulky body freed as she rose to her feet. "But yes, I am Henri. And you—you do not look like the *petit soldat* I knew. The paint, eet does not become you, *ma belle."*

She sank onto her heels and stared into those ill-assorted eyes, assessing the man she had not seen for many seasons. He was looking old, his hair and beard streaked with gray. His skin was almost as dark as hers, burned and weathered, toughened by his years in the harsh suns and winds of the plains. There was a glint in his eyes that she thought might be laughter, which puzzled her. What had he to laugh about?

"You are, I make no doubt, the *jeune fille des Cheyennes* about whom my young frien' talk. I thought that mus' be the young one I recall. You know one call Cleve? Weeth much pale hair and ver' bright gray eyes, ees it not so?"

In a handy mix of sign language, French, and the English she had learned from Cleve, she began to speak. "I, a warrior of the Ni-o-ma-ate-a-nin-ya, have come all this long way to find a wife. Among the women of my band I saw none to take my fancy, and my brother Singing Wolf has suggested that I go away to find another kind of wife, one who will be right for me."

She watched Henri closely, noting his grimace of silent laughter at this outrageous announcement. "This must be done by capture, I think, to be a proper thing," she went on. "If you would warn that pale-haired one of my approach, I must bind you fast, for he is a formidable warrior and I must catch him unaware. He will, do you not think, make a very fine wife for me?"

The Frenchman leaned forward, folded his arms over his belly, and laughed so hard she feared he might fall down onto the gritty stone. Gasping, hooting, snorting, he laughed himself out at last. When he raised his face to hers, it was streaked with tears of amusement.

"But of course! That ees the only propair manner in wheech to obtain a woman, as I, Henri, know so well! Follow me, *ma chérie*. I shall lead you to heem, and be sure that I weel not warn heem of hees peril! Thees ees a theeng I mus' see weeth thees eyes of mine!"

He turned again onto the dim path leading down the rough way, and Second Son came after him, keeping a watchful eye on every move he made. She had come too far to risk losing her mate now.

chapter

— 16 —

A warmer day had dawned. The clouds had dropped all their snow, driven away by a strong south breeze. The plains to the east of the river, just visible through the trees, were showing faint green traces amid their dead grasses as Cleve did the chores about the shanty and waited for Henri to return from his turn at watching on the black mountain.

The creek on which the shanty was located proved to be an interesting place for waiting, for mule deer came down to drink there, followed by slender-legged fawns. Henri did not hunt near his own home, he said, saving such tame game for desperate times. Cleve felt strangely content. His future, at least for now, looked favorable. He had brought supplies the Frenchman needed, and guided by the advice of Singing Wolf, he had managed to wangle a fifty-fifty partnership on the proceeds of future trapping as the two talked and dug one mass grave to dispose of the bodies of the dead and hid all traces of blood and battle.

By the time Henri was satisfied that Blackfoot, even if they dared to search so near the tower, would find nothing that would tell them what had happened there, Cleve felt he knew the old man fairly well. He liked him. He was fascinated by his ways and interested by the way his mind worked. But he didn't trust him worth a damn.

Busy stirring the beaver tail he had cut up into an iron pot over the outdoor fire, the young man almost unconsciously kept his ears alert for any change in the calls of the birds that were now returning to nest along the Belle Fourche. Since leaving Missouri, he had learned to keep a part of himself focused on the world around him, no matter how busy his hands might be.

The magpie downstream gave a shriek. Had Henri returned from his watch on the tower? That was not alarming, and Cleve didn't even go around the cabin to meet the Frenchman. He was weary with running and fighting and keeping alert when he really wanted sleep more than anything. He heard a soft step at the corner of the shanty and looked up into the trapper's eyes, which twinkled with unexplained mirth.

"Henri?" he asked, straightening his kinked back. "What is it? You look . . . funny—"

And there he stopped.

Another shape hurtled from concealment behind the bulk of the old trapper, screaming a war cry as it fell upon him. In one instant, Cleve found himself tangled with a catamount in human form, and he wrestled, cursed, heaved, and groaned as his wiry attacker used every dirty trick to subdue him.

From time to time he caught a glimpse of the face of this anonymous enemy, but that did him no good. It was painted in vertical black and white stripes, unrecognizable even to its own mother, he felt sure. Yet as he fought, he began to find something disturbingly familiar about the scent rising from the deerhide shirt and the glossy black tail of hair. He recognized the flipping and flailing eagle feathers that got into his eyes and his mouth as he struggled with the short stocky warrior.

Snip, hearing the commotion, came running. Strangely, instead of tackling this enemy, he sat down, tongue lolling, and watched the battle. Every time Cleve rolled over, the dog looked as if he were laughing. What was happening here?

With a triumphant grunt, the stranger bounced up from Cleve's last toss, which had landed him against the shanty, and charged again, this time tripping him and rolling him facedown into the grit and dead leaves of the clearing. Putting a foot on the back of the young trapper's head, the victor cried shrilly to the sky, and Cleve, bruised and trodden, began to laugh.

"Second Son?" he gasped, easing from beneath that small determined foot. "You little devil! What are you doing here?"

Lavallette sat down suddenly on the chopping block and let out a roar of laughter, but Cleve ignored him. Snip seemed equally amused.

The painted face turned toward him, the black eyes snapping with mirth. "You thought this to be some dreadful enemy from your past, did you not, Yellow-Hair? And it was only this warrior from the Burning Hearts, come to capture a wife."

For a moment, her words puzzled him. A wife? For another moment, all his early training rose up against the idea. Pa would die and go to hell before he'd see a son of his become a wife, particularly of an Indian. Ma would mourn as if he had died if she knew he had taken up with an Indian.

But this was Second Son. He had dreamed of her, thought of her, hurt for the sight of her. What did it matter whether he was her wife or her husband? It would all come to the same thing once they were together.

Then the humor of the situation overcame him. Cleve sat down by Snip and began to chuckle. That rose to a roar of laughter. Catching the dog in his arms, he looked up at Second Son, then over at Henri, still convulsed, his beard billowing with the force of his guffaws.

"You hear that, my friend?" he gasped to the trapper. "I have just been captured! I'm going to be"—he leaned against the wall for support, "this great and dangerous warrior's wife!"

Tears streamed down the Frenchman's cheeks, but he was laughing too hard to reply. Instead, he pointed to the girl, who was methodically wiping the paint from her face. "She ees the one who kill the man behin' you," he gasped. "I see the stripe, the paint, the scalplock, but nevair do I dream these warrior is woman, even though I know her from old time when I sit een her brothair's tipi and see her as young warrior."

As her features came clean of the paint, Second Son was smiling too. She turned toward Cleve, her expression a combination of smugness and questioning. "It is not customary, but I will ask. Are you willing to become my wife? I have brought horses, but you have no parents to give them to. This one does not qualify, I think." She bent to touch Snip, who was sniffing about her ankles, his tail wagging like a metronome.

Cleve stepped away from his prop against the shanty. "Am I willing? I'll be your dog, if Snip doesn't mind! I never thought I'd see you again, Second Son. Do you mean you came all this way to find me? What about your brother?"

She gave a last wipe, leaving a smudge under her left eye. "Singing Wolf advised me to go and capture a wife, Yellow-Hair. He knew my unusual problem, of course, and he and his wives felt this to be the best way for me to find one to share my life. But if you object, I will not hold you in captivity."

The young trapper grabbed her and hugged her tight. "You'd *better* hold me in captivity, warrior-woman. I'd rather have you than any miss in Missouri or a troop of cavalry. You just better bet that I'm going to make you the best wife any woman ever had!"

Henri, heaving with deep guffaws, rolled off the chopping block and buried his face in his arms. Snip moved to his side and nosed him to make sure he was all right, but he only laughed harder.

Cleve felt a deep satisfaction. With an experienced partner, he could hope to be both a survivor and a good trapper. With this unpredictable, incomprehensible woman, who was worth more to him than Ashworth's entire company, he felt that he might just learn to live happily here in the wilderness.

The thought of Missouri was lost in the past. Even

that evil buffalo seemed to have no power over him now. He had, at last, a family, someone who was bound to him by ties stronger than simple friendship. In time, they would have children, and he would become the sort of father he had wished his Pa could be. Only good things would come of this.

Second Son stepped back and looked down at the gurgling Frenchman. "You trust him?" she asked. "He is strange, that one. My brother welcomed him, but he never stopped watching him."

"I trust him about as far as any white man," Cleve said, without thinking. Then he realized that with those words he had sealed his future as completely as if he had stood before a preacher with this woman. He was now, he thought, truly a Cheyenne, free of the artificial rules that his own kind held so dear. There were other rules he would learn from Second Son, but they were ones he would choose rather than old restrictions inherited from a dead past.

I'm sorry, Ma, he said, deep inside where nobody could hear, *but I'll never go back to your ways now. You'd be shocked at what I'm doing, but out here the truth is plain and easy to see.* He felt an instant of sharp regret, saw Ma's face clearly, her expression sad, her gaze reproachful.

Then he buried his chin in Second Son's hair, which smelled of grass and spring leaves, and let the past and all his bitterness float away on the wind. He was complete again, part of a whole instead of a single lonely chip floating on the great ocean of the plains.

AFTERWORD

It is always difficult to describe a culture from the outside, particularly if it exists only as an evolved version, its actual details of attitudes and beliefs lost in the past. However, American Indian tradition and history, myth and legend, provide so fertile a field and the varied and interesting characters of the different tribes so rich a treasury for the storyteller that it is worth any effort to dig into that lost past.

The early whites who moved into the untracked West were no less interesting than the red men who lived there. I have used one such white explorer, very nearly just as he appears in the history books, to lead into my book. John Colter was one of the group accompanying Lewis and Clark on their expedition up the Missouri River to the Columbia. As the expedition returned eastward, it was met by an outgoing group, who asked that he guide them back into the country from which he had just come. He went back into the plains and the mountains where he spent several years opening up negotiations with different tribes on behalf of trapping interests, including that of entrepreneur Manuel Lisa.

His run was legendary and made him famous up and down the Missouri and far beyond; in fact, the run recounted here is only one of two, each all but incredible in its details. Accounts of those can be found in many histories of the mountain men.

Colter did return to Missouri sometime in 1810. He married but lived only a few years after taking a wife, dying of illness in a small town on the Missouri River. I have supplied him with a fictional cousin and her brood, but I have no information about any relatives Colter might have had in Missouri or elsewhere.

Other characters have no basis in historical persons, though they embody attitudes and characters who lived in this era. Cleve Bennett's father is such a character.

In the early nineteenth century, and for decades after, the family was the possession of the father, and even their lives were subject to his will. A father could kill a son with some impunity. A son who killed his father would have been damned by both God and man. So Jase could have gotten away with Cleve's murder, but the reverse would not be true.

In other cases I have taken actual people and situations and altered them for dramatic effect and the needs of my plot, some considerably and some only slightly. For instance, I have taken some liberties with the historical Ashley trapping venture, and for that reason I have altered the names and many traits of those involved, though the ad for the expedition that was in the newspaper has been changed only slightly, its text nearly that of the original.

The actual group did lose their horses to Indians, being forced to build a fort and spend the winter of 1822–1823 at the junction of the Yellowstone and the Missouri before reaching the Arikara villages where the attack upon Ashley's people took place in early June of 1823.

Perhaps the most satisfying element of writing this book has been the attempt at recreating something like the lifestyle of some of the Plains Indians. Although a great deal has been written about American Indians of all kinds, the truth of their lives prior to any intermixing with white men is now lost to us, except for tiny bits and pieces left through oral tradition.

Because federal regulations required that Indian culture, religion, language, and myth be stamped out among the captive peoples, great gaps are left in our knowledge of any tribe in its pure and uncorrupted state. In addition, early whites observing the Indians in their unaltered state were so conditioned to European habits and values that they did not comprehend the cultures they saw.

The Cheyenne (the name whites used being a corruption of Sioux *Shi-hen-na*) had been located in the upper reaches of the Great Plains for some generations at the time of this book. As most Plains Indians shared many skills, rituals, and traditions, it is possible to piece together a fairly convincing idea of their lives at that time.

An important though fairly infrequent part of their

ritual was the Sun Dance, among the Cheyenne a long affair performed in a specially prepared lodge around a painted post. It went on for many days, some of the dancers fasting or staring at the sun or otherwise punishing their flesh. Those wanting special favors from the gods sometimes offered what they called a Sacrifice, skewering bone splints through the flesh and muscle of their chests or backs and hanging from the post by thongs attached to the skewers until they ripped out of their bodies. This was not required of warriors and was purely voluntary, an offering in return for some unusual dispensation the dancer wanted. It is not unlikely that this ritual, apart from the Sun-Dance ceremony, might have been used to prove the courage of a would-be adoptee into the tribe.

There were among American Indians a small number of women who were warriors, hunters, and even chiefs. Accounts of these warrior-women were found in the oral tradition, though incoming Europeans did not understand or accept this. Because of cultural bias, they did not report accurately their encounters with such unusual warriors.

In several tribes, women owned all the property, from tipi hides to fields, if any, and warriors owned only their weapons and clothing. It was the work of women that provided the necessities of life and made it possible to live with some comfort and security in their harsh environment.

The advent of the horse on this continent began changing that, for the horse was property that men in particular coveted. Also, the incoming whites' constant demand for furs meant that the hunter, rather than the gatherer, brought in items more valuable to the family and the tribe than before. This single element altered the balance of power between Indian men and women and began pushing them in the direction of the Europeans with whom they bartered, reducing the status of women and elevating that of men.

Second Son would have been unusual among her people. In any culture, unanimous agreement upon a belief, regardless of its truth, is often found. My use of such a mutually held myth with regard to Second Son is, I think, not unlikely.

But it is not only the people that are fascinating to one interested in the West, old or new. The terrain itself, as well as the fierce weather generated there, has shaped history and human endeavor and is a source of stories that has no limitations.

The mountain that the Sioux called the Bad Gods' Tower is the volcanic cone located in eastern Wyoming near the Belle Fourche River. We call it the Devil's Tower, and it was used as a focal point in the motion picture *Close Encounters of the Third Kind*. A black stub thrust up from a grassy plain, it is visible for many miles across the grasslands, and it is ominous and forbidding. It makes a wonderful lookout, and I suspect that anyone wanting to find nooks and crannies from which to ambush enemies would have his choice of many.

The plains themselves are awe-inspiring, and the mountains rising at their western edge come as a shock. Anyone coming out of the great reaches of grassland is staggered at those cold white peaks shining on the horizon.

Weapons too play a large part in any tale of the historical West, from the bows and arrows, lances and flint knives of the Indians to the more sophisticated but still primitive flintlocks, muskets, and steel knives of the whites.

Cleve's Hawken, issued by the fur company, would have been one of the first batch produced by Jacob Hawken and his brother Samuel after they opened their business in St. Louis around 1822. Ashworth would have wanted the newest and best for his trappers, and he outfited in St. Louis.

The flintlock Henri gave Cleve would probably have been a flintlock Kentucky rifle, made in the late eighteenth century, already a bit old-fashioned. Henri's flintlock musket was a model 1816 U.S. Flintlock Musket, probably made by the Springfield Armory. This would have been a fairly new model in 1824, allowing for the time required for the weapon to find its way via traders and other trappers into Henri's hands.

It is easier to learn the secrets of weapons made of wood, bone, and stone. Primitives still use such things in some parts of the world, and there have been modern enthusiasts who have relearned the old crafts of chipping flint, shaping shafts, and trimming feathers for fletching. The information is there for one who looks.

People, terrain, weapons, and weather—those are the components of a good story. Here I have combined different elements of all these, and while the story itself is fiction, the background, the cultures, and the attitudes reflect, I hope, something of the reality of that place and that time.

If you enjoyed
WILD COUNTRY
by John Killdeer,
be sure to look for the next novel in his
MOUNTAIN MAJESTY
series,
THE UNTAMED
available soon wherever Bantam titles are sold.

•   •   •

Turn the page for an exciting preview of Book 2 in
the MOUNTAIN MAJESTY series by John Killdeer.

chapter

— 1 —

Spring was greening the grasslands beyond the Belle Fourche River, and buffalo, mule deer, and incredible numbers of smaller beasts were busy in the grasses, making hunting easy. Cleve liked to take his bow and stalk small game for the pot, perfecting his skills with the weapon as he provided meat.

Henri, his partner in their trapping venture, was a master hand with food, and Cleve had wondered if cookery was somehow bred into the bones of Frenchmen. Back in his early days on the Missouri with the Ashworth trapping company, he had learned that either of the older French trappers guiding the expedition could take anything but shavings and willow bark and make something edible out of it.

Henri Lavallette could put his iron pot to simmering on the tripod over the outside fire, drop into it bits of dried leaf from his store in the shanty, along with rabbits, woodchuck, badgers, even jaybirds, and what came out was tempting and tasty. When he added roots and such, it was better still.

Even Second Son, Cleve's Cheyenne wife, had to admit that the old trapper's stew and roast meat and bread made of pounded seeds was good. Most women would have been put out at letting a man do all the cooking, but Second Son was not a woman, not to her people and not to herself. She was a warrior and hunter of the Burning-Heart Band of the Tsistsis'tas, skilled at war, raiding, and tracking man or animal over difficult terrain. Such matters as food she left to women or those men willing to tackle them unless she was alone on a long trail and must prepare her own.

Only at night, alone in the tipi she had showed Cleve how to set up, using the hides her people had given him and the poles she helped him cut from the hills along the river, was she a woman. And then she was such a woman as even the Frenchmen who had spun winter tales of amorous adventure and conquest had never dreamed.

It was like making love to a panther or a she-wolf—tense and breathless, with a hint of danger. Sometimes when Cleve emerged from their tipi at dawn, he sported toothmarks and bruises. Second Son seemed proud of her marks of affection, which she bore, like the eagle feathers that dangled from her hair, as symbols of prowess. Yet she was not like those harlots the Frenchmen had described. To her, love was a thing to be enjoyed intensely in its own time, but it was not to be overused. Her people, she told him, did not make more children than they could feed.

His dog, Snip, bounced ahead as Cleve moved through the early light, swinging by their ears the three jackrabbits he had skewered with expertly aimed arrows. He was wondering what would happen if Second Son became pregnant. Would she tame down, as white women did when with child, or would she remain the wild, free creature he knew?

A whistle shrilled through the morning. An eagle? No. By now, he recognized even the most expert birdcall from human lips. This was a signal to those below from the one who watched on the black mountain looming over the river near Henri's cabin. Someone had been sighted on the plain.

Cleve tucked the rabbits into his belt and set off at a run. This was dangerous country. Even now—he had reckoned it up and figured it must be 1825— few whites dared the plains, except for the French *coureurs de bois,* who had been coming since their homeland had claimed the middle of this huge continent. A whistle meant that any sort of company might be on the horizon.

They had already encountered Piegan, and those nine dead were hidden in a mass grave beside the river downstream. Absaroka were moving, Second Son told them, as well as Kiowa, Pawnee, Lakota, and other tribes. Spring brought game and wild plants the Indians harvested. Almost any tribe might be found here where the river watered game and the Black Hills to the southeast offered riches in lodgepoles and woodland plants.

Her people hunted this land, though less frequently than most. The summer gathering of the entire tribe usually took place farther east where the stretches of plain allowed huge congregations of buffalo to gather. Could the newcomers be Cheyenne?

Cleve slowed as he neared the river, slipping between the fat cottonwoods, dropping into the cover of the riverbank, and approaching their camp with caution. One never knew who would be waiting.

This time it was Henri. "You hear the wheestle?" he asked, his oddly assorted eyes, one green, one blue, busy checking out the area. "Your woman, she nevair nervous, so when she seegnal, Henri, he get very careful, *n'est ce pas?*"

"That makes a pair of us," Cleve said. He dropped the rabbits onto the stump where game was dressed and took out his skinning knife, which Henri had given him after their victory over the Blackfoot. With expert motions, he skinned and gutted the animals, disjointed them, and dropped them into the ever-simmering pot whose tight lid kept the aromas from escaping to betray the position of the camp.

Then, at a nod from the Frenchman, Cleve pulled the ball from his rifle, reloaded powder, ball, and patch, and primed the pan after checking the flint. If they were to have company, it was best to be prepared.

Together, the two moved across the river in Henri's canoe, sliding downstream under cover of the bank until they reached the level of the black stub that formed the Bad Gods' Tower. Another whistle greeted them as they sank the canoe in an eddy in a shallow creek and climbed the farther bank. This one was a warning, sure enough.

Stooping, they ran across the rough ground between the river and the volcanic core that was the black mountain. The organ-pipe pillars of rock formed crevices and crannies from which an ambush was easy, and the slanting slabs of fallen stone gave access to the upper parts of the height. Cleve ran up such a sloping course, leaving Henri to dig in among the debris at the foot of the truncated cone.

The young man tucked himself into a handy nook and gave a whistle of his own, this one soft, aimed at a specific distance and not audible on the grasslands below. From around the curve and slightly above, he heard a twitter, a birdsound so natural that he could hardly believe it came from the lips of his wife.

Then she was beside him, crouching against him in his cleft of rock, her finger pointing to the plain lying between the tower and the distant hills. Moving specks made dark dots against the pale green grass of spring: Horses, he realized, some ridden, some riderless. A herd was being driven at top speed toward the west.

"Absaroka." Her breath was warm against his ear, and even in such circumstances, Cleve felt himself becoming aroused. But he controlled that, as he was learning to control everything. The Cheyenne were not driven by their bodies but used them as tools and weapons, relying upon endurance and determination for survival. This was not a country that forgave weakness or self-indulgence.

Now, on the very edge of his vision, there came another group of riders, charging furiously after the horses and the raiders. "Pawnee," came the whisper against his ear. "Very angry."

Cleve watched the race across the plain until the bunched horses and their pursuers were out of sight beyond the farthest swell. Then he turned to Second Son. "When those fellows come back, they're going to be mad as hornets. We're going to have to keep close watch. It's a good thing the beaver are shedding and we don't have to keep the traps out, but it's sure going to cut into our job of baling the plews. We need to get them ready. Soon as the weather steadies down and there's no more chance of snow, Henri wants to head out for Lisa's fort, up on the Yellowstone, and trade them. He's got almost too many for all our packhorses to manage, and that's dangerous with Terrebonne's fur thieves keeping watch on him."

"Terrebonne." Second Son's tone was flat, and Cleve wondered again what had happened between her and the trapper during an earlier winter when she had rescued that Frenchman from the snow. Something drastic had taken place, he knew, but he also knew better than to ask the question outright. Second Son would tell him if the time ever came when it was important for him to know.

"You might follow them up the river. Not on the horse, for that might betray you to them. Afoot. You run faster than I," she said, her tone practical.

She was never one to misjudge a situation because of personal pride; Cleve knew that, even so soon in their marriage. If she thought it sensible to keep watch on the Pawnee when they turned to come back along their tracks, that was the thing to do. She knew those people as he could not. She had stolen enough horses from them to understand their reaction to that sort of raid.

"Sure thing," he said. He slid down the slanting ramp, and his wife leapt lightly after him, landing in his arms at the foot of the slope. He gave her a quick hug. "You and Henri can bale up the skins, and maybe I'll be back quick enough to help. But you take care, hear me? That Frenchman may be old, but he's a horny bastard. I see him watching you sometimes."

Second Son's lips thinned into a tight smile. "I have had . . . experience with Fransay before. Do not worry. I am a warrior, remember?"

And it was true. Even in the mock battle in which she had won him as her "wife" she had been a formidable opponent. He had been hard put to hold his own, and when she set her foot on his neck, it had not been because he had thrown the fight in order to win her. He might be a lot bigger, but she knew tricks that even the *coureurs de bois* had never mentioned while instructing their young comrades of the Ashworth group about the world they were going into.

The two returned to the hidden cabin and the tipi they shared in a clump of cottonwoods beyond it. Cleve put on his stoutest pair of moccasins and packed his possibles bag with supplies he might need. He capped his powder horn tightly; it was also a gift from Henri. He had lost his own "white man's" supplies to the Arikara almost a year before on the Missouri. Jerky would sustain him until he returned.

But he also took his bow and arrows. He had found that often it was good to have a silent weapon that did not mark your position with a cloud of black smoke. Cub, nephew of Second Son, had taught him well during his long stay with the Burning-Heart Band.

When he set out upriver, he stayed on the other side for miles, running easily, aiming to intersect the track of the horse thieves and their pursuers. The ground was rough, but by now he had run, he felt certain, over half the Great Plains, and his muscles were hardened to it. His heart pumped steadily, and his breath came regularly, without effort. At long intervals he paused to rest and drink from the river, but he covered ground at a good rate.

He cut the track of the stolen horses just after dawn the next morning. While one unshod pony's track is much like that of any other, he was able to distinguish the hoofmarks because those coming behind were crumbled less at the edges than those ahead.

The Pawnee were still chasing their animals, fuming with rage, he was sure. If he waited downstream, holing up to be hidden when they came back, he would know just where they were headed. If they moved toward the tower or the river near the trapping camp, he could hightail it downstream to find one of Henri's spare canoes, which were kept at intervals up and down the Belle Fourche. That would shoot him down to his companions, at this time of year when the stream ran bank-full, faster than anyone could ride.

It was a long wait, and a spring storm did not make it more comfortable. Rain mixed with sleet scoured the grasslands and rattled like shot among the leaf-buds above his hiding place. The patch of bushes he had chosen was scant cover against such weather, but the cougar-hide cloak, light enough to carry on such a run, was a lifesaver. He huddled into its supple folds and waited with the patience he was learning from Second Son.

Night came and went, and near midday he felt the vibration he was learning to recognize. His ear to the ground, he heard the thud of hooves and knew that the Pawnee were returning. He must find a place where he could watch the direction they took from the crossing.

Cleve crawled through the cold wet bushes, icy grass touching his face and freezing his hands. There was a clump of cottonwoods that some windstorm had blown into a wild tangle spanning the river. Hidden at its edge, he could see without being seen.

The butt of the easternmost tree reared from the ground, holding up a great chunk of dirt and roots like a wall. Cleve maneuvered to get behind that, in the angle of trunk and rootball. There he waited for what seemed hours, the fringe of feeder roots sticking out of the upper edge and providing excellent cover.

At last, in midafternoon, he heard the line of warriors splashing up out of the stream. He stared out cautiously to see the Pawnee driving ahead of them something like half the horses they had lost the day before. They looked dead beat, the horses drooping, the riders not much better off. There had been a hot chase and a stiff fight.

Even as he considered the bedraggled group, he heard behind him a twitter that did not come from a bird. Then something lanced through him, pinning his left arm at the shoulder to the tree trunk. He was helpless, his rifle crushed between his chest and the tree. His knife was in his belt, but it too was out of reach unless he could free himself. Knowing too well the swiftness with which a warrior could loose arrows, he understood that any movement would bring another shaft that might kill him outright.

There was only one thing to do, and by now he had seen enough dead men to do it well. He gurgled harshly, flopped a bit, making the arm give him hell, and went limp, his eyes half open, his eyeballs rolled back as far as he could make them go. The swaddling fur would hide from his attacker the fact that his arrow had not found his victim's heart. If he had been forced to hang from the arrow, he couldn't have done it without betraying the fact that there was still life in him, but luckily he had "died" with his feet under him. He could take off most of the weight while still making it look as if he were dead as dirt.

His worst fear was that the warrior, whoever he was and whyever he had been here instead of with the rest of his band, would take the time to scalp him. That would be nasty. But he was caught, no two ways about it, and he just had to wait and see what happened next.

There came a long cry from the plain east of the river. The sound of movement was distinct as the scout climbed the tangle, looked down for a moment on his victim, and turned away. The tangle rustled and snapped as he descended the other side, and after some minutes Cleve heard the sound of another horse, very near, moving away into the icy grassland.

All very good. Still he waited, however, not trusting the wily savages not to have another scout covering the river. He should have expected this one, and he cursed himself as he worked quietly at the shaft holding him to the dead cottonwood.

That was no good. The head of the arrow had gone solidly into the wood, and there was no way he could get at it, even if he'd been able to reach the knife. He had to reach around behind, no easy task, and break off the feathered end.

He had the long Bennett arms, which turned out to be a blessing. With his right hand, he reached back, feeling demons with red-hot pincers at work inside his muscle as he moved, and snapped off the tough wood of the shaft, leaving the stub free. Then, with one desperate heave, he pushed himself backward, pulling the wood through the wound it had made.

That was not even a little fun. Blood was pouring down him, front and back, the hot flood soaking his deerhide tunic and leggings. He would freeze, for the wind was now coming down from the northwest in gusts that found their way even into the nook protected by the uprooted trees. This was one of those late storms that often brought snow to the plains and blizzards to the mountains. He tugged the cougar hide about him and turned blindly toward the Belle Fourche.

He had to get back downriver. Already he felt light-headed from blood loss, and he had a hard time keeping his wits enough to pack torn-off bits of fur from his cougar hide into the entrance and exit holes. He knew he'd better stop that flow if he intended to get anyplace, and though the packing was painful, in time it lessened the bleeding to a minor trickle.

He knew more or less where the canoe was hidden. Henri had drawn him a map in the dirt, showing the dead snag extending over the river, the sharp elbow of stone jagging out into the water, and the protected pool downstream from where he had sunk this vessel of his flimsy navy. If he could get there, the current would carry him down to the camp, and he knew Second Son would be watching. Not even a hawk in the sky or a badger under the ground escaped her attention.

The night was coming on fast, for the cloud cover still hovered close to the ground and the wind carried more sleet along its blast. Cleve clung to tree trunks to balance himself as he staggered stubbornly forward, his feet numb, his arm afire, his head floating mistily above, unconnected to the rest of him.

At last he fell headlong into a prickly mass of bushes, and only his upflung right arm kept him from losing an eye to the frozen twigs he tumbled into. Lying there on his face, panting with effort and breathlessness, he thought longingly of death. He was too cold, too drained of blood, too disoriented to find his way home.

Mama would worry. Tim and Gene would search the woods for him, but Pa wouldn't even look up from his chores. He would never get home again, no matter how he tried . . . and that old bull buffalo he had seen in a vision (had it been real?) that stared at him with wicked eyes from a frosty face . . . it was lost now, in the fog. Frozen fog. Icy twigs. Cleve gave a long sigh and closed his eyes, feeling the beginning of warmth steal up his legs.

Something brought him back, sharply, imperatively. Second Son! He would leave her, after just finding her. He would lose that closeness that was like nothing he had known in his life of abuse with Pa. Second Son was calling him back, and he had to go. Now.

He pushed downward with both hands and almost screamed with the sudden agony in his left arm. Rolling over, he managed to sit, then pull himself upward using his right hand and a nearby sapling. His breath came in long groans now, and he felt as if the ground dipped and wavered under his feet, but he lifted the right foot, set it down, pulled the left forward, set it in front of the first.

One step at a time, with terrible concentration, Cleve forced his failing body toward the river. Once there, he turned downstream, more by instinct than vision, for by now it was dark. But he could hear the water moving beside him, and when he came to the leaning snag, it rammed directly into his belly, bringing him up short.

Was this the spot? He stared toward the sound of water, but he could see nothing but oily swirls of lesser darkness where the eddies coiled. There was no way he could find a sunk canoe in the darkness with his head spinning and his eyes blurred with pain.

He was on the wrong side of the river, miles from his goal. He hadn't even Snip with him to guide him right, for he'd left the animal tied near the tipi to keep him from betraying his presence to the Pawnee.

He lifted a foot, set it down. Again and again and again he did that, bumping into trees, crushing through brush and patches of icy slush. If he had to walk back to his wife, then that was what he'd do.

He didn't really know when he fell. Darkness filled him, mind and body, and he was almost warm again, or numb, which came to the same thing, when something cold pushed against his cheek, a hot tongue licked at his nose.

He groaned. "Donnn do'at, Snip!" he muttered. "Gotta sleep. . . ."

The hard nose nudged sharply into his shoulder, and the wound in his arm came to life again, stabbing him with dull agony. Cleve opened his eyes, staring cross-eyed at the dog's nose, smelling the carrion the animal had eaten on the breath now panting, moist and hot, into his face.

Fumbling his wits together, Cleve struggled to sit and then to stand. The dog nudged close, trying to help, and before long the man found himself more or less upright, leaning against an invisible tree. "Good dog," he said, though even his tongue seemed to be numb now. "Keep goin'. Sec' Son, she'll come help inna while."

Snip whined anxiously, and his tail whipped against Cleve's legs. The dog yowled, as if urging him to walk again.

With his dog there at his side, it didn't seem quite so hard to lift those stubborn feet, to force his drained body forward. When he paused, on the edge of unconsciousness, Snip nosed him or nipped him gently on the leg to get him started again.

From time to time, he was forced to halt and lean against a tree or drop flat on the ground, unable to go on. And yet every time, when the dog decided it was time to move again, Cleve dragged himself up, an inch at a time, his wounded arm and shoulder weighted with misery, and went ahead through the darkness.

The last time he fell, he could not rise. Snip whined and whimpered, dug with his nose, nudged and worried at his master, but Cleve could only groan. At last he felt the dog lick his cheek with a wet tongue. The sound of pattering paws moved away over the frozen debris of the riverbank.

Then it was peaceful as the cold numbed him further, the blood leaked from his wounds around the tufts of fur he had stuffed into them, and morning began lightening the sky to a faintly paler gray. Cleve could think of nothing now, though he knew he was no longer in Missouri. Ma and Pa and the boys were lost in the past, along with that devil-buffalo.

Henri and Second Son were mere whispers at the edge of his thought. A sudden clarity gripped him, and he knew that he would die here on the bank of the Belle Fourche, his ambitions unfulfilled, his dreams lost forever.

That was good. Life had been, except for these few weeks with Second Son, a painful experience. Death, with all its unknowns, could hardly be more terrifying.

He settled silently into a doze that would end in the longest sleep of all.

And that was when he heard the call, shrill and clear, from downriver. A rapid beat of paws came rushing toward him, amid a flurry of hoarse barks.

Damn! He was going to live. Second Son would see to that.